172 HOURS ON THE MOON

JOHAN HARSTAD

172 HOURS ON THE MOON

JOHAN HARSTAD

translation by Tara F. Chace

atom

www.atombooks.net

ATOM

First published as *Darlah – 172 timer på månen* in Norway in 2008 by Cappelen Damm
First published in the United States in 2012 by Little, Brown and Company
First published in Great Britain in 2012 by Atom
Reprinted 2013

This translation has been published with the financial support of NORLA.

All characters and events in this publication, other than those clearly in the public domain, are fictitious and any resemblance to real persons, living or dead, is purely coincidental.

The NASA "Return to the Moon" artwork is intended to represent a fictional and futuristic organization and is in no way intended to imply any endorsement by or affiliation with the National Aeronautics and Space Administration.

Image Credits:
Pages v, 13, 120, 157, 242, 248, 320, 330, 341, 353: NASA/courtesy of nasaimages.org
Page 34: Ryan McVay/Getty Images; © Getty Images
Pages 51, 52, 89, 123, 341: © LACKTR
Pages 107, 113: © John Erik Riley
Pages 191, 192, 280: © Rodeo Architects
Page 259: ESA – European Space Agency
Page 276: The Ohio State University Radio Observatory
The photograph on page 259 is an artist's impression. The size of the debris is exaggerated as compared to Earth.

A CIP catalogue record for this book is available from the British Library.

ISBN 978-1-907411-51-9

Printed and bound in Great Britain by Clays Ltd, St Ives plc

Papers used by Atom are from well-managed forests and other responsible sources.

FSC
www.fsc.org
MIX
Paper from responsible sources
FSC® C104740

Atom
An imprint of
Little, Brown Book Group
100 Victoria Embankment
London EC4Y 0DY

An Hachette UK Company
www.hachette.co.uk

www.atombooks.net

172 HOURS ON THE MOON

JOHAN HARSTAD

CONTENTS

PROLOGUE: FEBRUARY 2010

"Gentlemen, it's time," Dr. [redacted] said, eyeing the seven men in suits seated around the large conference table. They were some of the most powerful people in the country, together in the largest meeting room at NASA headquarters in Washington, D.C. It was nearing eleven o'clock at night.

They would have to make a decision soon.

"So, what's it going to be, then?" Dr. [redacted] asked impatiently.

The cigarette smoke in the room was thick and impenetrable, making the atmosphere even gloomier. All rules forbidding smoking in government offices had fallen by the wayside as nerves came to a head.

"Well," one of the seven began, chewing on his pencil, "it's an incredibly risky proposition. You must know that. Is it really worth it?"

"People had already completely lost interest in the moon missions before the last launch in 1972," another one said. "Why do you think they'd be on board with us going back?"

"It could be done," a third said. "We could tell them there's a good chance of finding large amounts of tantalum seventy-three at the moon's south pole."

The room was suddenly buzzing, the tension starting to crescendo.

"You don't want to go back to the south pole, trust me."

"Of course not."

"It'll kill you."

"I'm aware of that."

"If you ask me, I say leave the whole place alone."

"Gentlemen," Dr. [redacted] interrupted, "do you have any idea how important a discovery tantalum seventy-three would be? Most current technology is dependent on this material. People would be throwing money at us."

"So we're going up there to search for natural resources? I thought—" one of the other men said.

Dr. [redacted] interrupted him again. "No, we're not."

The chairman of the Joint Chiefs of Staff cleared his throat. "Let me put the cards on the table for you, gentlemen. We are not going to the south pole of the moon, and whether or not tantalum seventy-three is found on the moon is completely immaterial."

Confusion spread through the room.

"I presume some of you are familiar with Project Horizon?" he continued.

The man who had spoken first asked, "You mean the research done in the late fifties? The plans to build a military base on the moon? I thought that was scrapped."

Dr. [redacted] shook his head. "The base isn't military." He looked at the chairman of the Joint Chiefs. "It's just a research station. Isn't that right?"

The chairman didn't answer. He gave the man a friendly look. "It's called DARLAH 2. It was constructed in the seventies under the name Operation DP7."

"But why... in the world... why haven't any of us heard of it before?"

"All information concerning DARLAH 2 was classified top secret until just recently. For security reasons." He paused for a second, pondering whether or not he ought to say any more.

Dr. [redacted] beat him to it, explaining, "DARLAH 2 was built from 1974 to 1976. But the base is in the Sea of Tranquility, where, as you know, Armstrong and Aldrin originally landed in sixty-nine. None of the other landings occurred there."

"Why was it built?" one of the men who had been quiet up until that point asked.

"We found something," Dr. [redacted] replied.

"Could you elaborate?"

"We don't know what it is. The plan was to continue our studies and station personnel on the moon, but as you already know, after 1976 we lost most of our funding. And as I hinted, finances weren't the only reason the moon program was terminated. The truth is that... what we found up there is not the type of discovery for which one receives money for further research. We would have been asked to leave it alone. So we pretended it never existed... and, anyway, the signal disappeared."

"Until it showed up again last fall," the chairman of the Joint Chiefs added.

"The *signal*? *It?* What the hell is *it*?" one of the confused men exclaimed. Dr. [redacted] looked at the man who had spoken, then leaned over and pulled something out of his briefcase. He set a folder on the table and pulled out a four-by-six photo.

"This picture was taken on the moon by *Apollo 15*'s James Irwin. The astronaut in the photo is David R. Scott."

"But... who's the other person in the background?" one of the men asked.

"We don't know."

"You don't *know*? What the hell is going on here?"

"There's a proper time for everything, gentlemen. All the information you're asking for will be made available once we've unanimously voted to proceed with the plan—which, may I remind you, the president himself is in full support of. Now, can we discuss how we're going to explain the fact that we've had an unused base sitting up there for forty years without anyone finding out about it?"

"Unused? Are you trying to say that no one has ever stayed at this base before?" one of the astronauts in the room asked. "What about the people who built it?"

"They were never inside. The modules were assembled on the surface by machines, not by people."

One of the men already on board with the plan stood up, smiling confidently: "We'll say we've spent forty years testing it, making sure it works perfectly."

"And does it?" someone else asked.

"In principle, yes," replied the man, whose smile wasn't quite so confident anymore.

"*In principle* isn't good enough, is it?"

"It'll have to do. We have to go back within a decade, before someone else gets there first."

Several of the men present still seemed skeptical, if not stunned.

"But who are you going to send up there? What are they going to do?"

"The first expedition will accomplish three simple things. One: They'll test the base and make sure it's working the way it's supposed to. Two: They'll research the possibility of mining rare Earth metals that will give the United States a huge advantage in the technology manufacturing market. And three — this is the most important of all, gentlemen — they will attract media attention, which will consequently secure sufficient financial support to continue our research and... get rid of any potential... problems."

"Problems like what?" someone asked.

Dr. [redacted] held his hand up in front of him as if to stop the words. "As I said, we'll get to that. The idea is to turn the whole thing into a celebration of the fiftieth anniversary of the first manned mission to land on the moon. We'll build new, improved versions of the classic Apollo program rockets from the sixties and seventies. That's guaranteed to make people feel nostalgic."

"But no one under the age of forty-five even remembers those Apollo missions."

Dr. [redacted] waited a long time before speaking. He was a very intelligent man, and having to explain every detail to these ludicrous excuses for public figures was grating on his nerves. Fortunately, he had played this conversation out in his head many times, and he had an answer for anything they might ask, including the perfect idea for getting the entire *world* interested in a new mission. "Gentlemen, what if we send some teenagers up there?"

No one responded. They all just sat there, waiting, assuming he was joking.

But he wasn't.

"You want to send *kids*? Why in the world would you want to put kids on the moon?" someone asked.

Dr. [redacted] smiled patronizingly and replied, "If we select three young people, teenagers, who get to accompany the astronauts, we'll get a whole new generation excited about space exploration. It will be nothing less than a global sensation."

"But...just a minute ago you were telling us there's something...*unknown* up there. And none of you seem able to say what it really is or what potential consequences we're facing. And you want to send untrained, innocent teenagers up there as, what, *guinea pigs*?"

"The benefits outweigh the risks," Dr. [redacted] replied. "The probability of anything happening is small in the specific area of operation, and the astronauts will have the opportunity to set up important equipment and perform the necessary studies. For the sake of simplicity, I think it's best to look at this as two missions in one. The first—our part—is to research the potential mining of tantalum seventy-three—"

"I thought you said we would not actually look for tantalum at all?"

"We won't." Then he went on. "The second part will be the teenagers' mission, which will be little effort for them. The media attention will be automatic. They'll portray this as a glamorous space version of a trip to Disneyland. And, best of all, my preliminary inquiries indicate that some major corporate sponsorship is almost guaranteed, which will likely provide the money we need for a second mission."

"There'll be a second mission as well?"

"I'm afraid so."

"You want kids to go on the second one as well?"

"No."

Dr. [redacted] held up two thick envelopes marked TOP SECRET. "Teenagers on the moon, gentlemen, is the solution we've been looking for. The door opener."

"But how will you decide who gets to go?"

Dr. [redacted] smiled again, even more slyly, and replied, "We'll hold a lottery."

1

THE EARTH

OPPORTUNITY—2018

"That's the stupidest thing I've ever heard," Mia Nomeland said, giving her parents an unenthusiastic look. "No way."

"But Mia, honey. It's an amazing opportunity, don't you think?"

Her parents were sitting side by side on the sofa, as if glued together, with the ad they had clipped out of the newspaper lying on the coffee table in front of them. Every last corner of the world had already had a chance to see some version of it. The campaign had been running for weeks on TV, the radio, the Internet, and in the papers, and the name NASA was on its way to becoming as well known around the globe as Coca-Cola or McDonald's.

"An opportunity for what? To make a fool of myself?"

"Won't you even consider it?" her mother tried. "The deadline isn't for a month, you know."

"No! I don't want to consider it. There's nothing for me to do up there. There's something for me to do absolutely everywhere *except* on the moon."

"If it were me, I would have applied on the spot," her mother said.

"Well, I'm sure my friends and I are all very glad that you're not me."

"Mia!"

"Fine, sorry. It's just that I... I don't *care.* Is that so hard for you to understand? You guys are always telling me that the world is full of opportunities and that you have to choose some and let others pass you by. And that there are enough opportunities to last a lifetime and then some. Right, Dad?"

Her dad mumbled some sort of response and looked the other way.

Her mother sighed. "I'll leave the ad over here on the piano for a while, in case you change your mind."

It's always like this, Mia thought, leaving the living room. *They're not listening. They're just waiting for me to finish talking.*

Mia went up to her room in the attic and started practicing. When it came to her music, she never slacked off. She'd been playing the guitar for two years, and for a year and a half she'd been a vocalist in the band Rogue Squadron, a name with a nod to the seventies appropriate for a punk band that sort of sounded like something from another era, maybe 1982. Or 1984. Even though she didn't always care about getting every last little bit of her homework done, she made sure she knew her music history better than anyone.

DO YOU WANT
TO GO TO THE

MOON?

ARE YOU BETWEEN THE AGES OF 14 AND 18?

SPEND 172 HOURS ON THE MOON AT MOON BASE **DARLAH 2**

NASA

RETURN TO THE MOON **NASAMOONRETURN**.COM

Her latest discovery was the Talking Heads, a band she had slowly but surely fallen in love with. Or, rather, that she was doing her best to fall in love with, because she could tell it was good. She still struggled a little when she listened for a long time. And she wasn't quite sure if the music was post-punk or rock or just pop, and that made the whole thing even more complicated. But it had such a cold, electronic eighties sound, she knew it would be a perfect fit for her if she could just get into the music.

She kept practicing her guitar for an hour and wrote a draft for a new song that worked off a riff she'd stolen from songs she was totally sure no one had heard. It would be okay to show up with that at her band's rehearsal tomorrow. After she'd played through it five times and was pretty sure she remembered the chords, she set her guitar down, plugged her headphones into the stereo, and pressed *play*. Music from the band she had decided to start liking filled her ears. She lay back on the bed and closed her eyes.

"What are you listening to, Mia?" her dad asked, raising one side of her headphones. He was trying to smooth over the negative vibe from earlier in the day.

"Talking Heads," she answered.

"You know they were really popular when I was young."

Mia gave him a look but didn't respond.

"You know, it's an amazing opportunity, Mia, the moon. I—*we*—just want what's best for you. You know that."

She groaned but tried to smile at him anyway. "Dad, please. Just drop it, okay?"

But he wouldn't drop it.

"And for your band, have you given that any thought? Don't you guys want to be famous? I don't think it would hurt Rough Squadron in terms of publicity if the vocalist were a world-famous astronaut."

"*Rogue* Squadron," she corrected.

"Anyway," he replied, "you know what I mean." And then he left, shutting her door carefully behind him.

Mia lay down on her bed again. Was there something to what he said? No, there wasn't. She was a musician, after all. Not some astronaut wannabe. She turned her music on again, and vocalist David Byrne sang: *"I don't know what you expect staring into the TV set. Fighting fire with fire."*

It was almost May, but the air was still chilly in Norway. The trees lining the avenue were naked and lifeless with the exception of a couple of leaves here and there, which had opened too early. Two weeks had passed since Mia's parents had suggested their silly idea to her.

Now she was standing outside school, scraping her boots back and forth over the ground as she waited for Silje to come back from the bathroom. Lunch break would be over soon, and around her other students were scurrying back into the building for fear they'd be late. But Mia was not in any hurry. The teachers always came to class a few minutes late anyway. They sat up there in the teachers' lounge eating dry Ritz crackers and drinking bitter coffee while they trash-talked individual students.

Mia felt her school was the kind of place where the teachers, with a few decent exceptions, should have gone into pretty much any profession other than teaching. Janitorial work, for example. Or tending graveyards. Something where they didn't need to interact with living people. Most of them had just barely squeaked through their teaching programs about a hundred years earlier. They had almost infinite power here, and they did their best to remind the students of that every chance they got — because they all knew that this authority disappeared like dew in the sunlight the second they left school grounds and headed out into the real world, where they were forced to interact with people their own age.

Silje came out of the bathroom. She and Mia were the only ones who hadn't gone back inside yet.

"Cool boots," Silje said.

"I've been wearing them all day," Mia replied drily. "Didn't you notice?"

"Not until now. Where'd you get them?"

Mia looked down at her worn, black leather boots that laced up just above the ankle. "Online. Italian paratrooper boots."

"Awesome," Silje said. "Well, should we go in?"

"What do you have now?"

"Math," Silje said.

"I have *Deutsch*. With 'the Hair,'" Mia said with a sigh.

They went back in and took the stairs up to the second floor.

"Are we rehearsing tonight?" Silje asked right before they went their separate ways.

"I think so. Leonora's going to call me as soon as she knows if she can."

"Let me know, okay? I can be there at seven. Not before."

"Seven's fine. Hey, I wrote a new song yesterday."

"You did? What's it called?"

"'Bomb Hiroshima Again,' I think. I haven't decided yet."

"Cool," Silje said with a laugh. "See you later."

Mia continued on to the third floor and walked into the classroom. The teacher wasn't there yet, so she skimmed through her German book to figure out what in the world she was supposed to have read the night before.

The Hair came sailing into the classroom with an inflatable beach ball shaped like a model of the moon in her hands. Mia rolled her eyes. *Oh my God, not her, too.*

But, yes, the Hair—this tiny lady with the freakishly big hair—had caught moon fever. She disappeared behind her desk and started blabbering on in German about how exciting the whole thing was and how great it would be if one of her students ended up being selected.

Mia rolled her eyes again. It was a known fact that the Hair had been at this school too long. She only taught German and home ec. And then there was her big secret, which everyone knew but which she thought was well kept: The Hair had never been to Germany. She had only ever left Norway once, to go to Sweden. And that was back in the summer of 1986 or thereabouts, and she had come home again after four days.

But maybe the fact that she was now standing in front of them with that inflatable moon under her arm wasn't as strange as one might think. The whole world had come completely unhinged this winter. The newspapers, the radio, the TV, and the Internet were flooded with moon mania every day, from trivia and data spouted by experts and professors and astronomers to competitions where you could win all sorts of stuff just by answering a few simple questions about space travel. Meanwhile, millions of teenagers were busy logging on or standing in long lines at registration desks in malls or grocery stores in just about every single town in the whole world to make sure that their names had been entered.

For safety reasons, NASA had decided that the three young people who would be chosen to go must be at least fourteen and that they couldn't be older than eighteen. They would also need to be between five feet four inches and six feet four inches tall, undergo a psychological examination performed by a certified practitioner in their hometown, and pass a general physical examination in order to obtain a medical "green card." All applicants should have a near and distant visual acuity correctable to 20/20 and a blood pressure, while sitting, of no more than 140 over 90. And then there were all the tests and training they would be put through in the unlikely event that they were among the selected few.

While these requirements restricted the number of candidates somewhat, millions of names had been submitted for the big drawing, and as the days and weeks went by, people were close to bursting with excitement. Gamblers put money on which countries the lucky three would come from and on whether the winners would include more boys or girls. Talk show hosts invited experts to speculate about nonsense like the effect of seeing Earth from space on people so young. And then there were the debates that were as numerous as they were endless about this moon base that no one had ever heard mention of before now.

What was it? Why was it there? What did it do? Could people really trust that it had been built with peaceful intentions?

The Hair reached the end of her speech and switched into broken Norwegian, which often happened whenever she spoke German for too long. "But listen to this. Someone representing NASA—yes, *the* NASA—called our school to check in with our students about signing up for the lottery. As I'm sure you've heard, any school with one hundred percent participation by their eligible students will be entered in a sweepstakes for a grant for technology upgrades. The representative from NASA said that a whopping ninety-one from your grade have already signed up and asked us to encourage the rest of you to do so as well. But only five of you from my German class have taken advantage of this incredible opportunity."

No one said anything.

"Well done, Petter, Stine, Malene, and Henning."

The four students who'd signed up smiled at her smugly.

"And Mia, what a nice surprise. Congratulations."

Mia stiffened completely and said, "I didn't sign up for anything."

"Well, according to NASA, you did."

Mia leaned over her desk and said loudly, "Well then, they must have made a mistake! I totally *didn't* sign up for that stupid-ass lottery."

"Calm down, Mia. It's nothing to be self-conscious about."

"I'm not embarrassed about it. It's just not true. And even if it were, NASA shouldn't be releasing that kind of information to anyone."

The Hair waved her hand dismissively and winked at her, as if they were both in on some secret. "Evidently it was a condition of the sign-up procedure that you give NASA permission to reveal your name as a participant in the lottery. But we don't need to dwell on this. It's up to each individual to decide if he or she wants to consider doing it or not."

"What's your point?" Mia railed, rage welling up inside. "I told you I didn't sign up for that thing. What the hell would I do in space, anyway? Don't you think I have better things to do? Screw the moon!"

"We don't use language like that in my classroom, Mia!"

"No, *we* don't talk at all in your classroom. *You* just go off on hour-long monologues about whatever bullshit you feel like!"

The teacher stood and pointed to the door. "You're excused from the rest of the class, Mia. I don't want you here. You can wait out in the hall."

Mia didn't protest. She brushed her German book off the edge of her desk so it landed in her backpack, got up, and left. The hallway was empty, and from the surrounding classrooms she could hear snippets of Norwegian, math, and English classes going on. Without thinking, she opened the door to her classroom again and stared straight at the Hair.

"Besides, everyone knows you've never been to Germany. Maybe that's something *you* should be embarrassed about?" For half a second her teacher's face became long and sad, as if she'd been sentenced to life in prison for a nasty crime she forgot she'd committed.

Mia heard cheers starting to erupt from the other students before she slammed the door shut and headed down the stairs and out onto the school grounds. She strolled over to the track next to the gym, sat down on the railing, and took out her phone to call her mother. An uncomfortable suspicion had started to take shape in her mind.

Behind her, about thirty students were running around the track. Mia didn't even need to look to know that this was their crazy PE teacher's doing. She was almost fifty, had a mustache, and had been teaching there since the dawn of time. She didn't accept the concept of excuses; even if you were paralyzed from the waist down, she demanded that you perform to Olympic standards. Several of the panting students in the back were obviously pale, a couple of their faces were light green, and it was only a matter of time before they keeled over and vomited.

Mia's mother answered just as the first stomach emptied its contents onto the track.

"Mia, hi. What is it? Are you at school?"

"Mom, did you sign me up for that trip to the moon thing?"

It was quiet on the other end of the line. Very quiet.

"Mom?"

"I... we, your dad and I, we... thought you'd regret it. Later. So, well, we, um..."

Mia interrupted her harshly. "Did you sign me up?"

There was another pause, but shorter this time. "Yes."

Mia groaned. "*What* were you guys *thinking*?"

"Mia, everyone else your age thinks this is an amazing opportunity. Why—"

"But I'm not everyone else, am I? You have absolutely no respect for the fact that my opinions are different from yours. Why don't you guys go yourselves if you're so excited about it? Because that's what it's about, right? Since you guys aren't eligible, you're signing me up as the next best thing. What do you think, that it'll make us all rich and famous? Is that it?"

"Mia, I think you're being unreasonable now."

"Unreasonable? What's unreasonable is doing it behind my back."

"Mia..."

But Mia had already hung up. Two students collapsed with a dull thud onto the grass behind her. Seconds later the PE teacher was over them, hauling them up as the vomit ran down their gym clothes.

Gym.

Mia didn't even like the word. And it didn't have anything to do with the kind of shape she was in. She could have easily outrun most of the kids on the track. She could swim laps in the pool with her clothes on and retrieve those lame dummies from the bottom or whatever they were being asked to do, without getting tired.

But it was all just a waste of time. Actually, compared to gym, a trip to the moon kind of made sense.

MR. HIMMELFARB

The old man sat shaking on a sofa by the window and looked around the room in confusion. There were old people sitting everywhere, on the sofas, on the chairs. A woman who was almost a hundred dragged herself across the linoleum floor with her walker in front of her.

What in the world are all these old people doing at my house? the man thought.

His name was Oleg Himmelfarb. And if he weren't profoundly senile, he would have understood that he wasn't at his own house anymore, and that the old people were there because they all lived in the same nursing home he did. And obviously he would have understood that he was an old man himself, and that he had only a year left to live.

But he didn't know that. Oleg Himmelfarb hardly knew anything anymore.

At one time, less than six years ago, he had been a fully functioning person, a charming grandfather and a man who still loved his wife and gave her flowers every single Saturday. During his long professional life, Himmelfarb had been a custodian with the highest security clearance at NASA's Goldstone Deep Space Communications Complex in the middle of the Mojave Desert.

But all of that was forgotten now.

Safely tucked away and preserved at Parson's Nursing Home outside Miami, the previously quite intelligent Himmelfarb had been reduced to a bag with eyes, a box no one really knew where to send.

He sat there on the sofa with his hands in his lap for a few minutes, until the aides came into the room. One of the nurses lifted him off the deep sofa and into a standing position.

"Do you have your balance now?" she asked him, without waiting for a response. Himmelfarb stood there, straight up and down with his hands at his sides as he waited to be told to move. The nurse waved at him and he started walking in the direction her finger was pointing. It was best that way. *Don't resist, just do what they ask.* At least that let him avoid thinking, because every time he did that, he got a headache. It was like his brain could no longer tolerate the strain of deciding what his body should do.

"Are you coming, Mr. Himmelfarb?"

The old folks were rolled into the room and arranged in chairs in a semicircle around the TV. Several of the residents jumped nervously when the screen lit up. One of the aides rose and said, "My dear residents, today is an important day, so we're going to watch something we don't usually watch. Is that all right?"

No one responded to her question. There was a bit of grumbling among the residents, but it was impossible to know for sure if that had to do with what she'd said or with things only they were aware of.

"Good," the aide continued. "I'm sure you remember the moon landing in 1969, right? Well, we're going back there now. As we speak, a global lottery is being held for all the teenagers in the world. NASA has set aside three spots on the upcoming flight for them. My son Scott already entered. So, cross your fingers — my son may be selected to be an astronaut this year!"

"Turn on the Weather Channel!" one of the old people whimpered.

The aide pretended she didn't hear that and smiled. The speech the president was about to make, and especially the chance that her son could be one of the lucky winners, meant a lot to her. She clenched her fists in her pockets and waited.

Then the president's face appeared on the screen. He talked about the dawn of a new era in the history of space travel. He talked about the three young people who would travel to the moon aboard the spacecraft *Ceres*, and he showed sketches of the moon base DARLAH 2, where they would live during their stay up there. He did his best to make it seem completely unremarkable that the government had kept the base a secret for all these years.

Mr. Himmelfarb straightened up in his chair and concentrated on the man giving the speech, but he couldn't quite follow what he was saying. Still, it was like something minuscule clicked deep within his brain when the president showed the drawings of the moon base. He'd seen those drawings before. But where? And why did it make him so nervous?

Suddenly, his whole body stiffened. He couldn't breathe.

In that instant, it was totally clear to him where he'd seen those drawings before, and his face changed from an empty, apathetic expression to one of blinding, white fear.

He screamed.

And his scream could be heard all the way out on the street.

It was the sound of a person who'd just realized that all hope was lost.

SHIBUYA, JAPAN

Midori Yoshida was standing outside the Shibuya 109 shopping center in Tokyo with her bags between her feet, checking her phone for messages while she waited for her girlfriends Mizuho and Yoshimi to finish their shopping. It was a little past five, and the warm April air was a pleasant change from the stuffy clamminess in the dressing rooms.

Her mom had called. Midori was just about to call her back when she changed her mind. *No.* She would call her later. It surely wasn't anything important anyway. It never was. When her parents did call, it was just to nag her about something they thought she should've done. Or they called when they were mad because she wasn't home yet. Not so strange, given that they lived all the way out in Yokohama and it took almost forty minutes to get there by train from Shibuya or Shinjuku station. And that was when it wasn't rush hour.

Ever since she'd turned thirteen, almost two and a half years ago, Midori had made the trip into downtown Tokyo at least twice a week, on Wednesdays and Sundays. After school on Wednesdays she went hunting for clothes—used or new—and also fabric, shoes, hats, bracelets, and small knickknacks she knew she didn't need but that she wanted anyway. Every single yen she earned from her evening job in the warehouse for her uncle's supermarket went toward these purchases. Her parents thought she was throwing away money she would need in a few years. But the way Midori looked at it, it didn't make any sense to think like that. What was the point of her doing well in five or six years if she wasn't doing well now?

The truth was, Midori had only just begun to feel like she was doing well, and she wouldn't give that up for anything. She had never understood why the bullies targeted her specifically from the very beginning of elementary school, because there really wasn't anything to justify it. Without any false modesty, she was much prettier than most of the other girls in the class. She didn't talk differently or act in any way that made her stick out. Her taste in music was maybe a little different from most kids' preferences, but it's not like she made a big deal about it.

The harassment continued all the way through elementary school, and when she switched to junior high, it just followed her, like a part of her identity. It's not that the bullying was particularly serious; they never bothered her physically, and at least it was only the girls who took out their frustrations on her. The boys pretty much didn't care one way or the other. But it was enough that Midori could never totally relax while she was at school. She could never be quite who she wanted to be.

But since she'd become a teenager, that had changed. She'd heard about a place in downtown Tokyo called Harajuku, where offbeat teens gathered on Sundays and completely took over the area for a few hours. They came from all parts of the city, and all they had in common was the need to show that they were different. Most of them wore clothes and costumes they'd sewn at home, a chaotic blend of colors and outfits. Some looked like they came from the future; others were dressed like European maids from the nineteenth century. There were rock-and-roll types from the 1950s, superheroes, hippies, and teenagers wearing suits or with hair dyed all the colors of the rainbow. Everyone who didn't fit in anywhere else was here. Together.

After just a couple of months she had made more friends there than she ever would have dared to dream and, just like that, her life had changed radically. Now whatever those anonymous girls in her class thought or said to her, she didn't care. And better yet, she started getting back at them. She struck where they were weakest: boys. It was fun to play baseball with the guys and go to cafés with them during lunch break. She could talk about music with them and swap the latest news about bands that were coming to Tokyo.

She knew all too well that eventually these boys would end up having lives that were totally different from the ones they were hoping for. Every last one of them would end up a salaryman, wearing a suit, just pushing papers from nine to five, before falling asleep, exhausted, on the train home to their bitter wives. And those bitter wives? Well, they were all those drab girls in her class who were throwing their lives away by going to this school to begin with. Deep down, in spite of everything, they knew that the same thing would happen to them as to so many Japanese women. They were expected to get married by the age of twenty-five. They were expected to quit working and take care of the home. And then they would sit there, neat and tidy in their cramped apartments, doing dishes and waiting for their men to finally make it home after hours of overtime and a visit to some cheap hostess bar for a couple of overpriced drinks with random girls who didn't have saggy boobs that hung down to their knees. They would sit there wishing they were somewhere totally different, living a totally different life.

Midori was not going to be one of them. No question about it. She had other plans.

And the young people down in Harajuku were her ticket. They helped her remember that they all had choices and that they were free to do what they wanted with their lives.

Midori's sister, Kyoko, who was seven years older, had certainly never been a part of the Harajuku scene, but she'd done what she could to avoid winding up in what she called "the Japanese trap." She'd escaped. She moved to London when she was nineteen to study, and since then she'd come home to visit only twice a year. But there was something else, too. She seemed happier every time she came. *It's very simple, Midori,* Kyoko had told her. *There's more than Japan, you know. There's a whole world out there. You can go where you want. You just need to make up your mind.*

And that was exactly what Midori had done. The day she turned eighteen and was done with school, she would leave Yokohama, leave Tokyo, leave this whole noisy country that was desperately trying to be modern while still clinging firmly to its conservative past.

New York, she thought. *It has to be New York. Obviously.* But she didn't know why. Maybe it was the movies she'd seen. The pictures. The music. She pictured how she, Mizuho, Yoshimi, and maybe even more of her Harajuku friends could travel across the Pacific together. They'd be the neo-*modan garus*, the new modern girls. They'd find a big loft in an old apartment building, and they'd have to ride a rusty freight elevator to get to it. They'd have people visiting all the time, friends who popped in from Japan. They would make art, clothes, music, movies, everything. And they'd get old together, never get married, and never dry up into boring middle-aged women. Of course they'd date people, and their boyfriends would certainly come and live in their little commune for a while, as long as they made sure they left again before they really settled in.

That's how it would be. In less than three years.

She just had to make it until then.

"Midori!"

She turned toward the sound and saw her girlfriends walking out of Shibuya 109 behind a load of shopping bags. They could just barely walk normally. She smiled at them and strolled over to meet them.

"Did you guys leave anything for the other customers?" she asked.

"Well, we didn't buy the dressing room. Or the cash register. Here, can you take a couple bags?" Yoshimi held out her arms, and Midori relieved her of part of her load.

"I've been waiting for you guys forever. If I were a man, I'd have a long beard by now." Midori laughed.

"It's your own fault you finished so fast, you lightweight, not ours," Mizuho protested.

"Hey, three hours is *not* 'so fast'!"

"Okay, so it took a little longer than we thought," Mizuho replied. "But maybe this will make up for it." Mizuho handed her yet another bag. They'd bought her the boots she'd been wanting for months.

"You guys are crazy!" she exclaimed happily, and hugged them.

"Should we go get coffee before the train?" Mizuho asked.

Midori hesitated. "I don't know; it's starting to get late. My parents called and . . ."

"You're supposed to be home already?" Yoshimi asked.

"Yeah."

"But then it doesn't matter. If you're already late, it's not like you can make it home on time, right?"

"I guess not," Midori said. "Okay, then, a quick coffee."

They headed for the Starbucks and sat by the big windows on the second floor, where they had a panoramic view of the gigantic neon advertising billboards on the buildings across the street. Below them thousands of people scurried over the big crosswalks.

"Coffee actually isn't good for people like us," Yoshimi said. "But it tastes good, so what can we do?"

"Why isn't it good for us?" Midori wanted to know.

Yoshimi and Mizuho replied in unison: "Because it stunts your growth."

Midori took a big gulp. "We're Japanese. It's not like there was any big risk we were going to be six foot five anyway. Cheers!"

They raised their disposable cups and clicked them together. And that was the exact moment Midori heard the music.

It was classical music, dramatic and loud. She saw how people clearly stopped out on the street and turned toward them.

"Quick, they're going to play it again now!" Yoshimi squealed enthusiastically, already on her way down the stairs.

"Play *what*?" Midori managed to ask before grabbing her cup and running after her friend.

"The NASA ad!" Mizuho called over her shoulder, and disappeared out onto the street.

The huge video screen located on the side of the building was playing a Hollywood-style ad.

"It's been nearly fifty years since the very first moon landing took place," it began. With pictures of the historic 1969 event as the backdrop, the voice-over explained that NASA was ready to send people back to the moon for a longer stay. Then the action sequence began. A rocket hurtled out into space with dizzying force.

The voice-over paused for effect as the pictures showed a computer-generated image of a landing module quietly setting down on the moon. Small astronauts climbed out and went to work. In the background could be seen the contours of a large moon base.

"For this exceptional expedition," the overly dramatic voice continued, "NASA has decided to make an equally exceptional offer to the next generation. Three young people between fourteen and eighteen will have the opportunity..." *pause for*

Hisamitsu
サロンパス
MOON?
MOON?
MV

dramatic effect "...to be part..." *another pause for dramatic effect* "...of this return to the moon!"

Midori couldn't take her eyes off the screen.

"*You* could be the first teenager in space," the voice urged. "Sign up at www.nasamoonreturn.com and be part of the most important lottery in history. *You. Are. Invited.*"

And with a vigorous fanfare, the NASA logo flashed onto the screen for a few seconds before it went black. And then a stupid car ad came on.

"Had you really not seen that before?" Mizuho asked incredulously. "They've been playing it nonstop on TV. It's everywhere."

"I signed up already," Yoshimi said. "Are you guys going to?"

"No way," Mizuho said instantly. "What the heck would I do up there? There's nothing to see, nothing to buy, nothing to do. Pretty much like Roppongi during the day."

"What about you, Midori?"

But Midori was already too lost in her own thoughts to even hear them.

This is my ticket, she thought. *It's three years earlier than my plan, and it takes me a little farther than I'd thought, but this is my way out. This is the way to New York.*

Yoshimi tugged on her arm and said, "Isn't it cool?"

Midori snapped out of it. "Totally," she replied. "Totally. We should definitely sign up. Definitely."

DUPLEIX

Sixteen-year-old Antoine Devereux found himself waiting alone on the Dupleix Métro platform. It had been a long day, one of the longest. The kind of day that just kept going and going no matter how much time you tried to kill. But the morning had been different. The morning had been just as beautiful as every single morning had been for the last five months after he had met Simone at that party at Laurent's up on Montmartre. Ever since they hooked up the following week, he'd pretty much given up sleep altogether. He didn't need it. Being with her was like being connected to an enormous battery. She was the kind of girl people could fight a world war over. And he almost wished he could move with her to a deserted island that no one ever visited, just so he could be sure no one else would discover how amazingly perfect she was.

But now it was too late.

Some idiot guy named Noël had shown up out of nowhere and put better ideas in her head. Well, different ideas anyway.

And in April, damn it, of all months. In April, in Paris! Could it be any more tragic? If someone decided to hand out a prize for being the biggest failure, he was guaranteed to win just by showing up.

He looked at his watch. The train should have been here ages ago.

Resigned, he left the station and decided to walk home. He headed toward the Eiffel Tower first. It was starting to get dark, and the tourists were cramming themselves into its elevators like sardines for the ride to the top. One time he and Simone had done that, too. It had been a little cheesy, obviously. No Parisian with any self-respect would go up to the top of that tourist trap. But you couldn't ignore the fact that there was something romantic about it, and Simone had loved it.

It had been a few weeks before Christmas. He'd waited for her in the bitter cold by the north foot of the tower. She'd been half an hour late, and his hands were almost blue when she finally showed up. Luckily she'd let him warm them up in her sweater while they rode the elevator to the top. Antoine had waited until the other tourists finished looking at the view and disappeared back down to pull a bottle of wine out of his inside coat pocket. They'd shared the ice-cold bottle of red and then she'd told him she loved him. But then that must have been in November.

Five months earlier.

Relationships should really come with expiration dates stamped on them so at least people would have a chance to get out before the whole thing turned totally rancid.

He kept going along rue de Rivoli. Most of the shops were closed for the night, and aside from the incessant, loud traffic, the long street was pretty much devoid of people. He thought about what she was doing right now. It had only been an hour since he was sitting on her bed in her apartment on the beautiful avenue de Suffren, but that was all in the past.

Was *he* there yet?

Was Noël sitting in her room? Had Noël just walked in and replaced him?

Was she happy, or was she still thinking about him? Not that knowing would do him any good. Part of him hoped she was sobbing and miserable, that she was regretting how she'd acted, that she would be run over by a train on her way to school tomorrow. Part of him hoped she would fall down onto the tracks and that the train wheel would slice her skull in half, that her guts would ooze out her mouth and her blood would spray up onto the terrified commuters. And then there was the other part of him, the part that still loved her with all his might. The part that wanted her to have the best life possible, whether with him or with someone who made her happier than he could.

Antoine painstakingly ran through the last several months to understand why she'd broken up with him. Was it something he did? Something he said? Or something he didn't do or didn't say? He desperately racked his brain for the answer, an obvious, clear solution that would make him turn around and go back, ring her doorbell and say, *Yes, I'm sorry for what I did.*

But sometimes it's already too late before you open your mouth.

The boat had simply sailed on their relationship. And it hadn't just left port. The whole pier had been torn down, the water drained, and the whole place converted into the world's loneliest parking lot.

Suddenly Antoine wished he could just disappear for good and never see Simone or this city or this world again.

"Pardon me. Do you have a light?"

Antoine stopped. A man in his forties in a suit was standing on the sidewalk in front of him, blocking his way. He was fumbling with a pack of cigarettes.

"Just a sec." Antoine searched his jacket pockets and found a lighter. He passed it to the man, who lit it.

"You wouldn't happen to have a cigarette, too?"

"Sure," Antoine replied, perplexed that the man didn't just take one out of his own pack.

"Thanks," he said.

"No problem."

The man nodded at an enormous billboard over the shop across the street.

"Don't forget about the deadline, eh?" he said, and started walking away. Antoine didn't have a chance to respond before the man disappeared down the street.

Antoine glanced at the billboard. It was black, with an enormous moon half hidden in shadows:

DO YOU WANT TO GO TO THE MOON?

He'd heard about the mission and that NASA was going to take three teenagers on a trip to the moon; a bunch of people at school were talking about it. But he hadn't given it a second thought.

And it was right about then that it hit him: *What were you just wishing a second ago? You wanted to get out of here. Well... you can't get farther away than that.*

He'd already decided. He would sign up. As soon as he got home. Damn it, he would go to the moon, as far away as he could possibly go.

Then she could sit there in her room holding hands with Noël until she got arthritis, for all he cared.

When he finally reached home, he didn't say anything to his parents, pretended like nothing was up, and forced a smile from deep down in his gut when they asked how Simone was.

"I was just thinking about Simone," his mother said. "Maybe you'd like to invite her over to dinner soon? Maybe this Sunday? We haven't seen her for ages, and she's such a great girl. Don't you think so, Arnaud? Arnaud?"

"Huh? What is it?" he heard his father yell from the living room, his newspaper rustling.

"I was just saying we think Simone is such a great girl, isn't she?"

"Yes, yes," his father's voice said from the living room after a brief pause. "A really sweet girl. You have to take care of that one, Antoine. You hear me?"

Antoine felt his heart rising into his throat and realized he might throw it up at any moment, bloody and useless.

"Yeah," he forced himself to say. "Yeah, I'll ask her."

Then he went into his room. He powered up his Mac and entered the address: www.nasamoonreturn.com.

With a few clicks of his mouse, he found tons of pictures and film clips from the old moon landings in the sixties and seventies, interviews, and information about the contest. Applicants had to be between fourteen and eighteen to enter, but of course he already knew that. He also knew he probably would have no problem at all passing the medical and psychological examinations. After all, he was in good physical condition, and no one in his family had ever been mentally ill or anything like that. His parents and relatives *were* kind of strange, true, but that wasn't the same as saying he was likely to suddenly snap and start hunting down his crewmates with an ax.

NASA's rigorous three-month training program was another thing altogether. Would he have the stamina to go through with it? From what he understood, it included daily running sessions, logic tests, stress tests, and a number of flights in the Vomit Comet, an aircraft that quickly climbed to thirty thousand feet, only to point its nose straight down and dive for the deck, giving passengers a chance to experience weightlessness for twenty-five seconds at a time. Or nausea for two hours straight, if they were really unlucky. Then there were the high-altitude flight chambers used to familiarize trainees with the symptoms of oxygen deprivation, or hypoxia, as it was called. And finally they would have to spend a substantial amount of time in the Neutral Buoyancy Laboratory at Johnson Space Center, where a 202-by-102-foot pool, complete with a mockup of the spacecraft and landing module, would train them to enter and exit the modules at a depth of forty feet, simulating zero gravity. This was definitely no joke. Not to mention the hundreds, if not thousands, of pages of theory they would have to read and learn before they left the ground.

But first he had to apply, of course. And then just wait. The three winners would be notified in mid-July, he read. They would have to be absent from school from April until June of the following year for the training and final mission.

The winners would be flown first to New York to appear on *The Late Show* and then to the Johnson Space Center in Houston, Texas, where they would undergo the training before the launch from Kennedy Space Center in Florida in mid-July. He'd have to postpone a few finals, but that shouldn't be any problem. Besides, it's not like he could have a better excuse.

According to the information, the three winners would spend 172 hours on the moon plus the trip from Earth and back, which would take just over a week. They would stay at the DARLAH 2 moon base (weird, he'd never heard anything about a base being built on the moon, and he knew a few things about space travel), and from there they would perform a number of experiments on the surface. Top-notch astronauts with years of experience would be with them at all times and ensure their safety every step of the way. And then there would be media coverage, of course. The contest winners would have to be prepared to do interviews on TV, on radio, and online before, during, and after their trip. They would have to answer questions online, write blogs, and go on an international press junket afterward.

Antoine looked at the list of cities they'd have to go to: New York, L.A., Chicago, Boston, Washington, D.C., London, Paris, Berlin, Stockholm, Tokyo, Hong Kong, Sydney, and so on.

Well, it's not like that would be so bad, Antoine thought, smiling faintly at the notion that he would get to see the whole world in addition to space.

Sitting there in front of his computer reading the information, it was like Simone had been blown out of his consciousness. His only thought now was that he had to win. His name had to be selected.

He quickly Googled the statistics. It turned out that only about 8.5 percent of Earth's population was between fourteen and eighteen. If it was true that there were about seven billion people on Earth, that would make about six hundred million teenagers out there. And if you then discounted the teens from various parts of the world who didn't have access to the Internet—or any other chances to enter the contest—the number of actual contestants might be as small as three hundred million.

So that was only three hundred million other people he had to beat.

The odds definitely weren't in his favor. Three hundred million to one. There was pretty much a bigger chance of just about anything else happening in his life. Like Simone calling him in the next fifteen seconds.

A quick search did not lift his spirits any.

According to one page he found, it turned out that:

The odds of scoring 300 points in bowling was 11,500 to 1.

The odds of getting a hole in one in golf: 5,000 to 1.

The odds of being canonized and thus famous for all eternity: 20,000,000 to 1.

The odds of becoming an astronaut: 13,200,000 to 1.

The odds of being attacked by a great white shark: 11,500,000 to 1.

The odds of being killed in a plane crash: 354,319 to 1.

The odds of being killed by parts falling from a plane: 10,000,000 to 1.

The odds of winning an Oscar: 11,500 to 1.

The odds of becoming president: 10,000,000 to 1.

The odds of hooking up with a supermodel: 88,000 to 1.

The odds of winning an Olympic gold medal: 662,000 to 1.

The odds of seriously injuring yourself shaving: 685,000 to 1.

The odds of being killed by a meteor landing specifically on YOUR house: 182,128,880,000,000 to 1.

That last one was basically the only one that was less likely than his getting to go to the moon.

Antoine sat there looking at the numbers for a minute. Then he leaned over his keyboard and entered his name, birth date, phone number, and address.

He thought about it one last time.

Then he hit *send.*

NADOLSKI

The experienced astronaut eyed the lunar lander with a certain skepticism. Commander Lloyd Nadolski was forty-two. He'd been with NASA for almost fifteen years and was one of the few astronauts who had completed three missions in space. Now he was in one of the hangars at Kennedy Space Center, NASA's launch center located on Merritt Island on the coast of Florida. And he was not impressed with what he was seeing.

"Well, what do you think?"

He turned to see Ralph Pierce approaching him. Pierce was the lead engineer responsible for constructing the lander *Demeter*. NASA had been working on it for years and had not finished the final version until less than a week ago. Nadolski peered at the vessel again.

"Can it fly?" he asked, not directing his question to anyone.

"It flies, Commander. I can promise you that. We tested it again last Friday. All systems are working perfectly."

Nadolski nodded without looking at Pierce and walked around the lander. It had been designed to look like the vehicles that were used in the 1969 moon landing and the missions of the early seventies. Would it withstand the stresses? Flying was one thing; being able to rely on it 100 percent in space was another. There was no room for errors up there.

As far as Nadolski knew, the decision to use the almost fifty-year-old design, as opposed to building something newer and better, had come from the top, maybe from the president himself. At least the marketing department was satisfied. The classic design looked familiar to a lot of people and would unquestionably elicit memories among the oldest audience members.

Ultimately that's what it came down to: the audience. And money. NASA's popularity had been sinking steadily in recent decades following a couple of serious accidents and some missions that were not exactly audience-friendly. The space agency had sent astronauts up to repair satellites, solar arrays, and particle detectors. There had been no indications that a manned mission to Mars was going to happen anytime soon. NASA's websites were getting as little traffic as a mothballed museum.

Nadolski scratched his head. It was hard to find sense in all this. The questions started nagging at him again, as they had periodically since he'd heard about these teenagers he was supposed to bring on the mission. Who knew how they were going to behave? What if they panicked? Messed around with equipment on board without anyone realizing what they'd done? Space was no place for children.

He shook off the thought. He'd been working at NASA long enough to know that its system of checks and balances was absolutely top-notch. And this time they had even less room for error. The worst-case scenario was that this mission would be the death knell for the whole organization.

"Well," Nadolski said after a long silence, "as long as it goes without a hitch..." He let this statement hang in the air before adding, "If it doesn't, I can promise you I'll come back more pissed off than you've ever seen me. Heads will roll."

Engineer Pierce forced a smile. "Don't give it another thought. I guarantee it'll do what it has to do." He turned and left the hangar while Nadolski stood there, giving the lander one last look. *You can only guarantee that*, he thought, *because we both know if it doesn't work, you'll never see me back here on Earth again.*

Nadolski cautiously kicked one of the wheel struts up by the chassis. It was a kick with almost no force, more like a nudge, but it was still enough that a little piece of the lander came loose.

Damn it....

He bent over, picked up the small, rectangular disk, and decided he'd give it to the evening shift before he went home.

PAPER

Mia was at the bus stop waiting for a bus that was already ten minutes late. Summer had already arrived, and it should have been a warm, sunny afternoon, the kind of day where you hung out on the beach with your friends until Norway's sub-arctic sun finally set around midnight and everyone stole home. Instead it was pouring rain, and her black hair was plastered annoyingly to her face. Mia was shivering in her thin jacket and mindlessly drumming a rhythm with her leg as she sat on the bench.

Her band Rogue Squadron had been around for almost two years now — one year and eight months, to be precise — but it still hadn't gotten anywhere. Sure, the band members were young; there weren't many people their age who'd been doing it as long as they had, but still. Mia must have written forty songs in that time, coming up with most of the chords and riffs. And all the lyrics. They had recorded a demo months earlier, but they had never sent it anywhere. Their Facebook pages were receiving a moderate number of hits at best. Their only gig had been one concert the previous year at Metropolis, which hosts a lot of underground music performances as part of Fantastic Underground 10. Things weren't going that well for Rogue Squadron. Something had to be done.

Mia spotted the bus winding its way through traffic. She stepped out onto the sidewalk and held out her hand to signal to the driver that she wanted to get on. She'd always hated having to do that—it looked totally ridiculous. What was the point? She was standing at the bus stop, wasn't she? But if you didn't hold out your hand and keep it there, stiffly, until the bus pulled to a stop, the bus driver would just drive right by.

Mia waved her arm a few times to be sure the driver had seen her. The bus stopped, and she used her left hand to shake the water out of her hair as she climbed on and set her coins on the tray in front of the driver.

"One youth fare to Madla," she said.

He looked at her, tired and uninterested. "Do you have ID?"

That was bus drivers' favorite sentence. There was money to be made asking questions like that. Maybe he could get one more person to pay the full adult fare. Never before in the history of the world was there a time when kids under sixteen had to lug around their IDs.

"Do you have a license to drive this bus?" Mia replied.

"Of course."

"Can I see it?" Mia asked.

"No. You're the one who needs to show ID if you want the youth fare. That's just the way it is, little lady."

Mia realized she was almost enjoying this. A little spat with the driver, delaying the bus and making all the passengers glare at her a little, suited her just fine right now. The driver finally gave up, took her coins, and returned her change.

"Take a seat," he mumbled.

"Drive safely," she replied, and winked before plodding down the center aisle and finding a seat in the very back of the bus.

Leonora, Silje, and Kari were waiting outside the rehearsal space when Mia walked up. They too were wet from the rain.

"Thought you'd drowned," Kari said irritably when Mia reached them.

"The bus was late. And there was a little argument about my fare."

"I don't know why you can't just bring your school ID or something," Leonora said.

"Well, what would be the fun of that?" Mia laughed, unlocking the door.

Their rehearsal space was in a warehouse in Kvernevik, and they shared it with two other bands that were almost never there. Which meant that Mia and Rogue Squadron had nearly unlimited access to it, and sometimes they spent whole weekends out there, playing until late at night and sleeping on mattresses on the floor. They didn't care that it was the most run-down rehearsal space in all of Stavanger, its walls imbued with old sweat and desperation from impossible solos and hopeless chords.

The room was in a subbasement below the actual basement

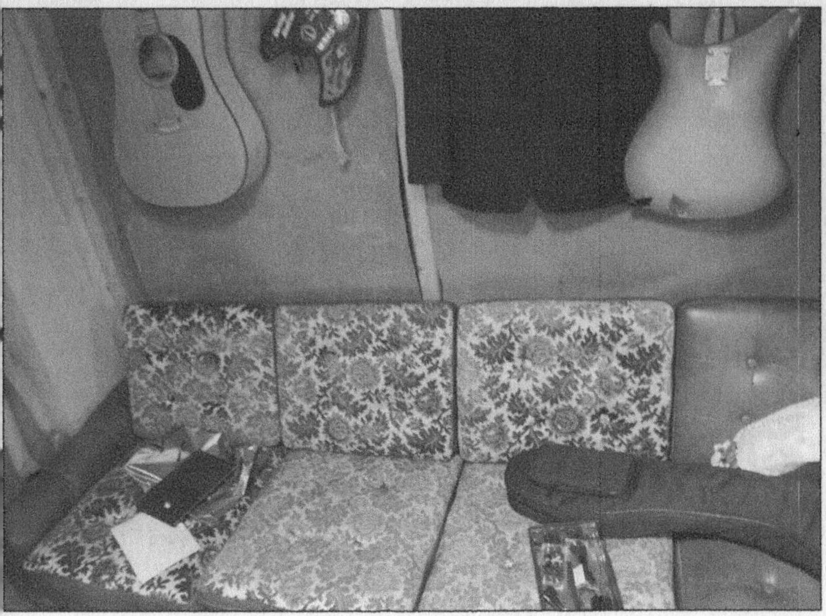

and didn't have any windows. Daylight was simulated by a string of overhead light fixtures and a floor lamp or two. It didn't help that Leonora chain-smoked, occasionally making it hard for the various band members to see one another through the haze. Plus, the floor was covered with empty bottles, wires, broken drumsticks, and leftover food.

They didn't usually talk much as they plugged in their guitars, tuned the drums, turned on the amps, and adjusted the settings. Mia finished tuning her guitar, moved over in front of her various effect pedals, and caught Leonora's eyes behind the drums. She gave the drummer a quick nod and then heard "*one, two, three, four,*" and she dropped her hand to the strings and started into the song "II."

It was one of their fastest songs and should have been great for a warm-up. Mia had written it on one of the first days in January, and it was about those two skyscrapers in New York that had been hit by airplanes in a terrorist attack.

Before the band even hit the last note of the song, Leonora quit playing without warning. The guitars kept going for a couple beats, as if they had to slow down before they could stop. Then there was total silence in the room.

It hadn't sounded good. Far from it. It wasn't that they'd played anything wrong. It just wasn't working. It felt like an enormous elephant had waltzed into their rehearsal space and sat down on them. The four girls avoided making eye contact.

"I just don't think we're getting anywhere," Mia finally said. "I don't know. In a way it's like... like we've been playing the same songs so long we're starting to get worse."

"What do you mean?" Leonora asked.

"I mean we've got to do something more than just sit here going over and over the same stuff. What if we gave a concert soon? Tried going into the studio? Something. I mean, what do we actually want to get out of this? Sometimes I wonder if we're just playing together because we're friends, and we could've just as easily been doing something different together instead."

"Like what?" Silje asked.

"I don't know. It's just that... I want this. This band is the best thing that's happened to me. *You guys* are. Sometimes I think this is the only thing I have that's worth anything. That at least I can think, *Okay, no matter what, I'm in a band*. But lately, well, it's like we're not getting anywhere."

Kari seemed grumpy and flopped back limply onto the sofa. "What are you really trying to say, Mia? That we need to practice more? I mean, we're already here every other day!"

"It's not about that," Mia protested. "But we need to decide what we want."

"All right, what do you want, then?" Silje asked, making every effort not to sound pissed off, so she wouldn't wreck the mood so early in the session. "If you could have whatever you wanted, what would you wish for?"

Mia thought about it. For a long time. But that was mostly for appearances' sake. Because she'd already figured this out a long time ago. She thought about this every night when she sat in her room writing songs. She thought about it before she fell asleep, and she pictured how it could be, all of it. Album covers, tours, airports. Hotel rooms.

"I would wish that we could live off Rogue Squadron," she replied. "That we would release our music and tour four months a year, at least. That we all lived together in a big apartment that was also our studio, an apartment in downtown Oslo. That we were a band that meant something to people."

The other three girls nodded tentatively at what she said.

"Okay, good," began Silje, who had always been the most realistic of all of them. "Then . . ." Silje stopped abruptly. Someone was pounding on the door. They all heard the sound of hands hitting the metal door one floor above them.

"Who's *that*?" Mia asked, looking at Kari.

"How should I know," she replied. "I can't see through concrete."

Leonora went out into the hall and let someone in. Mia heard a voice that she immediately recognized.

Mom, she thought. *What in the world is she doing here?*

For a second she was scared that something might have happened to her little brother, Sander. He was only nine and not quite like other kids, but she really loved the weird little guy who always had to wear a helmet when he was outside and who was always hoping winter would come so he could pull a knit hat over his helmet to hide it from view. Had something happened to him? Had someone died?

She didn't have time to think anything else before her mother hurried into the room and flung her arms around Mia's neck. "Congratulations! Oh, to *think*, my own *daughter*!" She practically squealed as Mia struggled for air in her embrace.

"What are you doing here?" Mia asked harshly when she realized that no one was dead. "What do you want?"

But her mother didn't hear the disparaging tone. She only heard her own excitement.

"Mia, you won! You *won*!"

"What did I win? What are you talking about?"

"You're going to the moon, Mia!"

As if someone were offering her an armed atomic bomb, Mia instinctively took a step back. Her mother was standing in front of her, holding an envelope in her hand. Mia could plainly see NASA's logo on the white paper.

At that moment she hated her mother.

Hated her for coming here and interrupting them. Hated her for pushing her way into the rehearsal room and embarrassing her and making her look like a little kid. Hated her for never listening. Right then Mia hated her mother simply for being her mother.

"Did you open my mail?" was all Mia could get out. The other three girls stood there silently.

Her mother was confused. That wasn't the response she'd been expecting.

"No, well, we, uh...your father and I..." her mother began, straining to find the right words, the way she always did when her daughter was mad at her. "Well, we saw that it was, well, uh, you know, that it said NASA on... on the envelope, and then... we wanted to make sure it was true before we drove all the way out here. I'm sure you understand that? Right?"

"Dad's here, too?"

"No, he's at home with Sander."

"Give me the letter," Mia said tersely.

"Oh, Mia, honey, this is a wonderful, wonderful opportunity. It's the experience of a lifetime," her mother said, handing over the envelope.

Mia held it in her trembling hands for a few seconds before she crumpled it and flung it at the wall.

"What part don't you get, Mom? Huh? What is so unbelievably hard for you to understand? I said I didn't want to go, didn't I? I said that a million times! What the hell is there for me to do on the moon?"

"Mia, honey..."

"You're interrupting our rehearsal, Mom. You have to go."

Mia's mother tried to hide that she was on the verge of tears. "We'll talk about it later, Mia. Right? Have a good practice session." She walked toward the door, then paused, her eyes on the floor. "You guys ought to clean this place. It's atrocious."

Then she left.

Mia and the others waited until they heard the sound of a car driving away.

"Shit. That is without a doubt the craziest thing I've ever heard," Silje exclaimed, staring at Mia.

"So the Hair *was* right when she included your name as one of the people who'd signed up for the moon contest?" Leonora asked, surprised, fumbling around in her pack of cigarettes for a smoke. "Why didn't you say anything?"

Silje just kept staring at her friend, totally dumbstruck. "Shit! You've got to be kidding me! You *won*?" she said in disbelief. "Do you get how many people signed up for that? There must've been over a billion."

Mia felt faint. They hadn't discussed the moon or the lottery since that day in German class. And now? Now she had been selected out of millions of entrants to go to the moon, even though she didn't want to, and all her friends were going to think she'd lied to them.

"It's not totally true," she said, trying to figure out what to say next. "My parents did it, you know? They signed me up for that stupid contest, even though I told them I wasn't interested."

"Is that true?" Leonora didn't quite know what to say.

"If so, that's lame," Silje commented. "I mean, if you clearly said you didn't want to go, you know."

"I did! A bunch of times."

"Talk about being all up in your business," Leonora said, taking a seat on the sofa and opening a bottle of water. "I mean, they got you a trip to the moon that you don't want. But still, wow! What are you going to do?"

Mia sighed heavily. "I don't know," she replied. "I really don't know."

Kari hadn't said anything since Mia's mother had knocked. "But, Mia?" she said.

"Yeah?"

"Why don't you want to go?"

Mia hadn't expected that question. She'd assumed that none of them would have any interest in the whole thing. "Do you get how far away it is? How much time I'd need to spend training? Or, I mean, the fact that it's not exactly risk-free. It's not like stopping by 7-Eleven. Or what about the fact that I don't give a shit about space? We live here, in Stavanger. Norway. Europe. What would I do up there? Look at rocks with two other nerds and wave at the camera for a week? That's not exactly what I was planning on spending my next year on."

Kari eyed her up and down, shaking her head. "Are you a total idiot, or what?" she asked slowly.

"What do you mean by that?" Mia didn't like the way Kari was talking to her. "I don't know what your plans are, but mine are all set," Mia explained. "In 2019, I'm going to be onstage, playing concerts. Maybe recording an album. At least a demo. I'm not going to throw away my time posing for NASA ads. They can just pick someone else."

Kari kept giving her that disapproving look.

"I signed up," Leonora admitted weakly. She put out her cigarette in the pyramid of butts on the low coffee table in front of her and lit a new one without a thought.

Mia turned and looked at her friend in surprise.

"Me, too," Silje added.

"And me," Kari said.

"But why?" was all Mia could manage to say.

"Why not?" Silje responded. "*Everyone* entered that contest. Don't you get how big this is?"

Mia let her eyes wander from Silje to Kari to Leonora. "But when the Hair read those names... there weren't that many people at our school that had entered. And she didn't say any of your names."

Leonora said, "I'm the only one who's in the Hair's German class with you. I entered when I got home from school that day. I mean, you'd already signed up, so I thought it would be cool. Maybe a lot of other people at school thought that and signed up later, after the Hair talked about it."

Mia couldn't make any sense of it. Did the whole band

have moon fever? She plopped down onto the sofa next to Leonora.

Kari sat up on the other side of her. "Anyway, it doesn't matter now. Mia won. Mia's *going to the moon*!"

"The hell I am! I'm not going anywhere!" she practically yelled.

The four girls sat silently on the sofas, staring at the walls, three of them wishing their names had been picked, the fourth feeling like she'd just been given some kind of prison sentence.

"I think it's lame if you don't go," Silje finally said, breaking the oppressive silence.

"What are you talking about? What are you, my mother or something?"

Kari crossed her arms. "We just think you should look at the big picture, Mia."

"We? *We?* Did you guys discuss this in advance? What kind of big picture am I supposed to be seeing?"

"Listen," Kari said. "You think Rogue Squadron is in a rut, right? You want — what was it you said? — you want to be able to live off the band, right? You want us to tour, record albums, hang out in hotels in Tokyo and L.A., right?"

"So?" Mia mumbled.

"So? Don't you get it? This is the opportunity of a lifetime, Mia! It's not going to get any better than this. Don't you get how famous you'll be? You'll be able to do whatever the hell you want after this. *Whatever. You. Want.* Want a record contract? *No problem.* Tour? *When do you want to start?* Quit school and live off the band? *Absolutely.* You'll be the first person under twenty who's been on the moon. You'll do hundreds of interviews, TV shows, and I don't know what else. Every single one of them will be a chance to promote the band. We're guaranteed to get to perform on David Letterman!"

"I thought he was retiring," Mia said drily.

"Screw that. He's been saying that for years now. But it never happens, does it? The guy is going to keep doing it until they have to drag his double-breasted suit out of the studio."

They laughed at that. A nice, quick laugh that dissolved some of the tension in the room.

"'We're pleased to have a great new band for you tonight,'" Kari said, doing her best David Letterman impersonation. "'A great band, and the singer—well, you all know her—just returned from the moon. From the Land of the Midnight Sun, please welcome Norwegian teenage astronaut Mia Nomeland and her amazing band, Rogue Squadron!'"

Kari, Leonora, and Silje clapped, and Mia had to smile a little as she played along for a minute.

"Think about it, Mia," Silje said. "If you go to the moon, you'll come back with, what, say ten great new songs you wrote up there? Maybe even a hidden track that you recorded on the moon. If that doesn't say recording contract, nothing does."

"Do you think they'll let her bring her guitar up there?" Leonora asked, laughing.

"Of course," Silje said. "But that's not the point. The point is she doesn't realize how good this will be for us."

"Well, it's not like we're Pink Floyd," Mia said, still not totally convinced. "Are we supposed to be some kind of space band now?"

Kari rolled her eyes and said, "No, of course not. We can be whatever we want. We can get whatever we want out of this opportunity. There's only one thing that has to happen."

"I have to go."

"Exactly."

"You're going to regret it for the rest of your life if you don't go, Mia," Silje said. "You're going to be working at the drive-through window at a McDonald's, wearing that stupid hat and ridiculous uniform, with a vacant look in your eyes and deep-fat fryer grease all over yourself, thinking about the opportunity you said no to."

"I say we put it to a vote," Kari said.

"Hey! Wait a minute!" Mia protested.

Kari held her hand up in the air. "Silje?"

Silje's hand went up.

"Leonora?"

She lit another cigarette and raised her hand.

"It looks like the majority has decided, Mia. You're going to be spending next summer in space."

A slow, stubborn smile was growing on Mia's face, and there was nothing she could do to stop it. They had a compelling argument, didn't they? That it could make all the difference for the band?

It's just a few weeks. How bad can it be?

She stood up, walked over to the wall, and picked up the crumpled NASA envelope.

She looked at the other band members.

"Okay," she said. "I'll go."

The rest of practice was some of the most beautiful music-making Mia had experienced.

Her decision to go had elicited a cheer unlike any she'd heard before. They played better than they had in ages, and they even wrote two new songs, "Which Way L.A." and "Super Fast Song." They planned two albums and dreamed their way around the world four times on endless tours in enormous tour buses.

They also played "II" again, and this time it was right on the mark. Leonora was pounding away on the last refrain when Mia signaled that they should take it one more time from the top, and this time she gave it everything she had. When they reached the end of the refrain, she just kept going, playing the same riff over and over again, faster than they'd ever practiced. Mia screamed into the microphone and tore at the strings harder than ever. One of her strings broke, but she pretended not to notice, kept going and going until there was only a wall of noise left, and she turned to the others and gave them the sign. They all counted to four in their heads and stopped at the same time. To the second.

And then it was over.

The room got quiet. It was as if the sound had sunk to the floor.

Without a word, they all set down their instruments and moved over to the sofas. Silje was the first to say anything. "Jesus, what was that?"

Mia looked at her fingers. The tip of her index finger was bleeding a little. "What do you mean?"

"That was totally awesome, if you ask me," Kari said. "We should do more of that. Like on 'Vintage Spandex.' That would work there, don't you think? Just hold on to it even more at the end."

"You guys, I think this is actually the start of something big," Silje said.

* * *

They were giddy and slightly dazed when they finally left the rehearsal space at quarter to midnight to catch the last bus home. They kept singing on the bus, and the driver flashed them nasty looks in the rearview mirror.

Mia was the last of the band members to get off the bus. She needed a walk right now, despite the heavy rain. A couple of cars passed her, the drivers paying no notice to her trudging through the empty streets, tugging the collar of her thin jacket up to cover the back of her neck. A girl walking through the rain in heavy paratrooper boots, even though it was the middle of summer. A fifteen-year-old girl with big headphones, nodding her head to the beat of the music she was listening to. And if the drivers had looked carefully, for the brief instant the headlights illuminated her face, they would have been able to see that this girl was smiling.

Because she had made up her mind now.

She was going. And she would make the best of it. Take the opportunities that came her way.

This is the beginning, she thought as she followed the sidewalk homeward and stepped into her front yard. *This is where the whole thing finally begins.*

MAIL

Midori watched the mailman, Takumi Watanabe, as he stood in front of the mailboxes in the lobby. He was holding the envelope in front of him with both hands. His black Lab named Bob stood next to him.

"Well, Midori-chan, it looks like you really *are* the luckiest girl I've ever met."

Midori didn't know if she dared take the envelope or not.

"I think you're the luckiest person I've ever met," Takumi repeated. He usually did that, repeated what he had just said. As if he didn't have that much to say, so he said everything twice to sort of fill the time.

Midori had never been particularly lucky. Not that she had necessarily been unlucky, either. One time she had even won a TV contest. After calling in and answering four way-too-easy questions from the idiotic host, she was told that she was the day's winner. But she had misunderstood the prize. It wasn't a Mac laptop but a special edition of the manga comic *Akira* that included all six books in a single two-thousand-page collector's volume. She sold it to a guy in her class that same week and spent the money at the Shibuya 109 mall instead.

"I think you're the luckiest person I've ever met," Takumi repeated for the third time. He obviously had more trouble than most people coming up with something to talk about.

Finally Midori stretched out her hands and took the letter. The envelope was white and made of very nice paper. Her name was written in beautiful (and correct) Japanese characters. And in the upper left she saw the NASA logo. The letter was post-marked "Houston, Texas, United States of America."

"Well?" Takumi prompted impatiently.

"I don't really know," Midori replied, weighing the envelope in her hand.

"You have to open it."

"I do?"

"Yes. The mailman's job is to deliver the mail. But I haven't seen the mail yet. Just an envelope. That's not the same."

"No, I suppose not." She hesitated a few more seconds. It suddenly occurred to her how momentous this was.

"Midori-chan? Show us the mail, please?"

The dog feverishly wagged his tail, just as impatient as his owner.

Midori opened the envelope and pulled out the typed letter.

Dear Midori Yoshida,

It is our great honor to inform you that you have been selected from among millions of teenagers to participate as a crewmember on the spaceship *Ceres*'s expedition to the moon in July 2019. The journey will take you and two other young people on a historic trip to the Sea of Tranquility on the near side of the moon, where the first astronauts to walk on the moon—Neil Armstrong and Edwin "Buzz" Aldrin—landed in 1969. The expedition will take fifteen days, with a seven-day stay at moon base DARLAH. Prior to that, NASA would like to invite you and your immediate family to the Johnson Space Center in Houston, Texas, for a three-month-long training program. All expenses for this program will of course be paid.

We ask that you take the next few days to carefully consider whether this is a trip you would like to be a part of. It will doubtless change your life forever. We ask that you discuss this thoroughly with your parents, as their full consent will be required.

A NASA representative will contact you next week to obtain your response to this invitation. You and your parent(s) or guardian(s) must carefully read and sign the attached confidentiality agreement prior to this call, as this news must remain strictly in confidence before public announcement.

We congratulate you again on winning.

Respectfully yours,

Dr. Paul Lewis
NASA Administrator

"Well?" Takumi said again, a little more cautiously this time. She'd almost forgotten he was there. She raised her eyes and they looked at each other. Bob cocked his head to the side.

"I... won," her mouth said, and she felt herself starting to wobble.

Seconds later, Takumi Watanabe was picking her up and swinging her around as he laughed and cheered, "You're going to the moon! You're going to the moon!"

Bob barked, confused at the sudden commotion. A couple of women walking by stopped for a second and watched the grown man swinging the girl around and laughing giddily.

"No more mail for you, Midori-chan," he almost sang. "That's outside of my delivery zone! Ha, the *moon*! Isn't this unbelievable?"

Midori couldn't get a word out. Maybe that was just as well. She might have disappointed him anyway, because the truth was that Midori wasn't thinking about the moon at all as she stood there in the mailman's embrace. She wasn't thinking about her unique opportunity or staying in the Sea of Tranquility. All she could think about was the place she would go before and after this absurd trip. Two words kept running through her head.

New York. New York.

She knew exactly what this meant.

You just got your ticket out of here, Midori.

Midori didn't mention the letter to her parents until dinnertime later that night. They were so excited, they invited the neighbors in for a glass of sake to share the news; and before Midori knew it, the apartment was full of well-wishers, all sharing words of congratulations, amazement, and delight. Midori was happy, too, almost jubilant. She knew that this meant the end of her life as she knew it. It was a colossal choice for a fifteen-year-old to make, but she'd made it as soon as she read the letter, and she was determined not to change her mind. She wasn't coming back to Japan.

She still hadn't quite figured out how she was going to take care of the practical details, since she would only be sixteen when she came back to Earth. She and the other two teenagers would wind up in New York after the press tour around the world, and then she could duck out of the spotlight for good. Of course, that would mean she'd have to hide from the authorities for a few years until she was old enough to go to college.... No, that was a terrible plan, she had to admit. Besides, she didn't want to leave her parents forever. They could be complete imbeciles sometimes—well, a lot of the time—but still. Disappearing from them altogether was too much.

But there was another option. And that was to exploit Daddy Tetsuo's weakness for the United States. He'd never been there, but he was always talking about how much he wanted to go. The Grand Canyon—that's what he wanted to see most. God knows why. As far as Midori could tell, the Grand Canyon was just a big valley with some mountains, and there were plenty of those in Japan, too. But he brought it up all the time, and always with a certain reverence in his voice. *Well*, Midori thought, *you can have your Grand Canyon. As much of it as you want.*

She wouldn't say anything to her parents about wanting to move away from Yokohama in particular or Japan in general until they were well into their post-moon world tour. Then she'd suggest that they go see this Grand Canyon place. And then, as they stood there looking at the (probably not all *that* majestic) view, she could let the words drop: *What if we just moved here?*

And maybe, just maybe, they would say yes. It was a possibility anyway, and for now she'd have to believe it could work. Her life simply depended on it, she thought. If not, the whole trip to the moon would be a complete waste.

The dawn light was already starting to stream in through her thin curtains when she finally fell asleep at five thirty in the morning. She would have preferred to keep working on her plan, but her eyes wouldn't stay open, and she wasn't thinking clearly anymore. She quickly disappeared down the long corridor of sleep, and at the other end she found herself on the roof of a loft in Brooklyn, with a cup of coffee in her hands and a view of the Manhattan skyline. She opened the skylight and called down to her friends who were sitting in the large loft apartment below, surrounded by the paintings and clothes they'd been working on. "We'll be right up," they yelled to her, and Midori left the skylight open, sat down with her back against a chimney, and squinted at the cool, infinitely beautiful September sun.

The letter was true to its word. A Japanese-speaking NASA representative called Midori three days later and popped the question:

"Do you wish to say yes and be part of this mission?"

Midori didn't hesitate before answering, "Yes."

"And have you discussed the matter with your parents?"

She was taken aback for a second at how formal and business-like the representative sounded.

"Um, yes," Midori replied. "Of course."

"Good. I'll need to speak to them now after we're through talking. With their consent, one of our representatives will come to Yokohama next week to meet with you and your family and discuss the details."

She felt dazed as she handed the phone to her father, who immediately began confirming arrangements with NASA.

No going back now, she thought.

Sure enough, a week later a deep-voiced American man wearing a suit showed up at the door of their fifth-floor apartment a few minutes after seven p.m. Midori's parents had probably been expecting the representative to give them more thorough information about what their daughter could expect, but it was obvious that the purpose of his visit was totally different.

The man brushed aside their questions with a few curt, vague answers before opening his briefcase and taking out reams of paperwork. Midori and her parents had to sign countless documents, insurance forms, waivers for this and that, release of liability forms in the event of this or that, and so on. It would have been completely impossible to read them all; all they could do was sign where the man pointed with his well-manicured finger, over and over and over again until he seemed satisfied, smiled, and bowed deeply before thanking them and leaving, just as quietly and emotionlessly as he had arrived.

Midori and her parents just sat there on the floor around the coffee table, slightly confused by everything they had experienced in the last hour. But the man hadn't left a business card or a phone number. For all they knew, he was already on his way back to the airport, headed for the next country and the next teenage astronaut-to-be.

That feeling lasted for the next several months, as if everything was going too fast. When the calendar finally said March, it felt like only a few days had passed. Suddenly it seemed to Midori that she didn't have enough time for everything. She turned in her application to postpone her finals at school, which was granted. She said a hasty farewell to her friends in downtown Tokyo. And now that she was on her way to becoming a celebrity, she had to make several rounds of visits to her relatives in Yokohama, along with the neighbors and her dad's colleagues, before everyone seemed satisfied.

Takumi Watanabe was the last person Midori said good-bye to, the very morning she and her parents left. Like many other neighbors and relatives, he was waiting outside their building when the Yoshida family was ready to head to the United States. Takumi was standing at the very back of the crowd, so he wouldn't be in anyone's way, and Midori had to push her way through the throng to reach him.

"Well, have a good trip, Midori-san."

It was the first time he'd ever used the grown-up suffix "-san" with her instead of the diminutive "-chan" suffix that people used for kids. She was sure probably no one else noticed it, but to Midori it meant a lot. Like they were really friends now. After all, they had shared the historic moment when she opened the envelope containing the letter. Maybe he knew more about her plans than she realized, because the last thing he said was, "Don't forget your way home. Your mail will be waiting for you here."

Midori didn't respond. Instead she bowed to him and started walking toward the car that was waiting outside the building.

Seconds later it started moving toward Narita International Airport.

ANTOINE

The letter had arrived three days ago, but he already felt like he'd always had it, and he couldn't remember anymore how he had reacted when it arrived and he realized what it was.

You're going to the moon, Antoine.

That's what it said.

Obviously he had been surprised. Happy, too. But there was no getting around the fact that part of him had been expecting it. Because the way he saw it, he needed it more than anyone else.

But he hadn't said anything to his parents yet about the letter. It wasn't because he couldn't trust them. Actually, they were nice people who both worked at the Sorbonne University, where they hung out with young people every day. Antoine was sure that helped them be virtually normal. They rarely embarrassed him, and he could also talk to them about pretty much anything. But telling them about this—that could wait. He wanted to keep it to himself for a while longer, enjoy the feeling of knowing he was the only one in Paris who knew about it.

He wouldn't be able to keep it to himself for very long, though. He had been told by phone that once his parents formally agreed to the plan, a representative from the space organization would be coming to visit them one day the following week. And it was already Monday now. So, it was time.

He found his jacket and decided to go for a walk before showing the envelope to his parents.

He had told his mother he was going over to see Laurent, who lived just behind Montmartre. But he wasn't planning to go there, not even in that direction. He was going to where he'd been the last several afternoons until late in the evening. He was going to see Simone. The initial shock of her leaving him had subsided a good month ago and been replaced by a sense that he would survive, although he would never be truly happy again. That sense of acceptance had come over him very suddenly.

But, strangely, the feeling had somehow vanished over the last week and been replaced by something worse. A relapse. It was as if his emergency anesthesia had worn off, and now there was just excruciating pain again. And the only thing that helped was thinking about how he would soon be as far away from this two-timing city as he could be.

The rain had picked up in strength, and Antoine shivered as he walked the short distance to the Eiffel Tower, paid a couple of euros, and took the stairs up to the first observation level. In a way he was lucky with the weather, because there were hardly any tourists there now. The first level was also the best for his purposes, because here there was very little for the tourists to aim the telescope at, aside from the neighboring buildings.

Which just so happened to be exactly what Antoine was planning to do.

He took out his bag of two-euro coins, slid the first one in, and adjusted the focus. He pointed the telescope at the third floor of one of the apartment buildings on avenue de Suffren.

She was home. Simone was sitting in her room playing her guitar.

If he really concentrated, it almost felt as if he weren't standing half-drenched on the first landing of the Eiffel Tower but in the warmth of her room. He stared at her hands, stroking the strings, and imagined that he knew which song it was. Every once in a while she would set down her guitar and put her head in her hands. Antoine hoped she was doing that because she suddenly realized that she missed him. But it could just as easily been because she was having trouble with one of the chords. Or because she had a headache…

Suddenly everything went black.

For a moment he was gripped by panic, but then he snapped out of it and realized that his time on the telescope had expired. He put in a new coin, and Simone came back into sight in the window.

She was wearing his favorite sweater. The blue one, which, along with her hair, made her face even more magnificent. He had been with her when she bought it on a freezing day in January. They were out walking around after school and she was cold, so they hurried into one of the big department stores. They were actually just planning to warm up a little, but then she felt like trying on some clothes, and he didn't have any other plans. As if he ever had any other plans when he was with her. Being with her *was* the plan. He was the one who'd found the sweater and…

Blackness. Again.

He put in a new coin.

Wait, wait, wait, wait, wait, wait! What was this?

Someone had just walked into Simone's room.

Antoine pressed his eyes even closer to the telescope. A branch from one of the trees lining the street outside her building hid the right side of her room, and he could only see half of the person.

Surely just her mother. Or her father.

No. It wasn't one of her parents. He'd have recognized them by now. And she was putting her arm around his neck….

Was she kissing him?

What the hell?

Everything went black again.

Antoine desperately took his eyes off the scope and stuck his hand into his bag of coins. But he was too eager. It slipped out of his hands, and all the coins rolled across the deck.

Without paying any attention to the guards, who were laughing at him, Antoine got down on his hands and knees and swept the money into a pile. He pushed a coin into the machine and took up his post again. Now he could see the other person clearly. He didn't recognize him, had never seen him before, but he still knew immediately who it was. Noël. *The new guy.*

Asshole! For a brief second Antoine seriously considered

waiting outside her building and murdering the guy when he came out. But it wasn't worth it. He wasn't even worth touching.

Simone sat down to play the guitar again, and the guy wormed his way in behind her. He put his arms around her and laid his head on her shoulders. She kept singing for a while before suddenly stopping, turning her face to his, and kissing him. The guy wrapped his arms more tightly around her and carefully tipped her off the chair and down onto the floor so they disappeared from view.

He stepped back from the telescope and gave it a shove so it whipped around in a circle with remarkable speed, slamming into the railing with a cracking sound. *Enough.*

At home the next morning, Antoine woke up with his parents standing next to his bed, looking worried. For a few long moments, no one said anything.

Then their faces melted into enormous grins.

Antoine stared at them for a second, not understanding, before his mother pulled out the envelope from NASA. They had found it.

"Congratulations, son. *Bon voyage!*"

The next several minutes were a single, long blur of hugs and cheers, plus a few nervous questions about where he had been in recent days.

But those questions went unanswered.

NARITA

It seemed like half of Japan was at Narita International Airport. But most of them weren't actually going anywhere. They had all come to see Midori Yoshida say good-bye to the old country on her way to the moon. The lightning storm of flashbulbs going off had started as soon as her taxi slowed down outside Terminal 2, and Midori suddenly felt claustrophobic. But in a way it was fun, too. All of these people were here to see *her*.

She had actually wanted to wear a shiny, futuristic-looking silver outfit that Yoshimi had helped her sew. She had worn it for a while down in Harajuku, and it had been a really big hit. But at the last minute, her father had pleaded with her to wear something more formal, and she eventually conceded and put on a long, thick gray skirt and a snug-fitting black jacket with a black shirt underneath. The only things that didn't go were the grubby Onitsuka Tiger sneakers she'd been tromping around Tokyo in for the last several months. They were her favorite shoes, and even though her father thought she ought to wear boots, or at least nice shoes, she had insisted that sneakers were the only way to go for New York City.

But even though a part of her was fascinated by the enormous crowd of people surrounding the taxi when it stopped in front of the entrance, another part of her didn't like it at all. It had happened too fast. One second she had been her totally normal self, hanging out with her friends in Harajuku and dreaming of someday moving to a place where she could do exactly what she wanted. And the next she was transformed into Miss Midori Yoshida, a national icon whom every newspaper and TV station in the country dreamed of landing an interview with. Soon she would sit down on the plane, land on the other side of the world, meet the international media, and shake hands with who-knew-how-many new people.

And then there would be... the moon.

The moon. There was no turning back now. Every single one of the thousands of e-mails she had received in recent months just confirmed it: The machinery was in motion. And it would be impossible to stop it. Midori was in a cold sweat in the backseat and tried to focus on breathing calmly, ignoring the constant flicker of the flashbulbs outside and the hands pounding on the windowpanes.

"Isn't this wonderful?" she heard her mother say just before they opened the door and got out of the taxi. "They came just for you, Midori. Just to see you."

Midori opened the door and set one foot on the asphalt. The clicking from the cameras increased.

Now it's really happening, Midori.

She climbed out of the car and forced herself to wave to the smiling hordes of people watching her.

The exploding flashbulbs blinded her, and she shielded her eyes with her hand, trying to block the blinding lights. She made her way around to the trunk, grabbed her suitcases, and smiled at her father, who was bursting with pride. Then she fought her way forward with her parents in tow and vanished into the swarm of journalists calling out to her.

"What are you thinking right now, Yoshida-san?"

"Are you happy?"

"Have you talked to the other two winners?"

"What's the first thing you'll do when you get to the moon?" "Are you scared?" "Do you have anything to say to the people of Japan?" "How have you prepared for this?" "What do you think this will mean for you personally?" "How much did you know about the moon before is there anything you're dreading are you ready to go will it be sad to say good-bye to Earth are you scared are you happy what are you thinking right now what are you feeling howareyoudoing doyouhaveanylastwordsfortheviewingaudienceradiolistenersfriendsfamily whatareyougoingtomiss?"

When they emerged on the other side of the security checkpoint, it was finally quiet. There was only a lone photographer to be seen. He must have bought a plane ticket just to be allowed into the international departures hall. He took a few pictures from a distance before shuffling off, satisfied. The switch from the overwhelming throng before security was discombobulating but nice. In here there were pretty much only sleepy businessmen on their way to or from insignificant meetings, and they were preoccupied with their own affairs, not even glancing up at the press photographer who passed by them an arm's-length away.

Midori's father stopped in front of a screen showing the gate assignments for departing flights. He looked vaguely confused.

"J5?" he mumbled to himself. "J5?" He gave Midori and her mother a puzzled look. "Where in the world is J5?"

Behind them to the right were gates 61 to 67. To the left, gates 71 to 77. Ahead of them to the left, gates 81 to 88 and ahead of them to the right, gates 91 to 99. There was no sign of gate J5.

"Are we in the right terminal?" her father asked of no one in particular, scratching his head. His face was turning red, and sweat was beading up on his forehead. Midori's father didn't like situations like this. He liked being in complete control of what was going on and where he was supposed to go. He pulled out a map of the airport.

"Well, we're in the right terminal," he declared. "I just don't get it. It should be here."

A group of Japanese men in suits passed the family, and Midori's father bowed to them and asked for help.

But they just looked at him with a puzzled expression. "I'm sorry," one of them said. "There's no gate with that number here."

"We're at Narita Airport every week. We'd know if it existed," one of the other men said before they continued on toward gates 91 to 99.

"What are we going to do?" her mother exclaimed miserably,

just loud enough to make people turn around and look at them. Midori was embarrassed.

"I'm sure it's here somewhere," Midori tried. "We just have to ask someone who works here."

But there were no airport employees anywhere to be seen. Had they all decided to take their lunch breaks at the same time?

Midori's father was now beet red in the face and losing his composure. "Wait here, wait here, wait here," he panted, studying his map one more time. "I'm going to take a little walk around and see if I can find someone who can help us. Don't go anywhere." He rushed down one of the hallways.

Midori and her mother stood next to the large departures board without talking to each other. *This is so typical*, Midori thought. *Every single time those two don't understand something, they totally freak out. We've got hours until the plane leaves anyway. There's no reason to get all worked up.*

The last several weeks she had been almost dreading saying good-bye to her parents. After all, she had been living with them for fifteen years and was used to having them around every single day. But now she knew that she was looking forward to it, too. Everything would be calmer without them. They were like two propellers just spinning around and around for no reason, spewing unnecessary advice and warnings.

How long did it take to fly to New York anyway?

Eight hours?

Nine?

Longer?

She was going to have to find some way to get through this.

Twenty minutes passed without any sign of her father. Midori's mother started talking in falsetto, fretting about what might have happened to him.

"I'm sure he's probably just talking to someone or waiting in a line or something."

"Don't you CARE that your father is missing?" Midori's mother practically yelled.

Midori immediately looked down, her face red. "Chill out, Mom. We've got plenty of time."

"But something's WRONG, don't you think?" Her mother was on the verge of hysteria.

Seriously? Midori thought. *How melodramatic is this going to get?* "Mom, he's not *missing.* He just went to ask for directions. What's wrong is all this yelling. Can't you see that people are staring at us like we're insane? Listen, he'll be back in ten minutes. I guarantee it. And if he's not, fine, we'll have them page him over the PA system. Okay?"

Her mother nodded weakly and pretended to calm down a little.

"I'm going to go to the bathroom now, is that okay? It's right over there," Midori said, pointing to a sign at the other end of the hall. "Just wait here. I'll be back in three minutes."

"Do you really have to go right now, Midori? Shouldn't we wait here until your father comes back?"

Midori stared at her blankly. "I have to go *now.* Not in ten minutes. In ten minutes I won't have to go to the bathroom anymore. Do you get what I'm saying?"

Without waiting for her mother's response, Midori started walking toward the restrooms.

* * *

It didn't look as though anyone had been in there for a while. No drops of water in the sink from people who'd recently washed their hands. No little bits of paper towel that had landed outside the trash. Only the door of the fourth stall was closed. Midori picked the second one and went in. She listened to the murmur of the air conditioner, which got her thinking about the sounds on the moon. There weren't any, as far as she knew. No air for sound to travel through. It was impossible to imagine. For her entire life she'd been surrounded by sounds. People talking, traffic noise, the wind... Would the total absence of sound feel claustrophobic?

For some reason, that made her think about the other occupied stall at the end. She hadn't heard a thing from there since she came in. Not so much as a shuffle of feet or a throat clearing. As she went to the sink to wash her hands, she instinctively leaned down to check if there was someone in the stall. At first glance it appeared to be empty. But when she leaned over a little farther, she saw two shoes. Feet.

There is someone in there.

There were hundreds of reasons someone might sit in the bathroom for a long time at an airport. If you were afraid of flying, for example. Or just needed a little time to yourself. *But... no one, absolutely no one, sits there so perfectly quietly for so long.*

Without really thinking about it, Midori suddenly knocked softly on the stall door. "Hello?"

No one answered.

She knocked again, just as softly this time.

"Excuse me, is anyone in here? Is everything all right?"

But there was no response.

Midori knocked a third time, a little harder now.

"Hello? Miss?"

Suddenly it struck her: What if the person was dead and there was a corpse sitting in there behind the door? Horrible images flickered over her retinas: a dead woman, her mouth open, her face white, with blood running out of the corner of one eye, staring at her. A millipede crawling out of her nose and making its way down into her blouse, where it disappeared into a brownish black gaping hole in her chest.

But the person wasn't dead. There was someone in there who now took a long, slow breath.

Right then Midori remembered something unsettling. Way back in elementary school, her classmate Kaname had started a rumor. One of the stalls in the girls' bathroom at her old school had been closed for several weeks, presumably because one of the older girls had thrown something in the toilet and thoroughly clogged the narrow pipes. Kaname had told Midori and her friends that the OUT OF ORDER sign hanging on the door was just a cover, something the teachers had decided to hang up to make sure that no one tried to open the door. *Actually*, Kaname had said, *the truth is that someone's in there.* He paused a long, long time for dramatic effect before concluding: *Her name is Hanako-chan.*

That's all he would say. They pressed him as hard as they could, but Kaname just shook his head, and Midori thought she remembered him looking scared. It wasn't until a week later that he agreed to tell them the rest. *Hanako-chan*, he began, *isn't alive, but she lives in the bathroom. Do you get it?* Midori thought she understood. *And if you knock on the door and say her name two times, she'll answer you with a "yes?" She'll ask if you want to play with her. And then... she'll open the door....*

Of course, the whole thing was a silly story from a little boy's imagination. But still, by the end of that week, none of the girls were using the school bathrooms anymore. They held it until they got home or snuck off school grounds and went over to use the bathrooms at the nearby train station. In the end, there were so many problems with students whose bladders were so full they couldn't concentrate that the principal was forced to get the toilet fixed and then personally take down the OUT OF ORDER sign and open the door. And of course, the stall was empty.

But Midori stared at the door in front of her now.

Kaname, you idiot. If only you knew how much that stuff stuck with me.

She stepped toward the door. "Hanako-san?"

Seconds passed.

"Hanako-san?"

"*Yes?*" the person behind the door suddenly whispered.

Midori jumped back and had to support herself on the counter to keep from falling. Her heart was hammering out of control.

"You're looking for gate J5, aren't you?" the voice continued in a whisper.

Midori couldn't get a word out. *How did you know that?* she thought.

"It's here, it's nearby, Midori. But you mustn't go there. You must promise never to go there."

Midori thought she heard another sound of movement in the stall and saw the door handle move.

With a massive effort, she tore herself out of her temporary paralysis and ran out into the hallway, back out into the departures hall again. She stopped for a second to get her bearings and look for her mother. She looked right and left. Then right again.

At the end of a narrow corridor she hadn't noticed before, a sign glowed over a door: J5, lit up in white against a black background. Then she felt a hand on her shoulder. Midori stopped and found herself face-to-face with her father.

"Look, you found it," he said with a smile, nodding in the direction of the sign. "Let's go, then." Midori was so bewildered that she couldn't say anything about what had happened in the bathroom. She didn't even notice that her father had bought a ridiculous T-shirt that read FLY ME TO THE MOON. He found it at a gift shop while he was looking around the terminal and had put it on right away, as a sort of last-minute declaration of support for his daughter. He hurried off toward the door at the end of the corridor, and Midori and her mother followed along noiselessly and obediently.

The corridor was empty and devoid of any signage. Midori felt uncomfortable and longed to tell her parents what the person in the bathroom had said, and that maybe they should go back, but she was scared that they would just start wondering if she was even healthy enough to travel to New York. Besides, her father was moving down the corridor so fast there was no time to think.

"This has to be it," her father announced optimistically. "This gate must be totally new, since they haven't put up any permanent signage. No wonder it was nearly impossible to find." He

Gate
J5
NEW YORK / KENNEDY

pushed the door at the end of the corridor and held it open for Midori and her mother so they could enter first.

To their great relief they stepped into a departure lounge that looked just like all the others up in the terminal. But all three of them were surprised to see that it was full of passengers, waiting impatiently to board the flight.

"How did all these people get here?" Midori asked, noticing that she could hear a little nervousness in her own voice.

But her father, who was taking the whole thing with remarkable calm, said, "I suppose they came a different way. I think we must have come through some sort of service entrance. Don't you think?"

Midori nodded absentmindedly and racked her brain trying to understand what had happened in the last few minutes. But it didn't make any sense, none at all, and she decided to just put it out of her mind. They were at the gate now; that was the most important thing.

But that person in the bathroom said…

Don't think about it, Midori. Don't think about it. You're going to New York now, think about that. Your life starts now.

THE PLANE

Antoine was sitting on the stairs outside his family's summer home in Cherbourg-Octeville, on the Normandy coast. There was only one day to go before he was supposed to leave for Houston with his parents. The training course at Johnson Space Center with the other two teenagers would start, and from there they would be busy nonstop until the big launch.

The day he had gotten the letter from NASA felt so long ago now. He had really acted like a crazy person with all that business at the Eiffel Tower, hadn't he? Luckily, that was all behind him. He turned his eyes up toward the sky, but it was too light out to see the moon. It was just the sun, the white March sun that shone down on the little coastal village, making everything look as if it were in black and white. *It begins tomorrow*, he thought.

Antoine picked up the photo album he had brought out onto the steps and opened it. His father had been the one to suggest they go out to Cherbourg-Octeville for the last week. It was almost impossible to be in a bad mood out here, where you always felt the ocean, breathed the fresh air coming off the Channel. And then there were the colors, the light.

The only thing that didn't fit in this idyllic picture was the worn photo album that had been sitting on the bookshelf in the living room and that he was now holding in his hands. As a child Antoine had avoided the album like the plague. He had flipped through it once, without knowing what it was, and after that he couldn't sleep for days. The album was from 1945, and an American soldier had sent it to Antoine's great-grandparents as a gift. When the Allied forces came ashore on the Normandy coast in World War II to start the final push against the Nazis in the summer of 1944, Cherbourg had been hit hard. Like many others, his great-grandparents had taken in soldiers and let them recover for a few days. One of the sheltered soldiers had later sent an album of photos that he and his division had taken while they were there.

Most of the pictures just showed jubilant scenes of soldiers hugging the local population, eating together, and smiling for the camera — but there were also a few pictures that showed the gruesome consequences of the war. The picture that had terrified Antoine as a child showed the entrance to the summer home with a bullet-riddled soldier slumped against the front door, his blood trickling down the two front steps. One of his fellow soldiers was sitting next to him with his helmet in his hand, looking sad. Antoine's parents had tried to tell him that the soldier was just sleeping, but he knew that wasn't true. The soldier was dead. As a boy Antoine had been sure that the soldier, or his ghost, was still sitting out there on the steps, and for two summers in a row he had consistently gone in and out of the house through the back door. But as he got older, he instead made a habit of browsing through the album each time he came, studying the bullet hole that was next to the door, reminding himself that his own problems paled in comparison to what horrors happened here more than seventy years ago.

He sat there looking at the picture of the soldiers leaving their landing vessels, coming ashore on the beaches not far from here. But the picture could just as easily have been taken on the moon. The soldiers waded ashore onto an unknown beach completely shrouded in smoke and fog. Somewhere behind them you could just make out a dark hill. And that was when it hit Antoine that he didn't know what was waiting for him where he was going either. Not that anyone was going to attack him up there, but still... Was it really as safe as his father thought it would be? How many other people had done this before him? Ten? Twelve? It couldn't be more than that, he was sure.

An uncomfortable thought—that maybe it had all been a mistake—started growing within him.

Antoine looked at the time. It was almost five. In an hour his relatives from the city would arrive at the summerhouse, and they would all spend the last night before his departure with his parents. His mother was already in the kitchen, preparations in full swing for the many courses she would serve. Antoine set the photo album down and strolled the little way down to the water.

That's where they had come from, those poor young men who

had been sent to liberate France. What were they thinking on their way in? Were they scared or calm, convinced that they wouldn't make it back home alive again anyway? He mulled that thought over but realized he wasn't able to fully process it. No, he had to come back from the moon in one piece. He wasn't doing it to put as much distance between himself and Simone as possible. It was more that he hoped that she would follow his experiences on TV and realize she still loved him. If not that, this whole thing would be a total waste.

And then he heard it, the sound of a plane. It struck him that the sound came practically out of nowhere, but now the rumbling jet turbines were very clear. The engines didn't sound normal and low, the way they should. They sounded more like a whine, as if the pilot were desperately trying to correct his course. Antoine tilted his head back and spotted a passenger plane…

… as it came crashing down from the sky.

He sat there, totally paralyzed with his mouth open, watching the plane tearing through the cloud layer, down toward the ocean.

No, no, no, no, no, he thought.

The next second seemed to take forever. He managed to stand up and turn around to see if there was someone he could call out to. But there was no one there, not a soul. He was alone on the pier, and the plane was heading for the surface at full speed. And then he saw that the tail was painted with the enormous letters QU.

That… that just couldn't be.

He had no time to think anything else before the plane

smashed into the waves a couple thousand yards farther out and exploded in a violent ball of flame with an infernal sound that forced Antoine to cover his ears. Seconds later the wave of heat hit him, and he had to turn away for a second. And when he looked back out at the water, he saw burning jet fuel floating on the surface. He heard distant screams and squinted out into the twilight.

There were people out there. Survivors! They were clinging to the wreckage of the sinking tail section.

What do I do now? What in the world can I do?

His whole body was trembling, the adrenaline was surging through him, and his pulse was racing so hard that he thought his heart would split just from the pressure. His legs felt numb and he was sick to his stomach, cold as ice. One single thought kept going around and around in his head: *I have to do something.*

But he knew there was nothing he could do. He didn't have a boat and couldn't swim that far into the turbulent water.

He stood there mired in indecision, staring out at the flames, where the plane's tail section was disappearing down into the depths. He thought it already seemed that there were fewer voices crying out. Maybe they were all drowning, all of them? He turned and ran back to the summerhouse to call for help.

The first sign that something was seriously wrong was evident almost immediately.

He came storming into the kitchen and encountered his mother, who was standing by the dish drainer smiling at him.

His parents hadn't heard anything.

How could they not have heard that? The sound had been deafening.

But they weren't the only ones who hadn't noticed it. No one else had, either. Antoine's mother rather reluctantly called the coast guard after listening to his story, but they reported back that there had not been any plane crashes in the area. Antoine's visiting relatives hadn't noticed anything unusual.

Eventually Antoine stopped talking about it, mostly because he was afraid they were right. That it had never happened and the whole thing had just been a far-too-lifelike hallucination. Because that would mean he was losing his mind, wouldn't it?

But he knew he hadn't imagined it. A plane *had* crashed into the English Channel, before his very eyes.

He had seen people die.

And he had seen those two inexplicable letters on the plane's tail section: *QU*. As somewhat of an airline buff, he knew that *QU* was the symbol for East African Airlines planes, but... they never flew here. They operated exclusively in Africa—and, besides, the company had filed for bankruptcy several years ago. The coast guard had been in touch with the airline's former owners, but they said the only plane they had ever owned had been sold to another company in Kenya, which had repainted the tail markings with its own logo.

Antoine was deeply anxious when he woke up the next morning. But he didn't mention it, and his parents also pretended to have forgotten the whole episode. The newspaper and the radio didn't mention a word about it, either. After breakfast he sat with his laptop in his lap Googling information about possible accidents in the area but found nothing. He also checked Wikipedia, where he read about topics like hallucinations and abnormal psychology, but none of what he read seemed to fit. The only explanation he could come up with was that he had had some kind of panic attack.

Antoine was still worried a couple hours later when they boarded the large Air France plane that would take them to New York. He couldn't get away from the nagging thought that what he had seen the previous night was a sign. A sign that he should stay away from the skies. A sign that it was dangerous up there.

He did his best to look on the bright side. *Think about the future*, he told himself. *Think about what's ahead of you, all the experiences you're going to have. The future begins now, you know.*

And with those words, repeated to himself until he could calm down at last, his plane took off over the French capital, destined for America.

NEW YORK CITY

The sky was dark and grayish blue over Manhattan as the Nomeland family's taxi sailed over the Brooklyn Bridge, heading for the posh Four Seasons Hotel on East Fifty-Seventh Street. There was something dark and gloomy about the whole city; this wasn't how Mia had imagined it. Her parents, either, she thought. The mood in the car was tense, and the few words that were spoken were colored by guarded nervousness. Until now it had all been like a game, like a great vacation awaiting them. But the seriousness of the situation had slowly dawned on them all:

This was no vacation.

They were taking a risk. Sending their daughter into outer space.

What if she never came back?

What about all the things that could go wrong?

They remembered the pictures on TV of the space shuttle *Challenger* shown over and over again in 1986. It had exploded in a sea of flames seventy-three seconds after takeoff, killing all seven on board. But not instantaneously.

The cockpit they were sitting in had not been torn to pieces in the explosion. There was a chance that they'd all lived for the two minutes and forty-five seconds it took until they hit the surface of the water with two hundred times the force of gravity—enough to annihilate them.

Did they know they were going to die?

Maybe.

Probably.

Actually, only her parents were thinking about that. Mia wasn't aware of that infamous accident. She hadn't even been born when it happened. What she was thinking about, as the taxi slowed down and parked outside the hotel, was her friends.

What were they doing right now?

Were they together, without her?

She didn't want to think about that.

Were they having fun?

But she couldn't stop herself.

A hotel employee opened the cab door for her, and she took her first steps out onto a wet New York sidewalk. The rain soaked her hair in seconds so it stuck to her face and made her look even sadder than she was.

"Well, here we are," her father said with a smile, elbowing her gently in the side.

Mia didn't smile back.

"Are you tired?" he asked.

She nodded.

They stood there for a second, both on the verge of saying something of what they'd been thinking about in the cab. But before they had a chance, they were interrupted by a bellhop who came out of the hotel and stacked their luggage onto a cart.

"Welcome to New York," he said, grinning. "Sorry about the rain. It's not always like this." He held an umbrella over them even though it was only a few yards to the entrance. "Follow me, please."

A couple of NASA representatives met them in the restaurant later that evening. It was surprising that they offered fewer details about the moon mission itself than all the media interviews and online chats and video blogs and TV shows and ad campaigns and the extensive world tour that would start as soon as they returned from the mission.

"Yes, this is an outstanding opportunity for her," her mother said.

"We're very grateful Mia was chosen," her father said.

"Obviously, it will change her life forever," one of the NASA men said.

"I'm going to bed," Mia suddenly announced, getting up from the table. Her mother, her father, and the two NASA men looked at one another.

"Now?" her father said. "You're going now? But we're talking about *you* here, about *your* trip. Don't you want to talk about it?"

"It's not like you guys will even notice whether I'm here or not."

Her father came up to her room twenty minutes later along with Sander. Mia was just finishing brushing her teeth when he knocked on the door.

"Mia? Are you going to open the door? There's someone here who wants to go to bed."

She walked over and let them in.

Sander smiled when he saw her and shuffled into the bathroom, where he started brushing his teeth right away. Toothbrushing was his specialty and he was very proud of it. His technique wasn't great and it always took him a while, since his toy lion needed a good once-over with the brush before Sander was satisfied. But at least he could do it by himself.

Mia went back to the suitcase by her bed and got out her things. Her father followed her and sat down on a chair.

"I'm sorry about that," he said.

"About what?" Mia asked.

"About... everything. That this wasn't what you'd planned for yourself. But you know, John Lennon once said, 'Life is what happens when you're busy making other plans.'"

Mia wasn't about to argue with John Lennon. After all, she was a musician herself.

"So, what about tomorrow?" her father went on. "Is there anything special you want to do, Mia? It's the last day before we go to Texas, you know. Maybe we should go see the Statue of Liberty? That would be something, wouldn't it?"

Boy, that would be ironic, Mia thought. Visiting the Statue of Liberty when she didn't even get to decide what she was going to do with her own life, let alone her summer vacation?

"Sure, why not," she replied, looking the other way.

Her father sighed and stood up. She felt bad for a minute. He was doing his best. It wasn't all his fault.

"Sorry." The apology tumbled out of her mouth.

He stepped closer and gave her a good hug. The intervals between hugs had gotten longer and longer in recent years, so it meant a lot to Mia.

"See you tomorrow, then," he said. "Good night, Mia."

"Good night, Dad."

Sander came running out of the bathroom and flung his arms around his dad, his mouth still lathered in toothpaste.

"Night-night!"

"Good night, Sander," his father said, picking up the boy and giving him an equally vigorous hug back. And then he had to hug the boy's stuffed lion, too. The furry fabric around its mouth was almost worn through from intense toothbrushing over the last several months. Grayish white cotton stuffing was poking out and made it look as if the lion was trying to cough up a hair ball or two.

Their father walked over to the door and turned toward Mia. "Everything's going to be fine," he said. "I promise."

She helped Sander get into his pajamas, and then he climbed into bed. She pulled the covers up to his chin.

"Sleep well, Sander."

It looked like he was thinking. "Are you sad?" he finally asked.

Mia nodded.

"Because you're going so far away?"

"No, not because of that."

"Then why?"

There was no point in trying to explain the problem to Sander. "Because I'm going away from you, of course," she said, sitting down on the edge of his bed.

"I could go with you. If you want. Lion, too."

"Sorry, but that won't work."

Sander thought about it for a long time. "But!" he said suddenly, lighting up. "I can send you letters."

She thought about how simple everything was in Sander's world. There were no limits for him. Everything was possible. Mail to the moon?

"Of course you can."

"I could write you one now," he said.

"But I haven't even left yet," she laughed.

"So you can take it with you."

"Okay."

Mia found a pen, some stationery, and an envelope and brought them back over to Sander. It struck her that she'd never seen him write anything other than his own name. And even then he usually forgot the *E*. But she gave him what he needed, left the reading light on over his bed, and let him be.

Mia couldn't sleep. Or had she slept? She fumbled in the dark for her cell phone and found it on the nightstand.

The clock said one thirty. That meant she'd been asleep for almost four hours. She thought she could hear her parents and the NASA men in the room next door talking loudly. She heard them clink glasses and there was laughter—loud, shrill laughter.

What were they talking about? *Her?*

She looked over at Sander's bed, squinting to make him out in the dark room. His breathing was regular, calm.

Quietly she pulled the covers down and slid her legs onto the floor. Her boots were waiting by the door, and after pulling them on and shrugging her arms into her jacket, she carefully let herself out of the hotel room and took the elevator to the relatively crowded lobby. A group of Asian guests was checking in, and several men in suits were sitting in the bar talking loudly to one another. She stood there watching them for a couple of minutes wondering what to do.

Suddenly it hit her that she could do anything. No one knew she was up. Sander was sleeping, and her parents were busy entertaining the NASA guys. What if she just walked out of the hotel, left them all? They'd never find her again, not in this city. She could disappear for good. Maybe she could go to Mexico? Find some new friends, start a new band, they could share a worn-down apartment in the middle of Mexico City. Why not?

Just the thought was enough to give her goose bumps. If she left, no one would even realize for hours that she was gone. They wouldn't notice until breakfast at the earliest, or when they knocked on the door to her and Sander's room. But by then she'd be long gone.

Mia walked through the revolving door, out onto the sidewalk. The doorman approached her the instant he spotted her.

"Can I help you, miss?"

"No, thanks, I'm fine," she replied quickly.

"Where are your parents, if I may ask?"

Mia turned and pointed to the bar. "They're sitting in there. I'm just going to go buy a pack of gum."

"I think they have gum at the front desk."

"Not the right kind," she responded.

"And what kind would that be?"

"A Norwegian kind. I doubt you've had it before."

"Norway, huh? Well, just don't go too far. This is New York City, not the best place for a tourist to be out alone in the middle of the night."

She nodded to him and started walking down the street, turning left onto Park Avenue. Above her towered enormous skyscrapers where only the very richest people could afford to live. A few blocks later she spotted Central Park, which she recognized from countless movies and TV shows. She knew it was enormous—much, much bigger than the park they usually went for walks in back home in Stavanger, Lake Mosvannet Park. Central Park was Lake Mosvannet on steroids.

She found an entrance on Fifth Avenue, and minutes later she was in the middle of the park, following the path that meandered along a little lake. Only the sounds of the traffic reminded her she was in the middle of a huge city. She started humming one of the songs her band had just written, the last one before she left. And then it hit her.

Her friends.

She looked at her watch. Two thirty in the morning. That meant it was about eight thirty in the morning in Norway. And that meant the others were at band practice.

Suddenly the same feeling she'd had in the lobby came over her again. She felt powerful. Free to do what she wanted. And what she wanted was to call them. Call them and find out how they were, maybe mention in passing that she was in Central Park.

Alone. *Well, I just felt like going for a walk. Needed to get a little fresh air. This city's not bad, you know.* She'd sound sophisticated, pretend being here was the most easy and natural thing in the world.

She'd left her cell phone in the room, so she started looking around for a pay phone. There wasn't much besides trees here. Almost no people, either. Just the occasional jogger off in the distance and a pair of young lovers staggering home along the path ahead of her. It took at least fifteen minutes for her to finally find a public phone.

She fished around for the coins she'd received as change when she bought a sandwich at the airport, and dialed Silje's cell number. Someone picked up on the other end. At first Mia just heard loud music, and a voice that was shouting to the others in the room: "You guys want to be quiet? The phone!"

"Hello?"

"Mia?"

"Yeah, it's me."

The voice shouted again, "Hey, everyone, it's Mia! Shh! This is so cool. How's it going?" Silje asked.

"Oh, fine."

"*Damn*, you're in New York City! That's crazy! What are you doing right now?" Silje asked.

"I'm in Central Park." Mia tried to sound all blasé.

"That is so cool. Is it amazing?"

"It's totally awesome," Mia said.

"Does it look like it does in the movies?"

Mia looked around at the park. "Yeah, actually, it does."

"Sweet."

"How about you guys?" Mia tried.

"Things are fine here. We wrote some new songs."

"Really?"

"I think they're really good. We've got to keep things going while you're gone, you know. The future won't wait even if someone's on vacation, right?"

Vacation? Was that some sort of accusation? Did they really think she didn't care anymore? Already? Or was Silje trying to make a joke? Mia wasn't sure.

"No, of course not," Mia said. "But... well, who's singing?"

"Kari. She wrote the lyrics and everything. I had no idea she could even write. And definitely no clue that she could sing. But she's a totally awesome singer, wouldn't you know it? Kari, you're a totally awesome singer!"

Mia could hear the other girls hooting in the background.

"*And* she can play the guitar at the same time!" Silje added.

"But... I'm still the vocalist, right?" Mia asked facetiously.

"Of course. We can talk about all that stuff when you get back. I mean, we'll work something out. But she's crazy good. You want to hear? Wait a sec...."

Mia didn't have a chance to respond before Silje set down the phone. It was quiet for a few seconds, then she heard them start one of the new songs.

And it was good. That was the problem. It was really good.

She stood there and listened to them for a minute, until the phone indicated that her money was almost used up. Then she hung up.

"No one home?"

Mia jumped. Someone was speaking English to her. She spun

around and was staring into the face of a homeless person, who was bending over a shopping cart. He must have been around seventy and was wearing a huge, filthy brown coat. But there was actually something really pleasant about him, despite the fact that he definitely hadn't bathed in several months. Or maybe years.

"Excuse me?" Mia responded.

"I said, 'No one home?'" The man gestured at the phone.

"Oh, no. Busy."

"That's how it is these days, you know. Everyone is busy all day. Not that I know why, but they are. So damn busy, all of them. It was different before. Have you ever been to Coney Island?"

"No."

"Playground of the World, it was called. It used to be an amazing place. Amazing. Now there's hardly anything left of it. When I was a kid, people from all over the world went there, and all the things you could do, all the rides, oh my God. There was a mechanical horse race, felt like it went on for hours, and over in Dreamland there was a railroad that ran through this mountain landscape, like the Swiss Alps or something. There were Venetian canals with gondolas, roller coasters, and Ferris wheels. And there was a one-armed lion tamer, Captain Bonavita he was called. It was the Playground of the World. That's what they called it. It was an amazing place. People came from all over the world to see it."

The man was starting to repeat himself, and Mia wondered if he wasn't senile. He disappeared into his own thoughts for a moment.

"We used to spend the nights there when we were kids. Slept on the beach. Under the stars. You can't do that anymore. I guess it's too dangerous nowadays. It's really sad."

"Maybe you should do it again?" Mia suggested.

"I wouldn't dare." He smiled at her. It was one of those sad smiles that made her heart cringe. "And you shouldn't be out here alone, either. What are you doing here, anyway?"

"I'm waiting for us to move on. My parents are back at the Four Seasons."

"Well, I have to tell you... best hotel in the city. I worked there once. As a doorman. But they fired me."

"Why?"

"I let everyone in. Probably shouldn't have. It's an expensive hotel."

"NASA is paying."

"NASA, you say? Not bad. Wait. You're not... yes, yes you *are*! You're one of them, aren't you?"

"One of who?"

"One of those poor kids they're going to send up into space."

Mia nodded.

"Nothing good will come of it, believe me. It's all about money, the whole thing. And who knows what you'll find up there?"

"What do you mean by that?"

"Just that you ought to let sleeping dogs lie. Take care of the people on Earth first. I think people ought to stay put. You know, uh, everything that goes up... must come down again."

He pulled an orange out of his coat pocket, held it in his hand a second before throwing it up into the air. It disappeared in the darkness, before coming rushing back down again and splitting open against the ground, some orangey flesh and pulp splattering over the asphalt path.

"You see? I think you ought to stay home."

"Little too late to suggest that now. It wasn't my idea. Going."

"It never is. It's always someone else's idea. Come on, it's time to get you back home to your folks."

"Are you going to walk me to the hotel?"

"Does it look like I have anything more important to do?"

"I guess not."

"Come on, then." He waved his hand toward the way out. "My name's Murray."

"Mia." He extended his dirty hand to her, and she shook it.

"Nice to meet you, Mia."

They strolled out of the park together. Several people they passed gave them weird looks, wondering if this disheveled homeless man was bothering her. A couple even stopped and asked her if she was all right.

And she was. Perfectly all right. Murray was giving her an impromptu tour, pointing to different buildings and educating Mia about their names and histories.

As she followed Murray pushing his shopping cart of possessions a few feet ahead of her, she now noticed that Murray had written something on the back of his coat in large black figures. She didn't know how she could have possibly missed it earlier. It looked like he had taken a gigantic felt-tipped pen and written across the whole surface.

"What does that mean?" she asked curiously when they stopped at a crosswalk.

"What?" he replied.

"The writing on your coat. '6E.' Is that your address or something?"

Murray looked at her in surprise, as if he didn't understand what she meant. "*What* are you talking about? *6E?* What is that?"

"That's what it says on your back," Mia said, pointing.

"It does?"

"Yeah."

"6E?"

"Yup."

Murray pulled off his coat and held it up in front of him.

"What the hell is this?" Murray asked Mia.

"Don't ask me. It's your coat," she said.

"But that's not my handwriting."

"Are you sure?" Mia asked.

"Am I sure? I know what my own handwriting looks like!"

"I was just asking," Mia protested.

Murray studied the writing on his coat.

"This isn't good," he mumbled to himself.

"What did you say?" Mia asked.

"Nothing. Best not to talk about it," he said, getting agitated. He immediately threw the coat in a nearby garbage can.

"Don't you want it?" Mia asked. "It's just pen, it'll wash out. I'm sure."

But Murray wasn't listening to her.

He's scared, she thought suddenly, and noticed the fear rubbing off on her. The writing on the coat was still visible from the parapet. From time to time he glanced over his shoulder as if he was expecting someone to be following him in the darkness.

What are you afraid of? she was going to ask, but didn't get the chance. When they turned the corner onto Haddon Avenue at last [illegible] Murray [illegible] said, 'It's best if you go on alone from here.' [illegible]

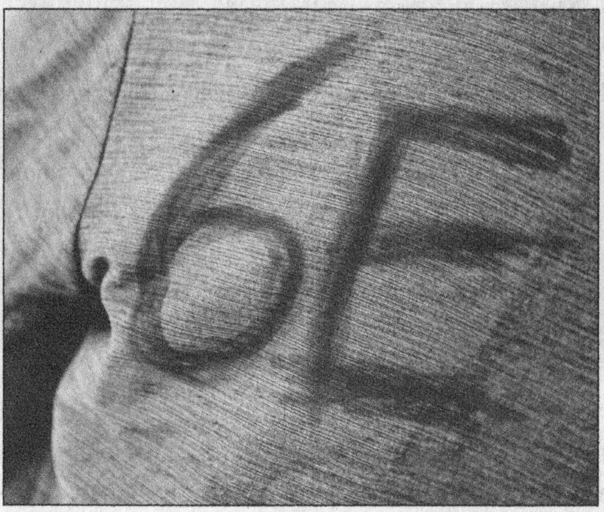

[illegible] she was gone. She was going to miss him, strange little [illegible]. She silently kicked off her shoes [illegible]

Something poked her in the side. She ran a hand down to her thigh, felt something, and pulled it up.

[illegible] envelope [illegible] Sawyer had written her [illegible] after all.

She was about to [illegible] it but changed her mind [illegible] she thought [illegible] trashcan. From time to time he glanced over his shoulder, as if he was expecting someone to be following him in the darkness.

What are you afraid of? she was going to ask, but didn't get the chance. When they turned the corner onto Madison Avenue at East Fifty-Seventh Street, Murray suddenly stopped and said, "It's best if you go on alone from here. The hotel is just over there. No point in anyone seeing me."

"You think they'd recognize you?"

"I don't know, but I recognize this place. That's bad enough."

"Okay."

"Take care of yourself, and make sure you come back again. Believe me, the moon is no place to stay. *Bad juju.*"

And with those words, Murray raised a hand in farewell, swung his shopping cart around, and plodded back down Fifty-Seventh Street again.

It was almost quarter past four in the morning when Mia finally tiptoed past her parents' hotel room and let herself back into her own. Sander was sound asleep and probably hadn't even noticed she was gone. She was going to miss him, strange little Sander. She silently kicked off her shoes, took off her clothes, and got into bed.

Something poked her in the side. She ran a hand down to her thigh, felt something, and pulled it up.

It was an envelope. Sander had written her a letter after all.

She was about to open it but changed her mind. *No,* she thought, *I'll save it for later, when I'm on the moon. When I miss him. That's what he'd want.*

She lay in bed for a while before she fell asleep, thinking about the band, about her friends. What would happen to it, to her? Would there be a band to come home to? Would she even be able to go back to Norway as the same old Mia?

One thing was for sure, anyway. When she got back to Norway, she would make her own decisions about her life. If a vocalist was what she wanted to be (and it was), then that's what she would be. And if she didn't want to go trotting around the globe as part of some NASA ad campaign, then she would refuse. Her mind was made up on that.

And she knew she could pull it off.

Because she'd spent a night on the town in New York City, and it had taught her something important: She was the one who decided which path she would take.

THE CREW

On that first day, Midori sat in a small classroom in the largest building at Johnson Space Center in Houston, along with the two other teens, who she knew were named Mia and Antoine. She couldn't understand why she hadn't officially been introduced to them yet, even though they had all been staying at that same hotel in New York. She had been the first one in the room, followed by some air force officers and folks from NASA. The instructors arrived minutes later escorting the other two people her age. But before any of them could say one word to each other, or at least nod at each other in recognition, the lesson had begun.

Midori had been told there would be a lot to learn, but when the manuals were tossed in her lap she realized she had been underestimating. The hefty volumes covered everything from an intense crash course in astronomy to how to eat, shower, go to the bathroom, walk, and move around in a weightless environment and on the surface of the moon, where gravity was only one-sixth as strong as on Earth. And there was an entire manual devoted just to safety and emergency preparedness. They'd have to study everything that could go wrong; nothing must be left to chance.

Midori stared down at her lap. There were three thick manuals there, labeled with the titles EXTRAVEHICULAR STAYS, DWELLING MODULE, and *CERES/DEMETER*. Those words meant almost nothing to her, so she glanced around. The other two teenagers, the girl from Norway and the boy from France, were also sitting there, randomly flipping back and forth through the manuals. She wished she could make eye contact with them. A smile maybe. Something that could lighten the mood a little. She felt a little lame, since she was sure the other two were moon nerds and she wasn't even remotely interested in it. Now she realized with dismay that she had to summon up the motivation to read and remember over seven hundred pages of dense information. Sure, NASA had translated her manuals into Japanese, but there were limits. She hadn't been tricked into a whole summer of homework, had she?

"Welcome." A man in a dark suit with light gray hair moved to stand in the front of the room. "My name is Dr. Paul Lewis. I'm an administrator here at NASA, and it's my great honor to welcome you here to the Johnson Space Center. And, first of all, let me tell you one thing: You three sitting before me today..." He paused for dramatic effect. "You are the three luckiest people on this planet." His face dissolved into an enormous smile. "And with a little help, you'll be the luckiest three people in space, too. Only a few people have experienced what you're going to experience. You'll be the youngest people to ever leave Earth's atmosphere. And you'll be the thirteenth, fourteenth, and fifteenth people to set foot on another celestial body. You'll be part of cutting-edge, pioneering research. And even more important"—he stretched his arms out wide—"you'll be part of history."

Midori looked down at her books. Maybe reading one of them would be enough.

Dr. Lewis continued: "As some of the luckiest people in the world, you also bear a great responsibility. I think you understand this. And I see more than just anticipation in your faces; I also see concern. And I see homesickness. It's nothing to be embarrassed about. Because you'll be going far away, farther than anyone you know has ever gone. You flew a combined total of over eighteen thousand miles to get here." He looked at the three teenagers. "Your ultimate destination is two hundred thirty-eight thousand miles away. And as you travel there, as you see Earth getting smaller through the windows...I guarantee you this: You'll miss home. But the things you will experience, the stories you'll have to tell from a stay of just one hundred seventy-two hours, will take you a lifetime to tell."

Midori glanced at the other two. She already got, even now, that they were different from her. They were both leaning over, their eyes wide, following the man's every word. She wondered how this was going to go. What if they were such computer nerds that you couldn't even really talk to them?

"So, what are we going to do here at Johnson for the next three months?" Dr. Lewis continued. "Well, we're going to train. We're going to teach you everything you need to know — about the equipment, about safety, about the spacecraft you'll be traveling on and the base you'll be staying at. Can any of you tell me what a module is?"

The European boy raised his hand.

"Mr. Devereux?"

"Modules are the units that make up the base on the surface of the moon," he answered in English.

Midori rolled her eyes. Apparently he'd read up on this stuff in advance.

"Correct," Dr. Lewis responded. "Let me show you." He signaled to one of the other suits in the room, and seconds later the lights were dimmed and the curtains drawn. Dr. Lewis pressed a button on the laptop in front of him, and a giant flat-screen computer monitor on the wall displayed a diagram of the moon base.

"DARLAH 2 is composed of four modules, located in the region called Mare Tranquillitatis. The Sea of Tranquility. The name is quite old, from a time when people thought the dark areas on the moon were filled with water. Today we know that the dark areas indicate lowlands and that the light gray areas are mountainous regions and higher terrain. We've marked the Mare Tranquillitatis landing area for you here."

SEA OF TRANQUILITY

Dr. Lewis pressed another button and displayed a picture.

"The reason we chose this specific site is that this is where the very first moon landing took place on July 20, 1969. No one has been there since. It will be your job to find the traces they left behind. Among other things, I can tell you that Buzz Aldrin left his moon boots sitting in the dust there."

Cool, Midori thought, deciding then and there that she would be the first to get hold of those boots. How cool would that be, to strut around Harajuku in those? She flinched a little. *Oh, that's right.* She wasn't going back there, was she?

Never.

Dr. Lewis presented them with a schedule for the upcoming weeks and then launched into a lecture on the history of the moon and its significance through the ages. Midori tuned out pretty much the whole thing when Dr. Lewis suddenly woke her up by turning on the lights.

"Finally, today I'd like to introduce you to the crew. You'll have the best available expertise with you on this trip, and they'll be responsible for everything. They'll be giving you assignments and orders, but they'll bear the ultimate responsibility for everything. Don't forget that. As long as you do what they ask, you'll have a fabulous trip. I promise you that."

One by one the crewmembers stepped forward and introduced themselves. Midori did her best to pay attention, but the session had already contained too much information all at once, and soon she had each person mixed up with the next. The only people she had no trouble keeping straight were the other two teenagers. Dr. Lewis called their names and they walked over to him. Antoine, the guy from France, was a very tall, lanky guy with dark hair and a big nose, sort of cute. (Very cute, actually, now that she thought about it.) And then there was Mia from Norway, a head taller than her, with black hair that hung down over her eyes. She was wearing enormous sunglasses and looked like a real goth girl. *Not exactly original, but cool anyway,* Midori thought. Then she went up, said her name and where she was from, shook hands with the other two and the crew.

"Well, that was it for today," Dr. Lewis concluded. "Now I assume you'd like to go back and see your families at the visitors' center. We'll see you back here at nine o'clock tomorrow morning."

Midori stood up, grabbed her bag, and started toward the exit. By the door she picked up an information sheet with the names of everyone who would be going. *Could be good to have,* she thought. *At least until I can tell everyone apart. If I ever can.*

RETURN TO THE MOON

EXPEDITION 69—RETURN TO THE MOON
JULY 18—AUGUST 8, 2019
SPACECRAFT: COMMAND MODULE CERES
LUNAR MODULE: DEMETER
ROCKET: SATURN V

CREW

CIVILIANS

YOSHIDA, MIDORI
AGE 16, YOKOHAMA, JAPAN

NOMELAND, MIA
AGE 16, STAVANGER, NORWAY

DEVEREUX, ANTOINE
AGE 17, PARIS, FRANCE

ASTRONAUTS

CAPT. NADOLSKI, LLOYD—COMMANDER (COM)
AGE 42, CLEVELAND, OH

LT. HALL, CAITLIN—*DEMETER* LUNAR MODULE PILOT (LMP)
AGE 32, NEW YORK, NY

CAPT. COLEMAN, ALDRICH—HABITAT COMMANDER (HCOM)
AGE 59, NEW YORK, NY

WILSON, SAMUEL—SPACE ENGINEER
AGE 34, DETROIT, MI

STANTON, PETER D.—SPACE ENGINEER
AGE 33, DULUTH, MN

ALONE

Mia squinted as she exited the building after the first class. Trucks and forklifts passed by her, and she could hear them grinding away in the hangars nearby. Johnson Space Center consisted of more than a hundred buildings arranged in an area large enough to house a small city. Even the practically empty parking lot in front of her would impress just about anyone with its vast size. That made her realize for the first time how expansive the field of space travel research had been and what a mind-boggling amount of money must have been involved.

Just then, one of the crewmembers she had just met walked out onto the steps. Mia couldn't remember her name, but luckily the woman held out her hand.

"Caitlin," she said.

"Mia."

"Nice to meet you, Mia. Where are you going?"

She wasn't sure. "I suppose I ought to get back to my parents," Mia replied. "But I'm not exactly sure where."

"I'm sure they're at the visitors' center. You want a ride?"

"You have a car?"

Caitlin blinked at her. "Um, yeah, of course I have a car. Who wants to go by foot when we're covering distances like this? Come on, let's go."

Mia followed her down the steps and around the corner to where her VW was parked. It turned out to be a rusty wreck of a car. Which actually was in keeping with Caitlin's style. There really wasn't anything about her that looked like an astronaut. She was younger than the rest, tall and thin, wearing worn jeans tucked well down into her boots. She had a faded T-shirt underneath a leather jacket that was cool enough that Mia wanted to ask her where she'd bought it. But she didn't.

"I can't get the door open," Mia said, a little embarrassed after lifting the door handle several times.

"Try giving it a kick."

Mia hesitated. "What do you mean?"

Caitlin came around to Mia's side and slammed her boot into the door. It opened. "Like that."

Mia sat down on the passenger's side and did her best to make some room for her legs among the huge heap of music magazines that had been tossed onto the floor.

"Just shove them aside, doesn't matter if you step on them. I've already read them anyway. Do you mind if I smoke?" Caitlin asked. Mia didn't have a chance to respond before Caitlin lit a cigarette and started the car. Seconds later she'd backed out of the parking space and was speeding along toward the visitors' center. A simple but very distinctive bass line poured out of the speakers, and Mia recognized the music right away.

"You listen to *them*?" Mia asked, surprised.

"You like the Talking Heads?"

"They're great," Mia said.

"'*Psycho Killer*,'" Caitlin said, singing along with the chorus. "Don't you just love when he does that? It's my favorite track."

Mia nodded and wondered if she should mention that she was in a band, too. But she decided to do that later. There'd be plenty of time once they were on the moon.

"So, should we see how fast we can get this old beater to go? I'm guessing seventy. What do you think?" Caitlin asked.

"No chance," Mia said.

"Good answer." Caitlin laughed loudly as she changed gears and floored it. The car shook as they raced across the asphalt toward the visitors' center. Mia was sure it would explode at any minute.

"Don't panic!" Caitlin yelled over the roar of the engine. "It can take it. Besides, this is nothing. Wait until you're sitting in the tip of the launch rocket — that's *real* shaking!"

Five seconds passed, four, three, two, one, and then Caitlin slammed on the brakes. The tires screamed as she turned the car into a parking space close to the entrance.

"There. Seventy-two miles per hour. Not bad for an old lady, huh?"

"You don't look old," Mia said quickly.

"I meant the car," Caitlin said with a smile. "But thanks anyway."

Caitlin had another errand to run nearby, so she said goodbye to Mia, pointing out the door to the visitors' center before disappearing in the opposite direction. Mia walked up the steps and into the spacious lobby. There were quite a few people inside, but Mia didn't see her own parents anywhere. She walked around the center a few times without finding them before she gave up and found one of the guards. He made a couple of phone calls but wasn't able to find anything out. After a while Mia decided to go back to the crew hotel and wait for them there. The guard made another call, this time for a driver, who picked her up in front of the entrance a couple minutes later.

The crew hotel wasn't actually a hotel. It was a large square building in the middle of the enormous base where they were all going to live for the next few weeks. It wasn't far to the hangars where they would be conducting the rest of their training and preparations. She knew that Sander and her parents were staying at a civilian hotel about a mile or so off base, and she could have gone there, too. But she figured they'd turn up pretty soon anyway.

Mia was given a key at the front desk and told that her luggage was already up in her room on the third floor. There was a letter for her, too.

A letter?

She assumed Sander must have written her another letter. He often did the same things over and over again once he'd mastered something. She still hadn't read his first letter.

"Here you go," the receptionist said, and handed her an envelope. Mia opened the letter right there, and read it standing by the front desk.

But it wasn't from Sander.

It was from her mom.

Mia folded the letter back up and stuffed it firmly into her back pocket. *Jeez*, she thought.

"Bad news?" the receptionist asked gently.

She looked him in the eye. "No, it's actually good. It's just unexpected."

Mia left the lobby and proceeded to look for her room. Her first reaction had been sadness. She felt abandoned. But at the same time she couldn't help feeling a sense of relief. And then happiness. A freedom her parents had indulged her with. It didn't get any better than that.

She found her room and let herself in, and soon the Talking Heads were blasting through her headphones as she lay comfortably on her new bed.

Dear Mia,

When we were standing at the top of the Statue of Liberty in New York that day, it suddenly hit me that you're not nine years old anymore. I don't know why I happened to think of it right then. Maybe it had something to do with where we were. At any rate, it hit me that maybe we haven't given you enough liberty, enough space lately. That might sound strange, but to a mother a child is never grown up. She's always your child, and maybe I've been thinking of you and Sander too similarly, and treating you too much the same. But you're not nine years old, like him, you're sixteen now and even though that doesn't mean you're an adult, you're still setting out on a journey that is really much more adult than anything your father and I have ever done. I know that this lottery wasn't your dream, and that it still isn't. I know that you'd rather be home in Stavanger with your band and that it cost you a lot to make the decision you did. But I still think this was the right choice, and that you will never regret it. It will change your life.

The point is, your father and I realized that you would probably benefit from a little time to yourself, without the three of us interfering all the time, so you can get a sense of what it feels like to stand on your own two feet. So we're taking Sander to Los Angeles for a while. As you know, Uncle Harald lives there and we'll be staying at his place. I think it'll be nice for all of us—a vacation for us and some time for you to relax. And you'll need that with all that's ahead of you. We didn't want to say anything to you until we'd left, in case you felt guilty and asked us not to go. I'm sure you understand. But you need to know that if we're thinking about this wrong and you really did want us to be here with you, all you have to do is call and we'll come back right away.

In the meantime I hope we can talk a little on the phone sometimes and that we can hear how you're doing. That would mean a huge amount to Sander, especially. He says hi. So does Lion, of course. You know how it is.

Finally I just want to say this: Dad and I and Sander are all incredibly proud of you, Mia, and love you so very much. Take care of yourself, don't wear yourself out, get to know the other kids who are going, and call us if anything comes up. I let Commander Nadolski know about this and asked him to keep an extra eye on you. Not that you need it, but . . . all the same. You're going to have an amazing, really amazing, trip.

We'll be back in plenty of time for the launch.

Hugs,

Mom

TAKEOFF

Mr. Himmelfarb was sitting on the edge of his bed, peering down at two brown leather shoes. That meant it was morning and he had to get up. Or it could mean it was nighttime and someone would be in soon to put him to bed. He looked out the window. The palm tree outside divided the sunlight into seven sharp rays that all hit him in the middle of his face. Was it at night that it was light out? Or was that during the day? It was best to wait for someone to come in and tell him what to do. It was hard for him to know how long he waited, but at some point one of the people dressed in white came into his room.

"There, I'm back," she said. "That didn't take so long, did it?" She gestured that she was ready to go. "Are you ready?"

He mumbled a response to her. He was ready. He was ready every day. Because every day was the same.

"If we hurry, we can catch the president's speech. Tomorrow's the big day, Oleg. They're going to the moon!" And with those words, she took him by the hand and led him down the white corridors, into the nursing home's TV lounge.

He had already forgotten how he reacted to seeing the drawings of the moon base, but there was something familiar about the rocket behind the formally dressed man standing in the TV lounge. Every time he tried to concentrate, it eluded him. How they had gotten that enormous rocket into the lounge without having to destroy the ceiling, he had no idea. They had certainly gone all out.

All the employees at the nursing home knew that Mr. Himmelfarb had been a custodian at the Goldstone Deep Space observatory, but no one knew precisely what he had done there or what he had seen over the years. Mr. Himmelfarb had been a very quiet and private man for his whole life, a man who stuck to his confidentiality agreement as if it were holy writ. Not even his now-deceased wife or his kids, who never visited him, had ever been told all the details of what his job had actually entailed.

When he first moved into the nursing home, his children had made sure to come see him once a week. But after his condition advanced, he became increasingly withdrawn from them, and at some point he finally stopped talking for good. And when he eventually no longer recognized them or even acknowledged their presence, they stopped coming altogether. The last thing Mr. Himmelfarb managed to think before he strolled into the deep valley of forgetfulness was how much he missed his kids and how glad he was that soon he wouldn't realize that they almost never visited him anymore. And that he loved them more than anything on Earth.

GOOD-BYE

July 16 had arrived. A couple of weeks beforehand they had moved from Houston to Kennedy Space Center in Florida, where the launch would take place. Kennedy Space Center was enormous, even bigger than the space center in Houston. It was located on Merritt Island, with Cape Canaveral Air Force Station as its closest neighbor. From her bedroom window, Mia could look out over the Atlantic and follow the waves as they slowly broke and washed over the beach down below. And if she leaned out the window and looked to the left, she could just barely catch a glimpse of the launchpad, where the almost hundred-meter-tall rocket was standing ready.

There were fewer than twenty-four hours left now. In only sixteen hours she would be out there. And the rocket would take off from Earth with her aboard. At a speed of eleven kilometers per second, they would leave Earth's atmosphere and be gone from everyone she knew.

She was in her room watching some American comedy on TV, but she wasn't laughing. She had done what her mother had asked in the letter and called once a week to tell them how she was doing. And like her mother had suggested, it had been good for Mia to have some time to herself, and the distance improved her relationship with her parents. For the first time in years they had long conversations, and the only difference was that now they took place by phone between Florida and L.A. They had talked about nearly everything—the expedition, the uncertainty about her band back home, and about Midori and Antoine.

There had been quite a bit about Antoine, especially in the last week. She hadn't noticed it herself, but she had a tendency to bring him up pretty much no matter what topic they were discussing. *Antoine said something about that yesterday.* Or *Antoine is good at that.* Mia also made sure she talked to Sander each time she called, but he didn't always say that much. Sometimes it was impossible to get him to make a sound. But that didn't bother her. She knew he was sitting there holding the phone, listening to her voice, and if he was too quiet she would just decide to tell him about the little details of her day instead.

Every once in a while she would go down to the lobby to check her e-mail or see if her friends were online, but the time difference between Norway and Florida meant they were never online at the same time, and the few e-mails that came just wished her good luck and didn't give her any information about the stuff she was wondering about: how the band was doing and what was going on back home these days. She never replied to the e-mails. So in the end she just wound up staying in her room, pulling a chair up to the window with the view out over Cape Kennedy, listening to the Talking Heads, and trying to write lyrics that were even better. Often she wrote only a few lines, which she would then scribble over and give up on, but she convinced herself that at least she was on her way, that this was just the beginning, and she would come back from the moon with lyrics that were really, really good.

She, Midori, and Antoine had been drilling with the crew the whole time. They went through all the maneuvers hundreds of times, crammed to memorize all the details, and practiced in simulators. She trained with the others in a big swimming pool to simulate what moving around on the moon would be like. She had forced herself to read the three manuals from cover to cover twice. She was ready to go. All that was left now was the wait. And dread.

She looked at the clock. It was almost like it was moving backward or had stopped altogether. As soon as they were in their places in the rocket, everything would be easier. Then it would be too late to back out, too late to turn back.

But there were still sixteen hours to go.

The countdown had begun.

16:14:32.

16:14:31.

16:14:30.

She tried to focus on the TV show, force herself not to look at the clock. The plot of this show was the same as always. Three or four people arguing about some trivial thing or other in a living room with a sofa in the middle. And about every ten seconds there would be a prerecorded, canned salvo of laughter from the audience so that at least there was some indication that the whole thing was supposed to be funny. For a while she thought about calling Silje to say good-bye, but she quickly rejected the idea. The last thing she needed was bad news, and talking to Silje or any of the other band members was almost definitely guaranteed not to improve her mood.

Mia looked at the clock again: 16:03:22.

Only eleven minutes had passed since the last time she'd checked. Time was a sticky, sleepy snail.

She put her headphones over her ears and quickly browsed through her computer files to the folder of demos the band had recorded at Leonora's house. She tried singing along to a couple of the songs to freshen up her memory, but it didn't go well. It was like they weren't her songs anymore. The music sounded foreign, as if it had been recorded in a completely different era. She turned it off in the middle of the song they had been the most satisfied with and browsed through the rest of the folders. Ultimately she found her way back to the Talking Heads. Unlike her own band's music, they didn't feel foreign to her. Just the opposite. Every time she listened to them lately, she felt like she understood them better and better. She put on one of her favorites, the song "Life During Wartime": *"This ain't no party, this ain't no disco, This ain't no fooling around."*

She had to concentrate now, had to be ready. She had to be prepared, push all thoughts of her family and friends out of her mind. *The moon*, she thought. *Focus on the moon.*

If you do well up there, you'll be able to spend the rest of your life doing exactly what you want.

She had the volume up to max, and the music was roaring in her ears. Maybe that's why she didn't hear the knock on the door. She suddenly looked up and saw Antoine and Midori smiling at her from the doorway.

"Everyone at Kennedy Space Center can hear you." Midori laughed.

Had she been singing out loud and not realized it? Mia was embarrassed and tore off her headphones.

"Sorry," she said.

"I'm sure no one minds. Anyway, it's great to hear you singing. It's so quiet around this place, it makes me paranoid."

"What are you listening to?" Antoine asked in his stereotypically French accent. *To what eez eet zat you are listening?*

"Talking Heads."

Antoine and Midori looked at each other. Neither of them was familiar with the group.

"Is that your band?" Midori asked.

Mia shook her head. She'd told them that she played in a band at home, but they hadn't heard any of her recordings.

"But you have some of your stuff on here? Your band's?"

Midori walked right over to the bed and picked up the headphones. She put them on her head. "Let's hear it, then."

Mia found their best song and pressed *play*. Midori was quiet while she waited for the music to start. Antoine moved closer, watching the two girls in anticipation.

"Wow, that is really cool," Midori said, tapping out the beat with her foot.

"You think?" Mia replied.

Midori started doing dance moves. "Are you guys going to put out an album or what?" she asked.

"I don't know."

"You have to!" Midori shouted, dancing her way toward the bathroom. "You'll sell millions. At least."

"Let me hear," Antoine pleaded, moving over to intercept Midori. She handed him the headphones, and soon he, too, was moving to the music. He was stiff and it was comical to watch, but the sight still made Mia incredibly happy. The doubts she'd just been feeling were suddenly gone. Of course their songs were good. Of course her lyrics and her voice were a big part of that. They could be big international stars.

And in that instant she became more determined than ever that when she got home to Norway, she would take the band to new heights. They'd be the best band in the country.

Midori and Antoine hung out in Mia's room all evening. Mia liked it, having them here with her. There was something safe about them, Antoine and Midori. They didn't need anything from her.

"Are your parents coming to the launch tomorrow?" Antoine asked.

"I guess so. I don't know. I actually haven't talked to them about it."

"How weird," Midori said.

"Well, *they're* weird." Mia laughed. "Are yours coming, Antoine?"

"Oh, yeah," Antoine said.

She actually knew that from before. Antoine's parents had been there every single day. They were the real nosy type. Mia thought NASA might be starting to get sick of them. But, of course they were nice enough people.

Midori's parents had also been at Kennedy Space Center every day since the training had moved to Florida. They were quieter, probably because they didn't speak very much English, so she hadn't really talked to them. The only time had been after the first and only press conference that had been held at the base. Media crews from all over the world had been there. Every single TV station and newspaper had interviewed them. Mia had left most of the talking to Antoine and Midori, and thankfully the crew had dealt with the hard questions. Mia's main contribution had been saying that she was looking forward to trying to walk on the moon with almost no gravity.

"Are you dreading it?" Midori asked.

Mia paused. "I'm not really sure. Are you?"

"I think so. How about you, Antoine?"

Antoine nodded his head slowly a few times. "Yes. A lot."

"Look at it this way," Mia began. "We go. We hang out for a

little while. We come back again. That's all it is. The only difference is we're going a little farther than usual."

"And we're traveling on a rocket that will burn off twenty tons of fuel the first second instead of by car."

"And we've been training for months about everything that can go wrong."

"Nothing's going to go wrong," Mia said, with no clue as to where all her sudden self-confidence was coming from.

"Are you sure?" Midori asked.

"I promise. I'll take care of you," Mia promised her.

"And what about me?" Antoine protested, annoyed. "Who's going to take care of me, huh?"

Mia laughed. "You have to take care of yourself. Besides, aren't you the oldest? You actually ought to be taking care of the two of us."

"True, true," he said, seeming pleased by the idea.

Mia looked at the clock. 12:32:56.

Time had started moving again. It was time to get some sleep.

"Mia?"

"Yeah, Midori?"

"Could I sleep here with you?"

"Why?"

"I don't think I'll be able to sleep down there in my room all by myself. Not tonight. Please?" Midori pleaded.

Mia nodded. "Okay."

"Hey!" Antoine protested. "Well, then I'm sleeping here, too. I'm not going to toss and turn alone in my room while you guys are sleeping in peace."

"Okay, fine." Mia laughed. "Go get your mattresses and then

you can sleep here. But no funny business, you got it? And Antoine, you wait in the hall while we're changing, and you keep under your own covers all night. Agreed?"

He smiled and pretended he was disappointed. "Agreed."

"Good, get going, then. I'm going to bed in fifteen minutes. And it's going to be quiet as a grave in here then."

Family and friends arrived for the launch the next day. Mia saw Antoine's and Midori's parents standing behind the fence at the launch center, waving. The astronauts' families were there, too: wives, children. But no Mom. No Dad. No Sander. She stood there by the truck for a few minutes looking for them, but they didn't show up. Then they were told it was time, and she climbed up onto the back of the truck.

That's when she spotted them, and realized they'd been there the whole time, almost hidden in the background, so she wouldn't be embarrassed by them. For a brief moment she knew she really loved them after all. They waved to her with their hands held high. And Sander was standing between them, with Lion in his hand, its head whipping from side to side as he waved.

Mia climbed on the truck and it rolled away from the people waving, carrying the crew toward the launchpad. The enormous Saturn V rocket grew even taller as they approached. It looked like it was poking a hole in the sky.

As the truck parked next to the rocket and disappeared into its shadow, she realized for the first time just exactly how big it was. It was like a ship—more like a giant aircraft carrier—standing on end.

It was almost hard to grasp. Only the uppermost section of the rocket was the actual spaceship. Only the little capsule located right above the top black stripe. The rest was just fuel. Explosive fuel. The capsule was an almost identical copy of the one they'd used the first time, in 1969. But then there had been only three people on board. The new capsule was twice as big, because now there were eight people. It was going to be crowded, and they were going to spend four days in it.

"Are you ready?" Antoine asked, glancing over at her. He looked like an adult, standing there in his full spacesuit with his helmet under his arm. "It's going to go fine," he told her, and smiled.

Mia didn't respond. She was staring up at the rocket. *Today is the start of a new era,* she thought. *The Mia the world has known is going to leave Earth now. And when I come back, everything will be different.*

And she was more right about that than she knew.

An elevator brought them level with the top of the rocket. Mia, Midori, and Antoine waited in the jetway between the capsule and the fixed service structure while the adults were seated and secured into their seats first. Then the teens followed. Mia was strapped in right next to Midori. The capsule was tipped at a ninety-degree angle, so they were lying on their backs as they sat in their seats. It was a strange feeling, like there wasn't any up or down anymore. Glowing buttons and screens and instruments with numbers flashing surrounded her on all sides. She lay there listening to voices crackling over her headphones as the astronauts spoke to the tower.

They were told there were fifteen minutes left until launch.

"How are you guys doing?" she heard a voice ask over the intercom. It was Caitlin. "Status?"

"Everything okay," Antoine replied.

"Everything okay," Midori repeated.

"Everything okay," Mia said.

"Good."

"Twelve minutes to launch."

"There's no turning back now." Mia wasn't sure who had said that. She didn't recognize the voice.

"Five minutes to launch."

Caitlin was studying the gauges and meters on the computer in front of her and reporting the readings to ground control.

"Two minutes to launch."

"*Ceres*, you're still clear for launch."

"One minute to launch."

"Still clear for launch. Will all departments confirm status?"

The different heads of the various ground control departments could be heard over the intercom as they gave their ready signals:

"TELMU, okay."

"Guidance officer, okay."

"FIDO, okay."

"EECOM, okay."

"GNC, okay."

"Flight surgeon, okay."

"CAPCOM, okay."

"Fifty seconds."

Commander Nadolski was pressing the buttons in front of him quickly and with complete focus.

"Thirty seconds."

"Fifteen seconds."

"Twelve seconds."

"Ten."

Antoine turned toward Mia and looked at her.

"Nine, eight, seven."

He held the eye contact. A nice, warm look.

"Six."

That may have been the exact moment she fell in love with him.

"Five, four — ignition sequence!"

"Three." He smiled at her from inside his helmet.

"Two, one —"

"We have liftoff!"

The pressure thrust them against their seatbacks. Antoine's smile turned into a grimace, and an overwhelming, rumbling sound filled the cockpit. The massive rocket engines pushed them up into the sky with incomprehensible force, until they came through the cloud layer, moving faster and faster. They had trained for this part of the expedition countless times. They had been given an introduction to all the systems and knew what all the sounds meant, what was happening from second to second. Everything was the way it was supposed to be. Still, a fierce wave of fear gripped her. She clenched the armrest and closed her eyes.

Please let me come back again, she thought.

* * *

The residents of Parson's Nursing Home were some of the millions of people worldwide who were following the launch during these exact seconds. All the old people who were well enough to sit upright were gathered in the TV lounge. The volume was turned up as high as it would go so the hard of hearing could follow, so when the countdown reached zero and the rocket engines blasted off it made the floor vibrate.

The nurses and aides clapped their hands, and some of the old folks cheered. Mr. Himmelfarb was looking anxiously at his shoes. *Ceres* lifted off the platform at Kennedy Space Center. He closed his eyes and tried to shut out all the noises.

The whole capsule shook as if it would fall apart at any moment. Mia thought she screamed, but there was too much noise to know for sure. She tried to turn her head to the side to look for Midori, but the pressure was too great — she couldn't move.

Then she heard a bang. She startled in fear for an instant.

"First rocket stage disconnected," she heard Nadolski say. "We're proceeding."

"Good to hear, *Ceres*. Good luck and God be with you!"

There was no point in resisting the force of the rocket. All they could do was let their bodies follow the ship's movements. And just as she came to accept all the head-pounding shaking, it became completely still.

Now she was able to see out the little window on her right side. All she could see was black, black nothingness.

Caitlin loosened her safety harness and turned to Mia, Midori, and Antoine. She fished a ballpoint pen out of the pocket next to her chair and held it up in front of them. Then she let it go. The pen bobbed slowly, weightlessly away from her.

Mia raised her right arm, gave the pen a careful shove, and watched it spin away toward Midori.

They were in space.

2

THE SKY

SEA OF TRANQUILITY

They had been cooped up for almost four days. Weightlessness was no longer a problem. In the beginning it had been hard to adjust to the new conditions, to make sure nothing was floating around in the command module and that all the guidelines for consuming food and beverages were being followed. Now they could move around effortlessly. The difference between up and down was no longer important; without gravity there was nothing to signal to your body if it was standing up or lying down.

Mia had been worried that this loss of reference points would make her feel sick, but it hadn't done that at all. Luckily. Not only would NASA officials have refused to let her go if they thought she would develop space sickness, but any potential vomiting in an environment where irreplaceable instruments covered every single available surface and there was no way to keep floating fluids in check would have had — to put it mildly — unpleasant consequences. The vomit would have floated around freely, sticky and slow, and they would have had to try to collect it with their fingers, bit by bit, before it got all over everything and everyone, creating an intolerable odor — and worst of all, threatened to potentially make the rest of the crew sick.

At night they hooked themselves into their bunks and slept standing up. They took up less space that way than if they slept lying down. During the day they squeezed into the little control room and watched while Commander Nadolski, Caitlin, Wilson, and Stanton did their calculations and inspections, made adjustments, and talked to NASA's ground control over the radio. It was one meaningless message after another:

"Houston, *Ceres* here. We're switching to 34/5, CR IN PX."

"Received, *Ceres*, switching to 34/5, CR IN PX. All clear to drain the DMV nozzle."

"Received. DMV nozzle drained, parallel symenology implemented. TVI is 74.56."

"54-5. Received. Would you read off the OTY readings for us?"

"Sure. One second. OTY is 54-5, 54-5, 54-5, 89-7, 89-8 . . ."

It had been exciting to listen to in the beginning, trying to guess what it all meant. But now the incessant chatter back and forth over the crackly lines had just become irritating. Mia did her best to block out the sounds.

The windows were fogged up. The breath of eight people was creating condensation in the capsule, and Mia had to wipe the glass at regular intervals to be able to see out. Not that there was much to see. The stars that had so engrossed and transfixed her the day before were starting to bore her. They weren't changing; nothing was changing. How incredibly strange to feel completely still, even though she knew she was actually traveling over thirty thousand miles per hour.

The first few hours after they'd left Kennedy Space Center had been the best. She had squeezed in around the biggest window with Midori, Antoine, and Caitlin and watched Earth as the space capsule orbited it. The sight had been indescribable. Not only had she been able to see the shape of Earth with total clarity, as if it were an enormous beach ball, she'd also seen whole countries—yes, almost whole continents. Italy really did look like a boot, and Caitlin had pointed out forest fires in Portugal to them. The smoke stretched over the terrain like white lines. It was weird to think that seven billion people lived on Earth, and yet it was impossible to see any buildings at all. Not one of the big cities was visible. It just looked deserted, the whole thing.

But Caitlin had known what she was thinking.

"It looks different at night," she'd said. "You won't see the lights where the people live until then. And how much of this planet is uninhabited."

It hit Mia right then that she still hadn't read the letter Sander wrote to her in New York more than three months ago. Those first several days in Houston were so busy she'd forgotten about everything other than the training. She had remembered to bring it with her when they left Houston, but then she had stuck it in her closet. In all the hubbub she didn't remember whether she'd brought it with her or not. But she had, hadn't she? She quickly looked through the small bag of private items she'd been allowed to take with her, but didn't find it. She wanted to dump everything out to make sure the letter wasn't hiding in with her journals and other things, but she knew that was impossible. Everything would bob around out of control and it would be complicated to get it all back again. It wouldn't be a particularly popular maneuver with the crew, either.

Resigned, she just had to accept that the letter from her brother was probably back in Florida. Maybe it was just nonsense, but for all she knew, it could be really clever. Sander might not be like all the other kids his age, but sometimes when she least expected it he'd surprise her with a sudden burst of inspiration. But the letter would just have to sit there for a couple more weeks. Unread.

Antoine was reclining behind Mia and dozing off. Nadolski and Caitlin were bent over a stack of papers, mumbling quietly to each other as they continuously made notes in black notebooks. Aldrich Coleman, the oldest person on board, was sitting with his head in his hands, looking out the window. He was a strong, fifty-nine-year-old man with a short beard and not much hair. It looked like he was even more bored than Mia, and that could well be the case. He didn't have anything to do at the moment, either. His job wouldn't start until after they had landed on the moon and gotten into the moon base. It would be his responsibility to make sure the base was functioning and that everyone followed the rules. But until then, he was just a passenger.

Midori was sitting just to Mia's left, reading a book. Mia tapped her lightly on the shoulder.

"What are you reading?" Mia asked, hoping to start a conversation to pass the time.

Midori lowered her book, turned it around, and looked at the cover, as if she wasn't actually entirely sure what she was reading.

"*Robinson Crusoe*," she answered. "Do you know it?"

"I know the story, anyway."

"Have you ever thought about what it would be like if you wound up on a desert island someday? Or what it would be like if all the people in the whole world disappeared, and you were the only one left, and the one thing you could rely on was yourself? Don't you ever think about stuff like that? That maybe you'll never get to see another person again?" Midori didn't wait for a response before adding, "I think about stuff like that all the time."

Caitlin came over to them and squeezed in next to Mia.

"How are you guys doing?"

Mia shrugged. "Okay."

"You see that screen over there?" Caitlin asked, pointing to a small video screen showing a glowing number 122. The girls nodded. "That means we're one hundred twenty-two minutes away from disconnecting with *Ceres*. And that, ladies, means that we're going in for our landing on the moon. So unless you have other, better plans, I suggest you start putting on your suits and moving your things over into the lunar lander."

She gave them a big, friendly smile as she said the last sentence, but neither Mia nor Midori noticed. They were already waking up Antoine and starting to wriggle their way back through the spaceship to where their airtight spacesuits were stored.

The next hour passed with tremendous speed. The suits were put on, tubes hooked up, and valves closed. Caitlin led them back through the spaceship to the oval hatch, gripped the large wheel in the middle, and spun it around. The hatch opened.

"Go on in. Be careful not to bump into anything. Sit down in the seats at the very back and buckle yourselves in." Caitlin disappeared for a second and showed up again with the others. One by one they pulled themselves over into the lunar lander: Midori, Antoine, Caitlin, Mia, Stanton, Wilson, and Coleman. Only Nadolski was left in *Ceres*, confirming final details with Earth.

"Okay, Houston, everything is ready for separation here. LOWP is set at 6658. *Ceres* will proceed in its preset orbit until we reconnect again in one hundred seventy-two hours. I'm moving over into lunar lander *Demeter* now."

"Received, *Ceres*. Good luck."

"This is *Ceres*. Over and out from here."

And then Nadolski entered the lunar lander. Mia was surprised to see that the screen back in *Ceres*—which had read 122 last time she'd looked—now showed just one minute remaining. Nadolski closed the steel hatch and turned the wheel firmly until it was sealed. He turned to the other seven who were crammed into the microscopic capsule.

"Hope none of you are afraid of close encounters." He laughed. "You look like sardines in a can."

Caitlin put on her headphones and the microphone. "Houston, *Demeter*. Ready to disconnect."

"Received, *Demeter*."

"We'll disconnect in five, four, three, two, one." She flipped a switch, and a quiet *clunk* was heard. "Disconnection successful," she reported.

"Okay, *Demeter*. You're all clear to descend."

Caitlin addressed her passengers. "Okay, everyone, this is it. We're ready to begin our descent and landing on the moon. We'll be landing in fifty-five minutes. As you all know, I'm the pilot aboard the lunar lander, and Commander Nadolski will be assisting me along the way. That means I must now ask the rest of you to be completely quiet until I tell you it's all right to talk again. We're going to need our full concentration. Is that understood?"

"Yes," Mia and Antoine responded in unison.

Caitlin did not look satisfied. "I ask again: Is that understood?"

This time no one responded.

"Good. Then we'll begin."

The fifty-five minutes that followed were more like a dream than anything else. It was as if they were all holding their breath. With the exception of muffled conversation between Caitlin and Nadolski and regular reports from the control center in Houston, there was complete silence on board.

Then, the view changed. From just being black nothingness, Mia could now see the gray surface of the moon through the one window. Every minute that went by, the contours became clearer and clearer. She saw mountains and valleys, hills, and crevices.

And then, as the lander rolled over onto its side, she saw the most exceptional sight she had ever seen: her very first Earthrise.

As the blue planet slowly emerged over the moon's horizon, suddenly she realized how far away from home they really were.

Caitlin turned to the three teenagers.

"Well, time to find your smiles! We're hooking up the cameras and will be transmitting live back to Earth from now on until we land." Nadolski flipped a couple of switches, and two video cameras switched on. "Wave at the folks back home," he said.

But none of them waved. They were way too busy watching what was going on outside.

"You're clear for landing," the control center in Houston announced.

"Landing in two minutes, thirty seconds," Nadolski reported back to ground control.

"Rotate three degrees down," Caitlin commanded, and Nadolski carried out the order.

"Two minutes to landing."

Mia could see the surface very clearly now, and she thought she'd never seen anything so lifeless. Everything was just gray. Gray, gray ash, absolutely no sign of life.

"One minute!"

Midori grabbed hold of her, holding her tight. Antoine seemed glued to the window.

"Oh my God," he exclaimed. "It's amazing!"

Caitlin stared at him sternly. "Antoine, quiet! Otherwise you'll have to walk from here!"

"Thirty seconds," Nadolski reported.

"Two and a half forward, drive a little to the left."

"Fifteen seconds, kicking up a little dust."

You could have heard a pin drop.

"Ten seconds."

You could have heard grass grow.

"Five seconds."

You could have heard God thinking.

"Contact. Engine off. Contact light on."

Caitlin was standing, facing Mia and Midori as she proudly announced to Mission Control in Houston and the millions of people who were guaranteed to be watching the live broadcast: "Houston, *Demeter* has landed in the Sea of Tranquility."

Mia looked out the window.

They had arrived.

ALDRIN

Captain Nadolski opened the hatch. He had checked each of their suits and made sure their helmets were properly secured. Coleman vented the air out of *Demeter.* Then Nadolski turned the big wheel and opened the hatch to the vacuum.

"Let's hope the moon shows us its most hospitable side" was the last thing Nadolski said before he turned around and climbed backward out the hatch.

Caitlin was the next one out. She struggled a little to find the ladder with her feet before she finally felt the step and climbed out. As soon as she had both feet on the ground, she aimed a video camera back up at the open hatch to film everything that happened.

And one by one, they climbed out and down onto the surface of the moon.

Midori had some trouble finding her footing. The suit felt

enormous and it made movement difficult. She had to constantly tell her limbs what to do before they would move, and even then they didn't quite seem to follow her orders. She suddenly felt a hand carefully pulling her left leg onto the ladder as she heard Nadolski say "I got you" over the intercom. The next minute she was standing with both feet planted in the gray dust.

The first thing that hit her was the silence. An overwhelming, dead silence, as if the only sound left in space was the suppressed sound of her own breathing. It gave her a feeling of having stepped outside the whole universe.

Midori wondered if her parents were watching right now. Probably they were. After the launch they'd been sent back to Houston along with Mia's and Antoine's parents, and now they were most certainly sitting somewhere at Johnson Space Center visitors' center bragging that that was their daughter. It wasn't hard to imagine her mother worrying incessantly as she thought about everything that could go wrong up here.

Mia considered saying a few well-chosen words as she climbed out. She had spent a lot of time trying to come up with something that seemed suitable for the occasion, something historic. But she hadn't been able to think of anything. Not a single word. And now, standing on the surface trying to slow down her heart rate and orient herself, she understood why. Her newfound respect for Armstrong and Aldrin only increased. No words seemed able to capture the beauty and eeriness of this place. But they had done it. Especially Aldrin. He had stepped off the LM and reported back to Earth the only possible words: *Magnificent. Magnificent desolation.*

Antoine was the last of the three to exit the LM. He had spent the most time at the neutral buoyancy lab back in Houston, and he exited the craft like a professional. No hesitation, no trouble; he just crawled out backward, found the ladder, and simply stepped down. He took a look around, as if to make sure he was in the right place before giving a thumbs-up to Nadolski. They were all here, all accounted for, ready to go.

And then a thought hit Antoine, without warning, but with great intensity. It was more of a statement of the truth than a casual reflection. *We don't belong here. Not at all.* But he kept his mouth shut.

Nadolski instructed them on the easiest way to move in the moon's weak gravitational field. "Imagine that you're under water. Remember what we practiced in the pool? Good. The easiest way to move is to lean forward slightly, but not too much. If you fall in these big suits, you'll need help getting up again. And for Pete's sake, stop jumping around, Midori!"

Nadolski let them practice for a few minutes before he gave Aldrich Coleman the sign.

"Okay. Everyone here? Then let's head to the moon base," Coleman said.

Mia hadn't even noticed it, but now that Coleman had them move away from the lunar lander, she suddenly noticed a large installation a few hundred yards away.

Coleman noticed that Mia was staring. "Yup, this is DARLAH 2," he said. "Isn't she beautiful?"

She shrugged, eyeing the white construction. It was hard to say what it looked like. An oblong and grossly oversized white shipping container, maybe. "I don't know if 'beautiful' is the right word, exactly," she replied.

"Oh, just wait. You'll come around. Once you've been there a few days. Besides, I can promise you that it's much better to be in there than it is to be out here in this desert."

"What happened to the first one, anyway?"

"What do you mean?" Coleman asked.

"I mean, if this base is called DARLAH 2 . . . well, then, where's DARLAH 1?"

Coleman's face clouded as he paused, and his voice took on a serious timbre. "We can come back to that" was all he said, and then turned away from her. He addressed the rest of the group: "Come on. We have to get inside before the sun gets too strong."

"Well, everyone," Mia heard Caitlin say over the intercom, addressing the people watching the live broadcast back on Earth, "are you ready for the great revelation? As you can see, we're safe and sound, and we're on our way over to DARLAH 2. This is the stationary moon base where we'll be spending the next one hundred and seventy-two hours."

As they slowly made their way to the base, Caitlin narrated with a history that had been kept secret from the rest of the world for close to half a century.

"DARLAH 2 is composed of modules built and transported to the moon by NASA craft. Four teams of six astronauts, with the help of lunar buggies and highly sophisticated robotics, assembled the base over a period of years in the mid-seventies in a program named Operation DP7. The existence of the program was kept secret from the public, as both NASA and the U.S. government feared the Soviets would not believe that the reason for building a permanent base on the moon had nothing to do with bringing weapons into space. It was intended as a research facility for mining rare minerals as well as acting as a staging area for future international expeditions to Mars, which NASA thought would be possible to undertake by the late nineties. The astronauts of DP7 operated out of the Skylab space station that was officially abandoned in 1974. In 1979, when the work on the moon was completed, Skylab was purposely made to reenter Earth's atmosphere, where it disintegrated over Australia. Interestingly, the astronauts never entered DARLAH 2 the entire time they were assembling it on the surface. The base's modules had been sealed so as not to corrupt the environment. The astronauts had to stay in the cramped compartment of their LM while on the moon, working in shifts. Unfortunately, NASA never sent men to Mars, so the base has sat here, unused, this whole time. A very well-hidden museum piece. Until now."

"Now?" Mia asked.

"Yes, NASA, along with the Japanese, European, and Russian space agencies, is planning to start using this place, finally."

"So we are going to Mars after all?"

"Not in the near future. You'd have to spend six months in that spacecraft to get there. Add another six months to get back. The plan is to use DARLAH as a base in the search for tantalum seventy-three, a very rare transition metal used in computers and the development of nanotech. But enough of that now, the more important thing is this: *you.*" Caitlin pointed to Midori, Mia, and Antoine. "These three young people will actually be the first people to visit the base since it left Earth, piece by piece."

She has a perfect voice for TV, Mia thought. *It's like she was made for this.*

"DARLAH 2 is two hundred and forty-eight by ninety-six meters, divided into four modules and an oxygen generator. The base has a living room, a communications room, six bedrooms, a bathroom, a storeroom, and an infirmary. It also has its own greenhouse connected to the oxygen generator, which not only takes care of reproducing oxygen but also provides enough food to keep astronauts alive for a very long time. The plan is for DARLAH 2 to serve as a residence for future astronauts who will conduct research on the moon and for astronauts who are continuing on to Mars."

Caitlin turned the camera to the ground and continued. "We now find ourselves at a historic moment, perhaps the most historic of them all. This is the exact spot where *Apollo 11* landed on July 20, 1969. Astronaut Buzz Aldrin's boot print is still clearly visible in the dust."

They stared at the imprint in disbelief. "NASA has decided to preserve Aldrin's footprint as an official monument to the first moon landing." Caitlin placed a transparent Plexiglas box over it to prevent any astronauts from disturbing the historic print. "Because of the vacuum out here, this one footprint could remain unchanged for millions of years to come. Just as all of our footprints could remain here for eternity, since there's no rain, snow, or wind to erase them."

A few meters from the footprint, Midori discovered something that she at first thought was trash. Several white objects were strewn in the dust. She took a few steps away from the group to investigate more closely. They seemed to be parts of a lander, not unlike the one they'd arrived in. Maybe they were left behind from the first landing.

"Caitlin!" she called into her helmet's built-in microphone. "Could you come over here for a second?"

Caitlin arrived quickly with the camera in her hand. "Well, look at that. The undercarriage of the LM *Eagle*. They left it here, you know. Armstrong and Aldrin. To save weight. The same with the rest that you see around you. They left everything they didn't need."

Among the remnants were two items that caught Midori's interest: a pair of moon boots. "And these?" she asked.

Caitlin took a step closer and zoomed in with her camera. "Yes. Those are Buzz Aldrin's actual moon boots. He left them here, too."

Midori was skeptical. "You mean he went back to Earth in just his stocking feet?"

"Well, he actually had a pair of thermoinsulated inner boots, but... yes."

"Are these going to be saved forever, too, by any chance?" Midori asked.

Caitlin thought about it. "Hmm, I don't know. Houston? What's the plan for Aldrin's boots?"

They waited a second for a response from ground control.

"There are no... uh... special plans for them, no," the response crackled back over the speaker.

"Great," Midori said, grabbing the boots. "Then I'm taking them. They're super cool. A little big, though." She turned around and carefully walked back over to the group.

"Houston, one of the kids just took Aldrin's boots from the surface!" Caitlin exclaimed.

It was quiet on the other end for quite some time. "Well,"

came the response finally, "he ought to have put a little more thought into where he tossed his things. Let her keep them. Until everyone returns to Earth, at least."

"Received," Caitlin said, walking back to Midori, who was just taking off her own boots to put on Aldrin's old pair.

"I wouldn't do that if I were you," Caitlin said calmly, taking hold of her. "The separate inner boots that Aldrin had are not a part of your equipment. You see, your inner boots are a built-in portion of your main boots. And under that you're just wearing socks. The temperature out here now is two hundred forty-eight degrees Fahrenheit. That's not a temperature to be getting undressed in."

"You're right." Midori stopped immediately. "Thank you."

"No problem. Come on, we're going in."

Midori followed Caitlin toward the moon base, and the rest of the group proceeded behind them, with Mia at the very back. She had noticed Midori grab the old moon boots and couldn't help but feel a little jealous. Italian paratrooper boots be damned—this was something totally different! But maybe she would at least get to keep the ones she was wearing now. Those wouldn't be so bad, either.

Every fourth or fifth step Mia turned around and looked at the footprints she was leaving behind. There were already a lot of them now, twenty feet trailing one another in the moondust. She wondered what Aldrin must have felt when he became one of the first to leave his footprint somewhere beyond Earth.

Mia didn't have time to think much else before Caitlin came to a halt. In front of them loomed an expansive grayish building with the NASA logo on it. It was only one story, but from what she could see, it stretched inward in all directions in a jumble of corridors and wings that extended several hundred yards from side to side. A large domed roof towered upward near the middle, and behind that she noticed the large oxygen generator — at least seventy feet high — that ensured they would have unlimited access to fresh air indoors.

Nadolski took the lead, entering a code on the keypad to the left of a large hatch marked HATCH 1, and then turned a large wheel to open it. To Mia's surprise, it moved absolutely noiselessly. She had expected to hear a scraping, moaning sound. *It's the vacuum that does that*, Mia thought. *That's why I can't hear it.*

This was followed by a thought — she had no idea where it had come from — but it forced its way into her consciousness and scared her to death: *In space, no one can hear you scream.*

After a moment's hesitation, Mia followed Nadolski into the decompression chamber along with the others. He shut the hatch behind them and equalized the pressure so they could take off their helmets and breathe the air in the moon base.

They were inside DARLAH 2.

THE NAME

They put Himmelfarb in the chair in front of the TV in his room. Sometimes they did that when there weren't enough aides working to keep an eye on all the residents. It worked like a charm every time. The old folks sat there neatly and politely and forgot all about time and place and the fact that they hadn't been bathed in several days.

Mr. Himmelfarb was excited and happy. He was watching a talk show, and the camera had just panned across the audience. Somehow, he'd gotten it into his head that they'd all stopped by to surprise him and have a cup of coffee with him in his room. He started rummaging around in his closet and cabinets for plates and silverware to serve the guests and arranged the dishware pleasantly on the bed. He threw away the flowers that were sitting on the windowsill and poured water from the vase into some cups.

"There you go," he mumbled inaudibly, turning his eyes toward the TV in concern. But the audience was still sitting there. Why weren't they getting up?

There weren't enough cups for everyone — that was the problem. He set his shoes, his hat, his radio, and the pictures from the wall in a row on the bed. He filled the vase and poured water into the shoes. *There.* He turned back to the screen again. Why didn't his guests want to stand up?

Mr. Himmelfarb slumped down onto his chair and sat there for half an hour before one of the aides came in to check on him and found his bed full of things. Her cautious hand settled onto his shoulder. "Have you had visitors again?" she asked gently.

Himmelfarb nodded silently.

The aide changed the channel, and the audience disappeared. "There. You see, now they've all left again, every last one." She didn't even notice that the old man was crying.

A new documentary about space had just started while the aide put everything away. There was hectic activity on the screen in front of Himmelfarb. Old, archived images showed researchers hard at work assembling various pieces of equipment and conducting tests. It wasn't easy to see exactly what they were doing, or where the pictures were taken, and the voice didn't say anything about that either. It was busy explaining the history of the American space program, offering statistics about the costs, size, and complexities of the program. Mr. Himmelfarb did not absorb any of this information, but still he remained glued to the screen.

A vague sense that he recognized a number of the faces smiling at him from a still photo took shape. He knew where the picture was taken, didn't he? It was from one of the hangars at Goldstone observatory, and the people in front had worked on a project that... What had it been about again?

He tried to remember. The person in the center of the photo had been in charge; the guy had scarcely been twenty years old back then. But... he'd been made responsible because... because he knew something, wasn't that it? Yes, that was it. He'd done some exceptional calculations at the university and had been summoned to Goldstone to work on what was simply referred to as "the moon question." What was his name again? Cohen? No... Kaufmann? No, that wasn't it, either.

Mr. Himmelfarb was beginning to get muddled again. It was hard to focus, but he kept trying. This photograph, what was it showing? He studied it more closely, trying to see past the people to that structure behind them.

The photo disappeared and was replaced by another one taken from a slightly different angle. The voice-over explained that it was the famous Lunar Roving Vehicle, the LRV, photographed along with the team who had designed and built it at the Boeing factory in Illinois. But that wasn't right. This picture was from Goldstone. No doubt about it. Mr. Himmelfarb kept searching for the name of that man, but now it was almost totally impossible. Collins? No. Kleinmann? He wasn't sure. A third picture was displayed on the screen, this time taken from the other end of the room. It was a photograph that showed the back side of the LRV and the backs of the "researchers."

But that wasn't what suddenly terrified Mr. Himmelfarb.

The fear came from seeing a half-open doorway toward the back of the photo. It wasn't meant to be an important part of the picture, but that was what caught his eye. It was just barely possible to catch a glimpse of a short man with a toolbox standing by the entrance to the room. His face wasn't clear, and you could only make him out if you knew he was standing there. But Mr. Himmelfarb recognized who it was. And he could tell that the person looked terrified.

The man in the photo was him.

"There," the aide said, switching off the TV. "You can't stay up all night watching TV, you know."

Mr. Himmelfarb sat there, staring at the black screen, but all he saw was himself. It looked like he was sneering back at himself from the reflection in the glass, the revolting sneer of a crazy man. He closed his eyes for a few seconds before opening them again. Now it was just his own sad face staring back at him. The loneliest person on the surface of Earth.

The aide's pager went off in her pocket and she fished it out. "Can you sit here for a little bit, Oleg? I'll come back and help you into bed in twenty minutes." She left the room without waiting for his response.

But Mr. Himmelfarb didn't even notice that she had left. It was like something tiny had just clicked in his consciousness. In a flash, the nerve endings in his brain sort of reconnected, really reconnected, and it washed over him, like a tidal wave of awareness.

This is where I live, he thought.

These are my things.

I live in a nursing home?

He slowly walked over to the mirror the aide had hung back up over his sink before she left, and looked at himself. Tears ran down his cheeks when he saw the ancient face staring back at him. It was as if year after year of missing his kids, his wife, his whole life, the person he used to be, were compressed into an overwhelming second of insight. The doors of his mind were wide open, and his brain was clear as the finest crystal.

Coleman. His name was Coleman. Not Cohen, not Kaufmann. Coleman.

And then came the landslide. He remembered everything that had happened at Goldstone the day that picture was taken. It washed over him, almost making him lose his balance.

He remembered Coleman, the reports, the events on the moon. He could clearly picture the grainy image the astronauts of *Apollo 17* had taken in the lunar highlands while doing their EVA. Coleman was the one who had shown it to him one afternoon in the fall of 1979, and just the thought of it made him shudder.

The picture had shown astronaut Eugene Cernan climbing onto the LRV. He looked awkward, as if he were in a hurry and couldn't get away fast enough. And less than a hundred feet behind him in the Taurus-Littrow valley was the reason. A dark silhouette, its contours blurry, but obviously not wearing a spacesuit, wearing ordinary clothes, was coming toward him. Mr. Himmelfarb had met Eugene several times. A nice guy, who unfortunately was never the same after the Apollo mission.

That might have to do with the fact that the figure in the background in the picture who was walking straight toward the rover bore a striking resemblance to Eugene himself.

DARLAH. They're going to start using the base.

But we agreed never to go back there.

Never.

He got his wallet out of his jacket and found his shoes next to the closet. Carefully, so as not to subject his frail body to any sudden movements, he leaned over and picked them up, sat down on the edge of the bed, slipped them on, and left his room. He walked down the hall as quickly as he could, heading for the pay phone by the stairs.

There's still time. They can still abort and come back if they haven't landed yet.

We have to tell them everything. All of it.

He didn't see anyone in the hallway. The few aides who were working were busy with patients in the other wings of the nursing home, which gave him unrestricted access to the pay phone in the hall.

His hands shaking, he fed some coins in, and dialed the old main number for Goldstone. It didn't even occur to him how remarkable it was that in his sudden state of clarity he could actually recall the sequence — but it didn't matter. The memory was futile.

"The number you're trying to reach is no longer in service."

Of course. It had been so long since he'd called there. Of course they'd have totally different numbers by now.

He flipped through the phone book attached to the phone by a metal cable.

K. L. M. N.

There it was. *N.*

NASA.

He found the number for Kennedy Space Center. Called it.

There was a recorded message. A menu, and choices. Too

many choices. It was confusing. He tried pressing *0* with the hope that an operator would pick up. No...just robotic, inappropriately cheerful recordings.

He looked at the time. There ought to be people there now.

He tried again, but no matter what sequence of numbers he used, he couldn't reach a human being.

Desperation and fear were starting to get the upper hand and he slammed down the phone. He felt his heart pumping faster and his chest ached. *Cape Canaveral,* it occurred to him. *I'll try Cape Canaveral.* He flipped through the phone book, found the number. Dialed.

A young man answered.

"Cape Canaveral Air Force Station, how can I help you?"

And with that Mr. Himmelfarb should have started explaining. He should have explained everything, all he knew, what they needed to do, why the mission had to be called off immediately. That he needed to speak to Dr. [redacted] in person, as soon as possible.

But he couldn't get a word out.

His memory was back, but the speech center of his brain wouldn't obey. Nothing would come out of his mouth besides muffled sounds, no matter how hard he struggled to pronounce everything correctly.

"Sir, is there something I can help you with?"

He gurgled and tried harder. But it didn't work.

Don't do this to me. Don't do this to me.

"Sir, are you still there?"

Let me just say one sentence. Let me just warn them. That's all I'm asking.

"Sir, I'm going to have to hang up now."

No, don't, don't. Just give me a little time.

"Good-bye."

Damn!

He felt an enormous wall of rage rising within him and almost blacked out. With more force than he thought his old hands contained, he attacked the pay phone using the receiver as his weapon. He struck huge cracks in the plastic enclosure, shards flying in all directions, and yanked on the receiver, ripping the cord out, but he didn't relent. The handset finally broke apart in his hands, the pieces falling to the floor. But Himmelfarb continued to smash the phone with his bare fists. He rammed his shoulder into the metal plate on the front, and coins tumbled out and clanked noisily to the floor. *It's too late*, he thought, raising both hands over his head. Pain shot up into his arms as he slammed his body into the pay phone. It came off the wall, dangled for a second, and then tumbled to the floor with a crash. Mr. Himmelfarb stood there in silence next to it until the aides came running. Still, he could think only one thing:

They couldn't go back.

They had to stay away.

Never go back there.

DARLAH 2

Antoine raised his hands to his throat, fumbling to find the fastener on his helmet.

"Let me help you. One second." Coleman came over to him and helped him undo the fastener. "There."

Antoine pulled the helmet off and took a breath.

There was something about the air. He noticed it as soon as they emerged from the decompression chamber into the first of the old modules. The air seemed old, stuffy, like it had given up on the thought of anyone ever breathing it. Nothing besides time had been moving around in here. The egg-white walls were covered with equipment and electronics that were clearly from the 1970s. Big LEDs in various colors and patterns blinked as they moved farther in toward module two. Outmoded computers were rattling off numeric codes and strips of information none of them could interpret.

Beyond that, it was disconcertingly quiet; only their footsteps on the steel grating on the floor made booming echoes with every step they took. It made Antoine feel like he was in a church, that he should be respectful and reverent. But then that thought was interrupted by another, darker one that he couldn't explain.

God isn't here. God doesn't even know about this place.

"I suggest we split into two groups," Caitlin told Nadolski. "I'll take the kids. You take Wilson, Stanton, and Coleman to the communications room and report back to Earth."

Nadolski nodded and looked peeved. Who was actually in charge here? He was, wasn't he? After all, he was the mission commander. And here was Caitlin, nothing but a pilot, seizing the reins.

"Fine," he replied tersely, motioning to the men that they should follow him. Caitlin handed Antoine the camera and asked him to film their trip into module two for the audience back on Earth. He moved to the back of the group and got them all in the viewfinder as they proceeded. Caitlin stopped at the first hatch and spoke directly into the camera:

"A number of you at home may be surprised that there appears to be gravity here in DARLAH. Because the base was built for long-term stays, one of the problems NASA struggled with was how to create artificial gravity. This was important to minimize muscle atrophy in the astronauts who would be spending long periods of time up here under near weightless conditions. A highly specialized system located below the floor in the computer room generates a local gravitational field of 0.97G. That's about the same as on Earth, where gravity is 1G."

The two groups of four were now lumbering farther into the base in their unwieldy EV suits. If moving around on the surface had been difficult in the beginning, the transition back to dealing with gravity again in the same gear was even harder. They had to walk slowly, setting one foot in front of the other, concentrating on keeping their balance. To the TV audience, it must have looked ridiculous. But for Mia, Antoine, Midori, and the other astronauts, there was nothing funny here.

The tension and anticipation was thick in the air as they walked through the base for the very first time. Every ten yards or so they encountered a new steel hatch that Caitlin would activate by pressing the button on the wall next to it. They could hear the hydraulic pumps that opened the hatches with a *pyiffff* sound, letting them into the next room. Inside, they could hear all of these sounds plainly and clearly. Caitlin explained that it was because the sound waves had air to move through, making it possible for the ear to perceive them.

"Everything in here is absolutely prehistoric," Midori complained as they made their way to the next safety hatch. "How can you guys be sure everything is still working?" She stopped in front of the hatch and eyed it skeptically for a minute, before she beat Caitlin to it and pressed the activation button. The door slid open. *Pyiffff.*

"Just because it's old doesn't necessarily mean it's bad," Caitlin retorted cheerfully. "Think of it this way. I'm thirty-two. Compared to you guys, I'm old, right? But that doesn't mean I don't work as well as you, does it?"

"But that's totally different," Midori protested, taking a breath. "It smells really weird in here. Stuffy, kind of."

"It'll get better, Midori," Caitlin replied, proceeding on through the hatch into module three. "Just wait until completely new air has started circulating through the modules. Then it'll be better."

"But you guys have tested this base, right?" Antoine asked. Midori's words had struck a nerve with him, and now for the first time on the expedition he was feeling a little less confident. "I mean, you're sure everything's working the way it's supposed to?"

"Absolutely," Caitlin replied gently. "It might look old, and I suppose it is old, everything you see here. But it's still in tip-top shape. Every single little piece and microchip was thoroughly tested before it was sent up into space. And after assembly it was checked again. So I can promise you that it works. Besides, do you really think NASA would take the chance of sending you guys up here if they doubted the equipment? Not to mention sending along a camera and broadcasting it all live to everyone in the whole world?" Her voice sort of quivered a little as she spoke.

"I don't know," Antoine said meekly.

"After all, you guys have to remember that the computers they had in 1969 were good enough for people to land on the moon. And the last time I checked, it wasn't like a PlayStation could do that."

The discussion stopped there. But to themselves they were all thinking the same thing: *How sure can you really be?* They continued the last little way to the B wing corridor without saying anything else to one another.

Mia and Midori got to share a room. Antoine was assigned the neighboring room. All the others would be living farther down the corridor. First a room for Caitlin, then Wilson and Stanton's room, then a single room for base manager Coleman, and all the way at the end of the corridor, Nadolski's room. On the other side of the corridor there was a big kitchen and farther down a spacious bathroom that they would all share.

Caitlin took them on a brief tour. The kitchen was strangely old and futuristic at the same time. It seemed like someone had tried to copy a 1970s science-fiction movie, everything all egg white with rounded corners. Two big doors along the one wall were labeled PANTRY and COLD STORAGE. Caitlin stopped in front of them.

"Here's our food supply," she said with a grin. The teenagers looked at one another.

"What do you mean?" Midori exclaimed. "You mean we're going to be eating whatever's in there?" She opened the door labeled PANTRY and peered in. Rows of shelves were covered with cans and boxes, all stamped with the logos for NASA and DARLAH. "But all of this is from the seventies, isn't it?"

"Of course," Caitlin said. "It's freeze-dried. Lasts practically forever."

"Well, I for one am *not* going to be eating that. You can just forget it," Midori fumed.

"That's up to you. But don't forget we're going to be here for one hundred and seventy-two hours, Midori. That's a whole week, you know."

That message seemed to sink in with Midori. She thought about it for a minute before she added: "Well, then I hope you guys have some Asian food stored up here, too, and not just a pile of hamburgers."

"I doubt you'll find sushi in there, if that's what you mean, but we may be able to dig up some noodles." Caitlin looked at the clock. "Okay, it's five o'clock. There've been a lot of impressions already. I suggest you go back to your rooms, so you can take off your suits and relax for a couple of hours. I'll come by at seven, and we'll go over to the living room in the A wing and meet up with the others before we head to dinner. Does that sound okay?"

None of them had any objections; they'd been longing to take off the suits. Only now did they realize how tired they actually were. Antoine trudged down the corridor behind Midori and Mia toward their bedrooms. All three stopped at the girls' door, and Antoine just stood there.

"Antoine?" Mia asked, looking at him askance.

He gave the two girls a gloomy look. "If either of you wants to have your very own room on the moon right now, you're very welcome to mine. It isn't exactly... how I envisioned it."

Mia took the hint and gave him a wry smile. "Okay, Antoine. Come on. Your girls will look after the poor little Frenchman who's afraid of being alone."

Antoine flung out his arms and looked around as if to say, *Can you blame me?* and followed them into the room.

Caitlin stood in the doorway for a second. "You guys have

two hours starting now, is that okay? I suggest you spend that time sleeping, not chatting. And Antoine?"

"Yeah?"

"No funny business with the girls, okay?"

"*Oui*, madame," he replied politely, and with a knowing smile, she left.

The bedroom was more like a little closet with a small, round window and an even smaller closet. Two bunks were mounted on the wall, one over the other, but there was no table, no chairs, nothing else.

"Where do they expect me to sleep?" Antoine asked.

"You were the one who insisted on being in here with us, weren't you?" Mia replied.

"You mean I'm supposed to sleep on the floor?"

The two girls looked at each other.

"You can sleep wherever you want," Mia said as neutrally as she could.

But the truth was that she wasn't indifferent. She knew very well what he would choose. She'd seen the signs in the last several days, how he was always nearby, following her every move.

"Well then, can I sleep next to you, Mia?" Antoine asked.

"Sure you can." She knew her response was too fast because Midori rolled her eyes and turned her back as she pulled off her bulky spacesuit.

Mia claimed the bottom bunk. She took off her suit and kept her underwear and T-shirt on before climbing in under the covers. Antoine followed right behind her. He carefully lay down next to her at the very edge of the bed. Midori climbed up and lay down in the top bunk.

But none of them could sleep.

Not that they tried, either. What in the world would be the point? You come to the moon and the first thing you do is go to sleep? That was the most idiotic suggestion in history.

Instead, the three teenagers stared out their little round window lit by the strong, clear light reflected from the moon's surface outside. It was so incredibly deserted. Almost beautiful. None of them could think of anything to say. They just lay there in awe of the view.

As time went by and no one spoke it was as if the view slowly changed. A veil of something threatening somehow came over the beautiful silence. They all noticed it, even though no one said it in words.

Perhaps that's what made Midori say, out of the blue: "Have you guys heard the story of Kuchisake-onna?"

"The story of what?" Antoine said.

"Kuchisake-onna, the slit-mouth woman."

"Nope. How come?"

"I just happened to think of her," Midori said from the bunk above. "She lived on Hokkaido in the eleven hundreds and was married to a powerful samurai. You know what a samurai is, right?"

"Of course," said Mia quickly, and then realized that maybe she didn't exactly understand it.

"A kind of merchant soldier for a nobleman, right?" Antoine tried to explain.

"More or less. Anyway: This samurai's wife was uncommonly beautiful, one of the most beautiful women in the whole country. She was also extremely vain. And unfaithful."

"I'm liking her less and less already," Antoine said.

"Yeah, I know, right? The samurai felt the same way, because he found out about her unfaithfulness. And he attacked her in revenge, sliced open her mouth from ear to ear while he screamed, 'Who's going to think you're beautiful now?'"

Midori let a few seconds go by before she continued. "According to the legend, she still roams around Japan at night. And her face is always covered by a surgical mask."

"I thought almost everyone in Japan wore surgical masks outside," Mia said.

"That's exactly the point," Midori replied. "A lot of Japanese people wear surgical masks when they're in places with a lot of people, to avoid spreading bacteria or catching a cold or stuff like that. That's why it's so hard to spot her. But you know it's her when she stops you and asks, '*Watashi kirei?*'"

Mia was about to ask what that meant, but Midori beat her to it. "Am I beautiful?" Midori translated.

"Ew," Antoine said.

"And if you say yes, she takes off her mask, shows her mutilated face, and asks: 'How about now?'"

Mia stuck her head out over the edge of the bed and looked at the Japanese girl in the bunk above her. "Midori, why are you telling us this? That's awful."

But Midori pretended she didn't hear her. "If you say no," she continued, "she'll kill you. And if you say yes again, she follows you home and kills you outside your house."

"In other words, she'll kill you no matter what," Antoine noted.

"No," Midori said. "There are two ways to get out of it. One way is to answer that she looks average. That will make her stop and think, which will give you enough time to get away."

"And the other?" Mia asked.

"The other way is to hold a container of hair pomade up in front of her face. That will remind her of the smell of a surgeon who once tried to help her."

"That's the dumbest story I've ever heard," Antoine remarked.

"It doesn't matter to me what you think, but know this: In the summer of 1979, three teenagers from Hokkaido inexplicably disappeared. They were fourteen, fifteen, and sixteen, on their way home from soccer practice. They were never found again. Even though the police searched the area for weeks, with dogs and uniformed officers. You know how I mentioned my uncle works for the Tokyo police in the Shibuya precinct? I was talking to him about this story last winter, and he was already aware of it. So I asked him to do a search in the database on the case, and you know what he found?"

Antoine was starting to look pale. Suddenly it was no longer the dumbest story he'd ever heard. Mia looked concerned. What worried her most wasn't the story per se, but that *he* was so clearly freaked out.

Midori slowly sat up in bed and climbed down to the other two, standing on the floor in front of them.

"He found a police report about a car accident that involved a woman. The car was found late at night. It was pouring rain and it was sheer luck that it was found at all, but it was. It had rolled over and was upside down on the shoulder, and when the policeman pulled her out, he discovered that her mouth was split from ear to ear. According to the report he wrote at the scene, she was conscious but didn't respond to the question when he asked her what her name was. All she said to him was 'Am I still beautiful?' Over and over and over again. He ran to his patrol car and called an ambulance, but when he got back she was gone. The same policeman was found dead later the same night. Right outside the front entrance of the apartment building he lived in."

"And where did this happen?" Antoine asked.

Midori fixed her eyes on his. "Where do you think?"

"Hokkaido?" He shuddered.

"Exactly. *Hokkaido.* Just a few hundred yards from where those teenagers were last seen."

Midori stood there lost in thought, as if she wasn't quite sure herself why she was telling the story. "Anyway," she said, suddenly back in her normal mood, "I just happened to think of that. I'm going to go to the bathroom. Don't make any babies while I'm gone, okay?"

And with that, she disappeared out the door.

Completely speechless, Mia and Antoine watched her leave. Neither of them moved. Mia noticed that Antoine was lying on the very edge of the mattress and that he was about to fall off onto the floor.

"You don't need to lie all the way over there if you don't want to," she said. "There's actually plenty of room."

He looked at her. "Are you sure?"

"Mmm."

He moved closer and Mia felt his foot touch hers. Instinctively she jumped and pulled her foot back, but then she regretted that and slowly pushed it back over to his.

"You know…I, uh, well, ever since, uh…" Antoine was

struggling to find the right words, but suddenly it was like they'd all been left in another room.

"You don't need to say anything," Mia said, putting her arm around him. And then he kissed her, more or less exactly 238,000 miles from the place where she'd thought it would happen.

ALARM

Midori had come back to the room just seconds after that first kiss had taken place, which effectively put a stop to any more. She hardly noticed that anything had changed while she'd been in the bathroom; but if she'd been paying attention to the details, she would have noticed that Antoine and Mia were making sure to be next to each other the whole time. And if she'd really been paying attention, she would have seen that he was giving Mia looks that meant he couldn't care less about the moon or the mission or all the fame in the world as long as he got to be around her.

Mia, for her part, tried as best she could to pretend to everyone else that nothing was going on. She had been thinking for a long time that something might happen between the two of them. But still, it happened so suddenly that she felt like she needed a little time before she would be ready to be teased by Midori or anyone else. But they would notice eventually, that was a given. Because sooner or later they would notice the little smile that was taking residence on her face. And for the first time, she was really, really glad she had come on this trip.

Antoine, Midori, and Mia were ready when Caitlin knocked on the door at exactly seven o'clock. The three teenagers followed her back through the long corridor that connected modules one and two via the computer room in the middle. Once they were in the large living room in module one, they met the rest of the crew, who were already waiting for them. Midori found a seat next to Coleman, while Mia and Antoine sat down next to Caitlin on the left side of the room.

Nadolski gave the dated decor a scornful look and took the floor. "Ladies and gentlemen, boys and girls, now we're finally gathered, all of us together, here in DARLAH 2. Welcome! As you know, base manager Aldrich Coleman is in charge as long as we're in here. I'm still responsible for the mission as a whole, but I want you to follow all of the instructions and orders Coleman gives you as long as we're indoors. Is that clear?" A bunch of *yes*es and *okay*s could be heard from throughout the room. "Good. Aldrich?"

Coleman stood up and moved to the center of the room. "Thanks, Lloyd. Well, I'll be brief. You know most of what there is to know about this place from the briefing in Houston, but let me repeat the most important things. DARLAH 2 is composed of four modules. Number one, which we're in now; number two, where you're sleeping and where the kitchen and bathroom are located; number three, where the computer room, greenhouse, and oxygen generator are; and number four, which contains the infirmary, equipment for going outside, and the decompression chamber. That was the way we came in. Module four was built and installed in the fall of 1976. The other modules are from the period between 1974 and 1976. By pressing the buttons near each safety hatch, you can move freely between modules one, two, and three, but I would ask you not to go into module four without permission from Commander Nadolski or myself. The same is true for the computer room, the greenhouse, and the oxygen generator in module three. Access to those is restricted and by permission only. I'm going to give each of you a map of DARLAH 2 so you get your bearings. Caitlin?"

"Yup," she replied, and went over to a cupboard, retrieved a stack of maps, and handed them out.

Mia took one, thanked her, and studied the drawings.

"Otherwise, what else is there?" Coleman thought for a moment. "Ah, yes. The room next to us is the communications room. This is where we'll maintain contact with Earth and where it'll also be possible for you guys to call home via radio if you need to. But only if it's absolutely necessary. This is not your average phone booth. We've also scheduled one press conference per day. These will be done via a linkup from the communications room. Nadolski will give you lists of which press conferences each of you will be attending. I shouldn't need to mention this, but I will anyway: Do your best to appear as positive as possible. Whether you're here to do your job or because you won a contest, we're all in the same boat. To resume..." He paused a little too long, searching for the right words. "To

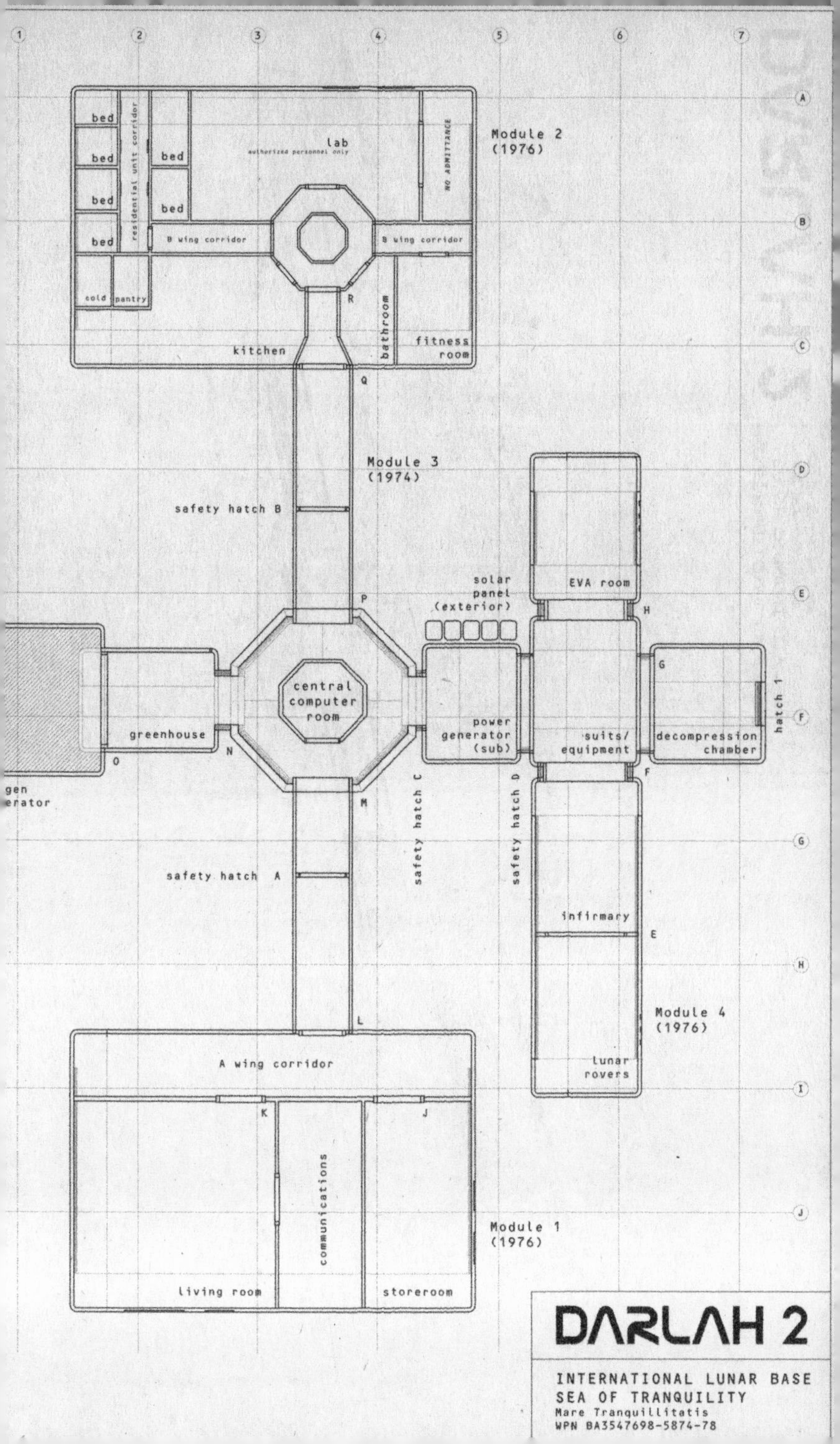

1
2
3
4
5
6
7
A
B
C
D
E
F
G
H
I
J
bed
bed
bed
bed
bed
bed
residential unit corridor
lab
authorized personnel only
NO ADMITTANCE
Module 2
(1976)
B wing corridor
B wing corridor
cold
pantry
R
bathroom
fitness
room
kitchen
Q
Module 3
(1974)
safety hatch B
P
solar
panel
(exterior)
EVA room
H
central
computer
room
greenhouse
O
N
power
generator
(sub)
suits/
equipment
G
decompression
chamber
hatch 1
F
gen
erator
M
safety hatch C
safety hatch D
safety hatch A
infirmary
E
Module 4
(1976)
L
lunar
rovers
A wing corridor
K
J
communications
Module 1
(1976)
living room
storeroom
DARLAH 2
INTERNATIONAL LUNAR BASE
SEA OF TRANQUILITY
Mare Tranquillitatis
WPN BA3547698-5874-78

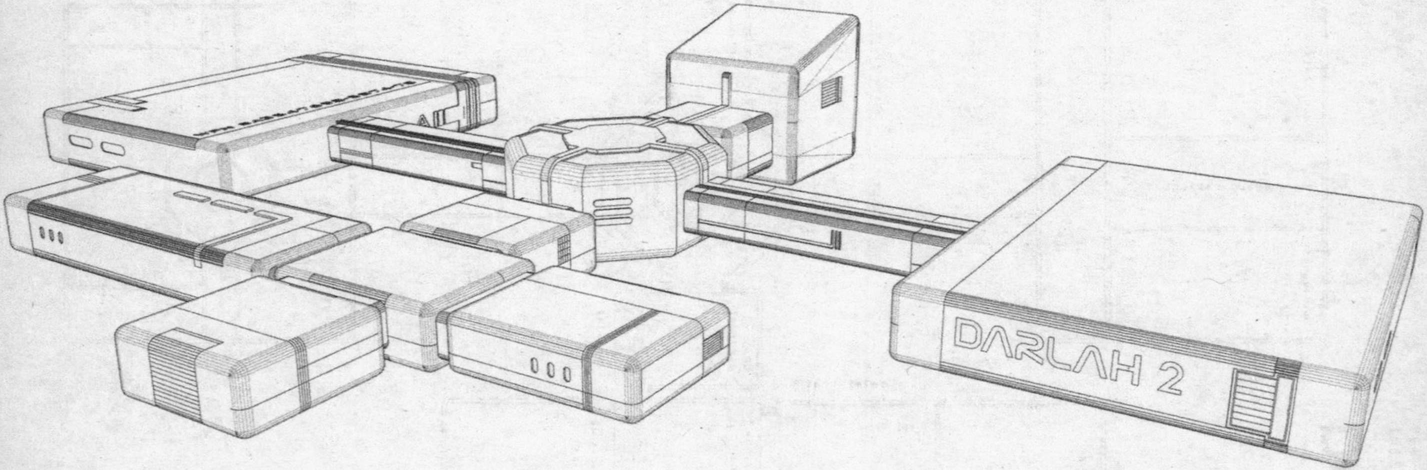

DARLAH 2

INTERNATIONAL LUNAR BASE
SEA OF TRANQUILITY
MARE TRANQUILLITATIS
WPN BA3547698-5874-78

resume studying the moon and procure support and financial resources for NASA to do just that."

It was at about that point that Mia started nodding off. Coleman continued to recount details about the base, what they were allowed to say during the press conferences, and what was classified information. He had a gentle voice, deep and pleasant, but also sleep-inducing. His tone reminded her of a car that just kept going and going in a straight line through the desert.

Nadolski took over from Coleman, and his rougher, more dynamic voice woke Mia back up again. Or maybe that was Antoine's fault, because he had just placed his hand on hers. Whatever had gotten her attention, she heard that rock samples would be collected, solar winds would be studied, and gravitation would be mapped in the areas from the Sea of Tranquility to Plinius and the big valley by the Sea of Serenity. And magnetism—there was a lot about that. Mia struggled to pay attention without quite pulling it off. Midori, on the other hand, was taking notes enthusiastically.

Antoine leaned over to Mia and whispered into her ear. "I was wondering, if you... well, if you'd like to come to bed—I mean, um, sleep in my room—with me?"

The thought made her surprisingly uncomfortable. Of course she wanted to share a room with him. But at the same time she had also been looking forward to sharing a room with Midori. And what would Midori think about having to sleep alone? On the way over from module two, Mia had felt like she was in full control of the situation, but now she suddenly felt like everything was moving too fast.

"Maybe," she said. "We'll see."

Antoine looked a little disappointed and leaned back in his chair. But he didn't let go of her hand.

Once again Coleman moved to the middle of the group.

"Okay. We've been through the most important things. Now I suggest that we all move into the communications room for our first press conference. There's half an hour set aside for it, and you'll all be asked questions by the journalists gathered in Houston. After that, we'll head over to the kitchen"—he flung out his arms—"and eat our first dinner on the moon together!" His awkward gesture seemed to emphasize how absurd and wonderful he thought it was to finally use this base that had been waiting for astronauts since the 1970s.

They moved into the communications room in a herd and sat down on benches in front of two cameras on tripods. The engineers, Wilson and Stanton, readied the equipment, and a minute later the broadcast was under way. Nadolski did most of the talking; the others commented on a couple of the journalists' technical questions.

Antoine was selected to speak on behalf of Midori, Antoine, and herself. Mia felt a little embarrassed about being shown on TV like this, as if she had suddenly been transformed into some kind of epic nerd. She thought about her friends, her band, the other people from her school who were surely sitting back home watching and commenting on every little movement she made. She instinctively pulled her hand back when Antoine tried to hold it.

"Commander Nadolski," a question from Houston began, piped through a speaker in the ceiling. "What will be the most important goal for NASA in the next one hundred and seventy hours?"

As Nadolski started answering, he was interrupted by more signals from Earth.

"Commander Nadolski," it came again, "what will be the most important goal for NASA in the next one hundred seventy hours?"

"Excuse me, we're obviously having some technical difficulties here. Coleman, I don't think Earth can hear us."

Coleman stepped over to the communications desk while Wilson and Stanton checked the microphone.

"I don't understand. Everything looks like it's working fine here," Stanton said.

"Try transferring the signal to one of the other channels," Wilson suggested.

Seconds ticked by.

"Commander Nadolski," the voice said once again. "I don't know if you can hear me, but my question was: What will be the most important goal for NASA in the next one hundred seventy hours?"

"We hear you, we hear you, we hear you!" a frustrated Nadolski shouted at the microphone, and then turned to his colleague. "Damn it, Stanton," he muttered. "What's going on?"

But Stanton didn't have a chance to respond. That very second the TV screens went dead, and the fluorescent lights on the ceiling blinked a few times before they also died. The room was completely black for a few seconds before the emergency power kicked on and bathed the room in a dark red color. Mia glanced nervously at Caitlin, who in turn was staring at Nadolski.

And then the alarm went off.

"What is it now?" Nadolski growled. "Is there really nothing that works here?" He flipped the radio transmitters off and on, but nothing happened. Coleman ordered everyone back into the living room.

"*Danger. Danger. Local power generator failure. Error code F548,*" an automated, metallic voice droned over the alarm system.

"What the . . . ?"

Sixteen eyes stared at one another in the dim red light, flitting around the room, as if everyone were waiting for someone to take charge.

"We have to go outside if we're going to fix it," Coleman said quietly, making it clear that he was not entirely comfortable with the thought. "The local power generator is outside, between modules three and four."

"We'll do it," Stanton and Wilson said. "We'll fix it."

"Are you sure?" Coleman asked.

"Yeah. We're going now," Stanton affirmed with grim determination.

"We'll need help putting on our suits," Wilson added.

Coleman didn't give them a chance to change their minds, responding quickly, "Caitlin will help you with that. The rest of you wait here."

Mia grabbed Antoine's hand again.

"Didn't I say everything here was ancient?" Midori complained in a low voice. "No wonder it broke before we even touched it!"

"Midori! Not now," Nadolski said, giving her a stern look that made her — and everyone else — stay quiet.

Nadolski asked everyone to sit down. "It's not supposed to

be like this, of course. But there's no danger. Really. This will be resolved quickly. Coleman"—he gestured to the aging astronaut—"will you come with me?"

The two of them went out into the corridor together. Nadolski stopped right under one of the red lights, and in the gleam from it he asked: "Tell me, Coleman. Can you explain one thing to me?"

"What?"

"If the emergency power turns on...and the system comes up again..."

"Yes?"

"Then why doesn't the radio equipment work?"

Coleman stared at him. "I don't know," he responded. Nadolski squinted hard at him, as if he didn't quite believe that Coleman was telling the full truth.

Back in the living room, the three teenagers sat in silence, but they were all thinking the same thing: When the emergency power kicked on, then it was serious.

If the main power didn't come back, they may never make it back home.

REPAIR

Stanton and Wilson followed Caitlin to module four. The red emergency lighting flooding the corridors made the whole place seem unreal. To Stanton it was like a warning that he never should have said yes to the man who came to see him that Saturday two years earlier. Hadn't his wife asked him not to do it, too? Yes. But then, he had never really believed that anyone would give him the opportunity anyway.

Peter D. Stanton had been an astronaut at NASA for six years, but he still hadn't logged as much as a single second in space. There weren't many spaceflights that required a man with his particular engineering background, and the two expeditions that he had been selected for had been canceled because of budget cuts. Stanton had been content to be an astronaut who never got to experience space, even though his name was on the crew list for the next lunar expedition. But that was years away, and Stanton had been at NASA long enough to know that there was no point in getting his hopes up. A lot could happen in that amount of time.

For many people in the space program, being an astronaut without having left Earth was synonymous with being a failure. But Stanton didn't see himself that way at all. Preparation for a space mission took an extraordinary amount of time. Astronauts hardly saw their families for a full year before they left; month after month of sixteen-hour workdays was the routine. And that didn't fit into Stanton's calendar anymore. Now he had a lot more time to spend with their three young daughters, aged three, five, and seven, because for a significant portion of the year when he lived up north in his home state of Minnesota, he almost never got home from work later than three in the afternoon. Stanton had found a balance in his life that made him truly happy, and as he followed Caitlin to module four, he wished again that he'd made a very different choice on that fateful day two years earlier.

It had been a totally normal Saturday morning in August. Stanton and his wife, Yvonne, were walking down an aisle in a Walmart, with the kids in tow, looking for canned tomatoes. When the man in the dark suit showed up, Stanton knew right away who it was. He didn't know him personally, but he'd heard a lot about him and knew he was way up the ladder in the NASA hierarchy. But Stanton couldn't imagine what in the world this man was doing all the way up here in the upper Midwest, and as he and Caitlin approached module four, it hit him that he'd never asked, either.

The man had shaken Stanton's hand and then turned to

Yvonne and said, "Excuse me, but would you mind if I borrowed your husband for a second?" The man never waited for a response.

Without hesitation, Stanton followed him through the store and out into the parking lot. It was raining. The man had two black umbrellas in his briefcase. He opened one and handed it to Stanton before opening the other above his own head.

"Let me get right down to it, Mr. Stanton. We don't have much time. Here's the issue: I'm sure you're aware that NASA is planning to send people back to the moon."

Stanton nodded.

"We've decided it will take place imminently. Five astronauts will be going. And three teenagers."

"*Teenagers?*" Stanton asked, giving the man an odd look.

"Yes. The plan is to send them up in July, two years from now. The rocket will be a — well, what should I call it? — an upgraded version of the Saturn V rockets from the Apollo program from the sixties and seventies and..."

"You're going to use an old launch rocket?" Stanton asked, incredulous.

The man waved his hand. "No, no, no, it's brand-new. It just looks like the Saturn V. The same for the command module and the lunar lander. Upgraded, somewhat enlarged versions of the ones from *Apollo 11*. You know, TV loves stuff like that. But anyway, yes, where was I? Right. The mission will include a hundred-and-seventy-two-hour stay on the moon and utilize DARLAH 2 as its habitat."

"Dar... what?"

"DARLAH 2. An unused lunar base by the Sea of Tranquility. Built back in the seventies." Stanton raised his eyebrows. He simply could not believe what he was hearing. "You'll learn the who, what, where, when, and why of *that* later, Stanton. The immediate issue is that our engineer, Riley, has to withdraw from the mission. His wife is expecting his third child."

"Good for him," Stanton replied, still baffled by everything the man had just said. He hardly knew where to start asking questions.

The man looked peeved and remarked snidely, "Yes, of course, let's all put on paper hats and throw him a party, eh? Anyway, that's not the point. The point is this: Mr. Stanton, we would really like to have you on the team next summer for this moon mission. Are you in?"

Stanton didn't know what to say. What was the man saying? That he could go to the moon after all? But he had given up on that. Totally and completely.

Or had he?

Yvonne found the two of them out there in the parking lot and realized instinctively, in the way only a spouse could, what the conversation was about. She wasn't going to risk losing her husband to space. She'd finally helped him forget that dream. She rushed up to them, shaking her head vigorously. "No. Whatever it is you're asking, he won't do it."

The man from NASA pretended not to notice. "I'm sorry to have to be so impatient, but I'm afraid time is of the essence. So, Stanton, what's it going to be?"

If only he'd listened to Yvonne that day.

Caitlin, Wilson, and Stanton reached the equipment room a minute later. Heavy spacesuits in a variety of sizes hung on the walls, along with boots, gloves, helmets, and oxygen containers. Caitlin quickly found the equipment they needed and started getting them into their suits.

"We need tools," Wilson announced. "And the plans for the generator."

Caitlin disappeared into the next room and came back with what he'd requested. She helped them hook up their oxygen tanks and asked them to put on their helmets before she sealed them into their suits. Then she took them by their arms.

"Can you hear me?"

They both nodded.

"Good. Do you see this gauge on your left arm? That shows how much oxygen you have available. We haven't had time to fill them up completely yet, so there's only thirty-five minutes in each. Pay close attention to your gauge and maintain radio contact, okay? I want reports on everything that happens in there."

Stanton eyed Caitlin uncertainly. "What do you mean, *in* there? We're going outside."

"You have to go outside to get to the hatch that provides access to the generator. It's one level below us, which means you'll have to climb down the ladder and follow the corridor in. Use the flashlights and look for any obvious breaches in the power supply before you start troubleshooting. And please, remember, guys—I know you know this already, but under no circumstances can you take your helmets off down there. There's no air supply to that room, and you'd suffocate in seconds. Do you understand that?"

Two helmets slowly nodded.

"Then it's time. Come on."

Stanton and Wilson followed Caitlin into the decompression chamber, where she asked them to get ready. She went back to the equipment room, sealed the hatch, and started the procedure that emptied the chamber of air. After that she opened the outer hatch, and the two men made their way outside.

The sky above them was blacker than anything they had ever seen before, and yet the sun was reflecting brightly on the gray surface.

They felt very far from home indeed.

Stanton and Wilson carefully made their way around the outside of module four, looking for the hatch to the power generator. They spotted it right away, right at ground level, just outside the building. They found a wheel on top of the stainless-steel hatch, and together they tried to rotate it. But it was fastened tight, as if it were sealed shut, and their clumsy astronaut gloves didn't make the job any easier. They had to squat down and force the wheel with all their strength—but finally the hatch opened.

Wilson shone his light down into the hole.

Did he see something?

He strained to see and felt sweat trickling down the back of his neck. *Yes.*

There.

There was a ladder there, just as Caitlin had said. It extended forty to fifty feet down into the darkness.

The two men exchanged glances.

"What do you think?" Wilson asked.

Stanton leaned over the hole. "I'll go first."

"You sure?"

"Yeah. Wait until I'm down before you follow. I'll give you the go-ahead."

"Okay. Caitlin, do you hear us? Stanton is climbing down the ladder now."

"Received, Wilson," a female voice came crackling through the comm speakers in their helmets. "Stanton, watch your oxygen tank when you enter the opening. You don't want it to get stuck. The opening's quite narrow."

"Yes, I see it. I'll be careful."

He kneeled down by the opening, backed into place, and set his feet on the top rung.

"I've got a foothold. I'm climbing down now," Stanton reported. He cautiously jiggled the oxygen tank on his back through the opening and climbed down, rung by rung. The actual hole was scarcely bigger than he was with all his equipment on, but with a little acrobatics he made it down to the bottom of the ladder. He turned his light inward and saw the narrow corridor Caitlin had mentioned. It couldn't be more than twelve feet long, and he caught a glimpse of the generator at the end.

"I'm down. Everything okay," Stanton reported. "It's tight, but there's just enough room for two."

"I'm coming down," Wilson replied, and began his descent.

In the meantime, Stanton investigated the corridor more closely. Thick cables covered the ceiling and the walls, but as far as he could see there was nothing wrong with them. He continued down the corridor, checking his oxygen gauge. Still twenty-eight minutes left. There wasn't any to spare, but it ought to be enough. He noticed the beam from Wilson's light behind him and was relieved to see that his colleague had made it down safely, too.

"Found anything?" Wilson asked.

"Nada. Let's take a look at the machinery."

They moved over next to the generator and ran their lights over the panel.

"Would you…are you seeing the same thing I am? Do you see that? There?" Wilson asked, pointing to where the main switch should have been. Half the panel appeared to have been smashed.

"Yeah," Stanton replied, stunned. They shone their lights up at the ceiling but didn't find any signs of anything that could have fallen and hit the panel.

"It's just destroyed, Wilson."

"Wilson, what's the status?" Caitlin's voice came over the intercom again.

"One second, we're investigating. It seems that…"

"Maybe we can hook things up somewhere after the panel? Remove the cover? That would make the job easier, don't you think?"

"Guys, what's going on?"

"Caitlin, we have a problem."

"A problem? What problem?"

Stanton passed on the information: "We're going to try to take off the cover to see if we can circumvent the switch."

"Check your oxygen," Caitlin reminded them. "How much time is left?"

"Twenty-two minutes," Stanton reported.

"Okay, see what you can do."

Wilson pulled out two screwdrivers from the tool bag. Stanton took one and started loosening the left side while Wilson went to work on the right. They both worked as fast as they could, but it still took them close to ten minutes to get the whole cover off. It still wasn't looking good. Whatever it was that had hit the panel, the force had been so great that it had destroyed nearly all the wire connections and circuit breakers and made one big salad out of them.

"I'm not sure we can make it, Stanton," Wilson said. "It's totally destroyed, and time's running out."

"Wait a minute." Stanton pushed Wilson aside. "Let me try it. Pass me a pair of pliers. And get the blowtorch ready."

"What are you going to do?"

"We'll open it up and cut our way into the main breaker. With a little luck, we can solder in a new line."

Wilson seemed frozen.

"Wilson? The pliers?" Stanton urged.

"We're not going to make it," Wilson responded, stunned.

Stanton refused to listen. "The pliers, please."

"Stanton, look at your gauge. Eleven minutes. And we need at least six to get back to DARLAH. I'm sorry, but this lunar mission was just canceled."

"Damn it, Wilson, don't give up. The pliers, *now*! Every second counts!"

"Caitlin, we're coming back," Wilson reported. "There's nothing we can do."

"Received," they heard Caitlin say.

Deep down Stanton knew Wilson was right. Soldering in a

new line would take time. A half hour at least, maybe more. If they could even find the right place to attempt the hookup. The only choice was to head back. He couldn't even bring himself to think about what the others would say. And the teenagers, those poor young kids…

"Stanton, we have to *go*. Now!"

Grudgingly he followed Wilson back to the ladder. Wilson stopped on the first rung.

"Stanton?" he said slowly. "I didn't close the hatch when I came down."

"So?"

"It's closed now."

They looked at each other.

"Maybe it…" Stanton bit his tongue. It hadn't blown shut; nothing blew shut in a vacuum. "Are you sure?"

"Totally sure. Seven minutes left on your oxygen gauge. Let's get this baby open."

And they tried. And tried.

They could have slammed their bodies against the hatch until they nearly killed themselves, but it wouldn't have changed a thing. Because that hatch was locked.

From the outside.

"Caitlin?"

She heard the panic about to overwhelm Wilson's voice. He was hyperventilating in his helmet.

"What is it?"

"Bad…news. The hatch. It's locked."

Caitlin refused to believe what she'd heard. "But that's impossible," she protested.

"We have five minutes of oxygen left, Caitlin."

"Are you sure? Try again! Hurry!"

Wilson's voice became hysterical. "We've tried everything! It's *locked*, goddamn it! Do you hear me?"

Caitlin felt the desperation grip her. "What about the blowtorch?" she asked. "You can cut your way out!"

"That steel is way too thick. You know that."

"We're coming out there to get you!"

"There isn't time. Four minutes."

"There's time. There *is* time! If you breathe calmly, as little as you can. Stay completely calm, understood? Nadolski and I are coming!"

"Caitlin?" That was Stanton's voice.

"Yes?"

"It's going to take you twenty minutes to suit up and get out here, maybe another few minutes to open the hatch." Unlike Wilson, Stanton was completely calm, almost relaxed. "It looks like our tickets were just one-way. I'm sorry about this, Caitlin. So awfully sorry. But I think it's best if you guys go home now."

"Stanton? Stanton? Do you hear me? Stanton? Wilson? Damn it! Respond! Do you hear me?"

They heard her. But there was no point in responding. They slowly climbed back down the ladder again, without saying a word to each other. They walked back to the generator and sat down side by side. Stanton held Wilson's hand. They looked at each other, smiled weakly. Then they put their hands on their helmets, opened the latches, and took them off.

Stanton had just enough time to picture one last thing before the vacuum rendered him unconscious.

He pictured Yvonne, that day she'd bought a new bicycle at the flea market. One of those old bikes with the fat tires. She had been standing in the garage pumping air into the tires when he got home. A second later she was sitting on it, riding around him in tight circles repeating that it had only cost her five dollars.

A totally, completely everyday event in the life of any old person.

And yet now it was as distant as could be.

DINNER

Mr. Himmelfarb was sitting at the dinner table in the nursing home, trembling. His fever had gone up over the last twenty-four hours. He had cold sweats and was staring vacantly into space, the plate of mashed potatoes untouched in front of him.

The staff seemed to think there was a simple explanation for his attack by the pay phone. Perhaps he was exhausted from believing that the people on the screen were really in his room with him. But if they could have seen inside his head, if they could have seen what he had seen, they surely would have handled it differently. They probably would have dropped whatever they had in their hands and run for their lives, out, away, gone.

But all they did was make sure the TV was taken out of his room and make sure he didn't wander into the TV lounge with the other residents. Now there was next to nothing for him to do other than sit in his chair and stare at the wall. And until recently he would have been perfectly content to do just that. But something had changed in Himmelfarb's head. His body was nearing its end — his breathing was more labored, his face looked haggard, and a steady stream of drool dangled from the corner of his mouth — but that thick, dogged, impenetrable fog in his brain had burned off somewhat and left him more lucid than ever.

He didn't like it at all.

Himmelfarb still hadn't so much as even tasted his food. All he'd done was to move the end of his spoon back and forth through the potatoes in a pattern that only he was aware of. He was in the process of dying, yes, and yet he understood everything. This new moon mission had nothing to do with fundraising or public relations. It had nothing to do with scientific lunar research.

His mind told him that he had to warn the staff, but it was no use. The words were there, but he couldn't get them out. They just came out as gurgling, drooling saliva.

He pictured those poor teenagers who were inside DARLAH now. What would become of them? He didn't want to think about it. It wasn't his problem. It wasn't his fault, was it? Or was it? He never had told anyone what had happened.

You should have done that forty years ago, Oleg. You're going to burn in hell for this, you know that.

There was nothing he could do.

He coughed. Again. He coughed with all his might, and two small drops of blood landed on the tablecloth in front of him without anyone noticing.

He was going to die now. And he knew it. He coughed again, and more drops of spit landed on the tablecloth.

Now they were looking at him. All of them. Thirty-two eyes stared as he carefully set his spoon down on the tablecloth, pushed his chair back from the table, stood up, and quietly said, "No one is going to survive."

The sound of his voice forming the words surprised him most of all. He was talking. He was doing it. There was still time! Time to say everything, all of it!

After that he took a couple of wobbly steps backward, spun around, lost his balance, and fell.

One of the aides had already stood up when he pushed his chair back from the table, and she almost grabbed him before his head hit the floor. The last of the senses that was still working in the old man's body, his vision, was suddenly replaced by an inky blackness.

Custodian Oleg Himmelfarb was no longer a part of this world.

It wasn't long before he was removed and the only one left in the dining room was the aide who had tried to catch Mr. Himmelfarb. The other patients had been moved into the lounge, where they were immediately placed in front of the television. To everyone's relief, the Weather Channel was turned on.

The aide had only been working at the facility a few weeks, and this was the first death she had ever witnessed. And yet it didn't frighten her, because ultimately it was the most natural thing in the world for the elderly to die. After all, when you got right down to it, that was why they were here, even though most of her job had to do with convincing the old people of the opposite.

She stood up to go into the break room. But something stopped her. Something caught her attention from the corner of her eye.

Mr. Himmelfarb's plate.

It was still full of mashed potatoes.

But in the middle of it she could see that he had written something. Letters, some kind of code, scratched into his food. She saw the spoon resting next to his plate, still with a bit of potato left on the narrow tip.

She read what he'd written:

6EQUJ5

SILENCE

Just hours before, eight people had been sitting in the living room. Now there were only six, but the silence that surrounded them seemed colossal. Caitlin had been forced to walk the somber path back from module four, and she had to struggle to keep her own hysteria at bay.

When she found herself face-to-face with the rest of the mission crew, they all realized right away that something was wrong, but none of them had thought anyone had died.

The news didn't go over well.

Some cried, including Antoine. Midori was almost inconsolable. Others, like Coleman, had shut down completely. Nadolski, too, was just sitting there staring at the wall. Mia didn't hold back her emotion and screamed at him, and then at all of the astronauts, insisting that they had no choice but to go out there and rescue them.

She didn't fully believe yet that there wasn't anyone to save.

The two men under the hatch out there didn't exist anymore. They were just two bodies, lifeless, doomed to lie in that airless cold until the next mission arrived. The decision to leave them was a hard one to make, but Commander Nadolski didn't actually have any other choice. Neither DARLAH 2 nor *Demeter* had a refrigerated storage room. It would fly in the face of every regulation, not to mention good common sense, to bring those two bodies and store them in the warmth for the four days the return trip would take. Who knew what bacteria could spread during that time?

Mia looked around the solemn room, everyone hunched, heads in hands, hopeless. The red lighting, indicating the emergency power was still active, only increased the dark mood. Just a few hours earlier she had been sure her life was finally going to start, and that Antoine was the one who would put it in motion. Now she was surrounded by people who were supposed to take care of her, and none of them was up to the task. And on top of everything — the silence.

Only the sound of the fans in the air system could be heard. A regular, low hum.

Someone finally stood up. Nadolski. He moved to the middle of the room, rubbed his hands over his face.

"There is absolutely no logical explanation for this. That hatch, like everything else here, had been tested, retested, and tested again."

"And when was that?" someone said. Mia didn't catch who.

"That's not the issue," Coleman said. "Losing the radio signals, even the video signals to Earth, now that's one thing. That I can understand."

"That you can *understand*?" Nadolski interrupted.

"I can accept that. It's happened before. On one of the Apollo missions, for example. What I can't understand is that the whole generator could be destroyed by natural causes. And that the hatch the engineers opened could close and lock itself shut behind them."

"What are you trying to say, Coleman?"

"I'm not trying to say anything, Nadolski. I just think we should be . . . careful."

Mia turned to look at Antoine. He looked pale, and she took a firm hold of his hand and set it in her lap. Who cared if anyone noticed? None of it mattered anymore.

"Fine. We'll be careful. Now listen up. This is the issue: On behalf of myself, the mission, and NASA, I deeply apologize that we find ourselves in this situation. We have just lost two good men, Sam Wilson and Peter Stanton. Their deaths are shocking and incomprehensible, but we can't cave in and give up because of this. The way things stand now, we need to focus on solutions, not problems. Coleman?"

"Yes?"

"We're still running on emergency backup power. How long will that last?"

"According to my calculations, twenty-two hours. Twelve hours after that the oxygen generator will stop working."

"Okay. We have just over thirty hours to get out of here. That means we're calling off the mission, effective immediately. I can't imagine anyone has any objections to that?"

No response.

"Good. We don't know what NASA and ground control think about that, since all communications are down. But we don't have any choice. We are, as you all understand, on our own. That means the following: Coleman, you'll get the kids into their suits. After that, take them down to the infirmary in module four. Caitlin, you're coming out to *Demeter* with me to prepare for departure. We'll meet in the infirmary in exactly eight hours. Which is to say three twenty-five a.m. Miami time. Let's hop to it."

Mia stood up and looked at Midori. Was she scared, too?

"Mia?"

Someone was talking to her. She tired to figure out where the sound was coming from.

"Mia, please!"

She turned from side to side, dazed.

"Mia, let go!" It was Antoine. He was standing right next to her. She loosened her grip on his hand, which bore obvious red marks from her fingers.

Coleman led the teens down the corridors, back to their rooms. He did his best to calm them down and explain how much training all the astronauts had been through for situations like this.

But no matter what he said, it didn't help in the least.

Because all three of them saw that there was way more fear in his eyes than there was in their own, and they realized he didn't believe a word of what he was telling them.

* * *

Nadolski led the way outside the base, with Caitlin following right behind him. They could clearly see the lunar lander *Demeter* a few hundred yards ahead of them. With every step they took, fine dust swirled up around their boots and slowly settled back down onto the surface again.

For Nadolski this was the most important day of his life. He had built his whole life around the space organization, and now everything he had ever done before was suddenly pushed into the background: the girlfriend he had married twelve years ago, the kids he had had with her, all of it was packed away and suppressed. His only objective now was to get his crewmembers home safely. That was his great mission in life. He would be welcomed as a hero. Not that that was the most important part, but he *did* want that, didn't he?

Yes.

He had to bring these people back.

No matter what.

Demeter was a welcome sight, standing there like a white monument in the gray landscape. Nadolski let Caitlin climb up the ladder first. She was just preparing to open the hatch when she bumped into something with her elbow. And the hatch swung open.

Oh no, she thought. *No. Not this, too.*

"Caitlin?"

She climbed in and helped Nadolski the last little bit, until he was in, too. She waited a few seconds before doing anything else. Postponing it. Then she grabbed the hatch, pulled it shut, twisted the locking wheel, and let go. She waited a few seconds, it felt like an eternity.

And the hatch slowly swung open again.

No no no no no no no.

She tried again. And again it swung open. Caitlin swore to herself.

Nadolski thumped her on the shoulder. "Problems?"

She turned to him. "The hatch is destroyed." Both of them knew what this meant, but she said it anyway: "We won't achieve compression."

She made one last attempt and then swore again softly as the hatch failed to lock and swung open. The whole lunar lander hungrily opened itself up to space.

Nadolski dropped down in the pilot's seat and swore. "Caitlin, tell me: What are the chances that damage like this could occur to these types of hatches?"

She flung out her arms. "I have no idea. One in billions, I would think. We never even practiced this in the simulator. I'm beginning to—" She cut herself short. "Nothing."

"You're beginning to what?"

Caitlin hesitated for a long time before responding, "I'm beginning to think we weren't supposed to come back to the moon."

He didn't respond, thinking hard. He had an idea. It was risky, but it was worth a try.

"What if we keep our suits on and take off anyway, with the hatch open? If we fill the rear compartments, everyone will have enough oxygen until we reconnect with the spacecraft in orbit."

But Caitlin just shook her head. “That won’t work. The hatch is linked to the computer for takeoff. It won’t let us take off until the hatch is sealed.”

“And we can’t reprogram it? Or override it?”

“No! I’m sorry, Nadolski. It’s just not possible.” She paused. “It looks like…” She forced the words out in a near-whisper. “We might be stranded.”

It was as if the word “stranded” triggered something in Nadolski. He stood up.

“Absolutely not! Not as long as I’m the commander. Come on. We have to go back to DARLAH.”

Mia was sitting in the infirmary with one arm around Antoine and one around Midori when Nadolski and Caitlin returned. She tried to make eye contact with Caitlin to get an idea of what was going on, but Caitlin looked away. Stared at the floor. Nadolski didn’t look at the teens, either. He whispered something to Coleman and motioned to Caitlin to follow him.

“Coleman, Caitlin, and I have to discuss a few details. The rest of you wait here. And no one leaves this room without my permission, is that *completely* clear?”

The teens nodded, even though the order was totally unnecessary: None of them could move.

The three astronauts came back just a few minutes later and made a brief statement:

“Take off your suits, hang them up in the equipment room, and meet us in the kitchen in module two. We’re going to be here for a while.”

DARLAH 1

They had been told that the lunar lander was unusable.

Midori had helped Caitlin prepare a simple soup for the six of them who remained, but none of them had much appetite. The now cold soup had remained pretty much untouched. Mia was sitting with her head resting on her hand, drumming her fingers on the edge of the table, and Antoine was sitting across from her staring into space, going over in his mind everything they'd just heard.

Coleman had been the one to address the group. "Commander Nadolski and I talked. There is a solution. We can't guarantee that it will work, but the way I see it we don't have any other choice." He looked the rest of them straight in the eyes. "It will require hard work from everyone." He wasn't quiet for long. It seemed as if he hadn't quite decided if he should say it or not. But then he said, "There's another DARLAH base."

Ever since Houston, Midori had been wondering why the base they were going to was called DARLAH 2, but she had decided not to ask for fear of sounding stupid. Odds were it was just a number that didn't mean something significant. Like with cars. They always had numbers and letters, like 340 SL or 240 GTI or whatever. They were all meaningless to her.

"What I'm about to tell you now is strictly classified, you have to understand that. Not even Commander Nadolski knew about this before now. Under normal circumstances I would have had to ask NASA and military leaders for permission before I said a single word, but because of the situation, I don't have that option right now. Therefore I can only urge you, in the strongest possible terms, never to mention a word of what I'm going to tell you to anyone. If you do, the government will fully and completely deny everything, and you will be considered an enemy of the state. You'd be refused entrance into the United States, and all doors will be closed to you. None of us would be able to guarantee your safety."

Mia was uncertain for a moment. Maybe she ought to step out of the room? Was this essentially a death threat from the U.S. government? She pictured existence as number one enemy of the United States, a life in hiding, always on the move, in constant fear that at any time someone might show up at her doorstep, ready to finish her off. But what choice did she have? It's not like she had anywhere to go.

"DARLAH 1 is a military installation that NASA built for the U.S. Air Force in 1974. It's a hundred feet below the surface, about seven miles from here. It was built at the same time as DARLAH 2's module three. The installation contains six nuclear missiles, each with an explosive force equivalent to fifty megatons of TNT. If that number doesn't mean much to you, I can tell you that's equivalent to three thousand times stronger than the bomb used on Hiroshima. The missiles were installed by the Nixon administration during the Cold War and were meant to be one final defense if war broke out between the United States and the U.S.S.R. In other words, if the war extended into space. People believed back then that that might happen."

Coleman paused and inhaled. *Believed back then that that might happen*. What was he thinking, saying that? He'd been practicing this explanation for a long time, and he was really trying not to talk too fast, which would clue everyone into the fact that he had just memorized this whole thing. Because not everything he was saying was true. The information about the missiles was certainly true, but neither they nor anything else at DARLAH 1 had been built to protect them against the Soviets. The installation and the missiles were installed to annihilate the entire moon if that became necessary. As a final solution.

But he wasn't about to say anything about that now.

"DARLAH 1 also contains an evacuation pod," he continued, "a minivessel created as a means to get off the moon and back to Earth if anything should go wrong. Unfortunately for us, the pod only has room for three people, which was the number of astronauts people thought it was feasible to have living up here permanently. That rules out our using it. Besides, there is some uncertainty about whether or not it is still in working condition."

Midori wondered why, in that case, Coleman originally

hadn't seemed uncertain about the "working condition" of the rest of this stupid base.

"And now for the last and most important item," he went on, finally getting to the point. "DARLAH 1 is primarily a power station, and both the missile base and the evacuation pod are merely additional equipment. A high-voltage line is supposed to run directly from DARLAH 1 to DARLAH 2, an emergency cable in the event that DARLAH 2 should end up in the situation we find ourselves in now. Thus we need to send a team over to DARLAH 1 to activate the power station. Then we can get the power back up and hopefully also radio communications so that we can call for help. But I ask all of you to be prepared for the fact that we might be up here for a long time."

Mia asked the obvious question on the teens' minds. "What do you mean by a *long time*?"

"Possibly months, maybe close to a year. Until NASA can send up a rescue team."

Mia listened anxiously to what Coleman was saying, and those final sentences settled like stones in the pit of her stomach. No one was coming to get them. Not for a year. She thought of everything she would lose, that she would never get to see for the foreseeable future: the woods, the ocean, beaches, streets, cities, cars, people.... She thought of her friends, who would go on with their lives without her. The band, concerts she wouldn't get to be part of. And after the battery in her iPod ran out, and that would be soon, it might be a whole year before she heard any music again at all. That thought was unbearable, and actually made her feel worse than the thought that she might never make it home again.

She ran her hand through Antoine's hair. *At least he's here*, she thought. And Midori. And Caitlin. That was a start. And maybe, just maybe, things would be fine, if the promises that they really would be rescued held. At least she'd get out of a couple of years of school.

You had to look on the bright side.

But looking on the bright side has a nasty habit of leading to disappointments.

The six of them were still sitting in the kitchen a couple of hours later when Nadolski was ready to select who would join him on the expedition to DARLAH 1.

"Unfortunately there are limited options at this point," he began. "I... well, I hope you understand how difficult it is to say this, but... we need Caitlin and Coleman here at DARLAH 2. Once I activate the power station, they'll have to work together to immediately reestablish contact with NASA to apprise the agency of our situation. This is our most pressing need, and for one of them to come with me will cost precious minutes during which we could be receiving advice from Houston. That means..." He closed his eyes and let that sink in. "That means that I have to ask one of you three to come." He looked at the three teens. "It's not an ideal situation. None of you should be asked to do something like this. My God, none of you should be in this situation in the first place. But I think everyone will agree that the problem here requires drastic measures. And it would be simply reckless of me to go alone, with just one rover, in case something should happen—"

Antoine suddenly stood up. "I'll go."

Mia instinctively grabbed his shirt and pulled him back down into his chair. "What are you *doing*?" she whispered urgently, feeling her throat tighten. "That's out of the question."

Antoine looked at her gently. "But, Mia, don't you remember what Coleman said? We're all going to have to work hard. This will be my contribution. I have to go. You know that."

Nadolski studied the French boy carefully. It seemed as if he understood the situation. He'd said he was scared. But they all were, and what the boy said was true.

"Thanks, Antoine. Thank you." Nadolski turned to Coleman. "Coleman, you'll be in charge of the group while we're gone. Caitlin, make sure everyone has food and water. And you should all get a little sleep, four hours each until we return. Coleman and Caitlin will sleep in shifts. Antoine Devereux, report to the rovers in module four in forty-five minutes."

The meeting was adjourned.

SIMONE

The sun had not yet fully risen over Paris when the rain woke up the seventeen-year-old girl. She wasn't sure how long she'd been asleep, but it was still predawn outside and she felt like crap, the way she always did when she woke up after just a couple of hours of sleep. It was a feeling she had grown accustomed to lately. It had been like this for more than two weeks, but she had no idea why. She went to bed early, ate healthy foods, and exercised three times a week. She went for long walks through the city with Noël and drank tea half an hour before bedtime. Nothing helped. If anything, her sleep problems had gotten worse.

She rubbed her eyes, aching from the lack of sleep, and dragged herself out of bed.

"Awake again?" she heard a sleepy voice ask. She turned toward Noël, who was lying in her bed, and nodded silently before turning her attention to the window. It had been raining for four days straight, and soon the park over by the Eiffel Tower was going to be one big puddle.

She and Noël had been together for a little over a year now, and things were still going well between them. She thought so, anyway. He'd been here for more than a month now, living in her room, eating dinner with her parents. Every day. Being with her. Every day. All the time. His clothes hung in her closet or lay strewn over her floor; his books, too. And the glasses he was always bringing up from the kitchen but never took back down again. In the evenings he would sit in her chair and watch her TV, with the remote control in his hands.

Come to think of it, it was almost as if he had quietly moved in and slowly but surely taken over her room, pushing her out of it. She stood there by the window wondering if maybe, ultimately, it was Noël's fault she couldn't sleep anymore. But she rejected the idea right away.

It wasn't him. It was something else. A person she had thought was out of her life for good.

This was about Antoine.

And in a way she had known that all along. But why? It didn't make any sense. They had broken up more than a year ago, and she wasn't in love with him anymore. She'd gotten over that ages ago, and she hoped that by now he had, too. They'd given it an honest go, but it just hadn't worked out for them. Shit happens. And then you move on.

She wasn't sure she'd succeeded in doing that yet. Noël was snoring behind her in the bed, a sort of rasping, slow snore that would drive anyone crazy if it went on for long.

The rain picked up, as did the noise from Noël. Simone shuffled across the floor, sitting down on the low armchair by the stereo. There was an old wine crate next to it with her records in it. Simone had always liked the warm, clear sound vinyl albums made when she played them on the record player her father had given her. She flipped through her albums, most of which had also come from her father, and absentmindedly let her hand select one from the wine crate as she turned on the record player. And when she realized which record she'd randomly grabbed, she felt almost sad.

It was Cannonball Adderley's jazz album *Somethin' Else*, which had been a gift from Antoine. For a second she wasn't sure if she wanted to play it after all, but finally she decided to put it on.

The piano and drums started cautiously, hesitantly, as if they were sneaking around, before an angry wind player got involved for a brief instant. That disappeared and it was quiet again for a few beats, and then there was a brief pause, a musical moment for contemplation. And then it came: The muted trumpet sounded like the saddest instrument in the world, and here it was on this very record. *Les feuilles morts*, the dead leaves. It was as if summer was gone and fall was hobbling across the countryside, meeting winter halfway.

The music seeped out of the speakers and settled like a soft coating on the walls without waking Noël, and Simone sank back into her chair, found a pack of smokes on the floor next to her, lit a cigarette, and closed her eyes. It was the most beautiful record of them all, and she remembered the day Antoine had given it to her. They'd been to the theater on rue Laplace to see an old French movie called *À bout de souffle*, and that was exactly how they both felt — breathless — like they'd discovered something totally new.

Weird to think about how great they were together then. And how it didn't last that long.

It had been worse for him, poor guy. After they broke up she had discovered him standing on the Eiffel Tower, up on the first observation deck, by those big coin-operated telescopes. She knew how he'd pointed one of them at her apartment building. Later that night she had snuck out and gone over to the tower, taken the stairs up, and found the telescope, untouched since he'd left it. She put a euro in and saw, not surprisingly, that she was looking right into her own room. She made the same trip a few times later on, too, just to confirm her suspicions that he was down there every night. Every time she climbed up to the telescope, it was pointed right at her room.

One day, several months later, when she decided to check out the telescope again, it was pointed in a totally different direction. Of course, that could mean that someone else had been using it in the meantime, but without really knowing why, she took it as a sign that he'd found other things to kill his time with. And now, now when she almost wished he were standing out there in the rain watching her again, she knew he was gone. He'd sent her a text message right before he left for New York. It was the only thing she'd heard from him since they broke up.

Hi Simone. I'm going to the moon
in July. That's totally the truth. Hope
you're doing well. See you on the dark
side of the moon.

And now he was up there somewhere, far, far away. She had of course heard about the contest and the spaceflight, like everyone else. She'd toyed with entering herself. But she never did. She figured her chances were so minuscule it wasn't even worth trying. But he had done it. Which was strange to think about.

What was he doing right now?

Who was he with up there? She thought she remembered hearing that the other two winners were girls. Had she seen pictures of them? So much had been written about them online since their names had been announced. And *Le Figaro*, the paper, had been reporting from the United States almost every day. But, no, she couldn't picture the girls.

Maybe she ought to get in touch with him when he got back? Or would it seem like she was just doing that because he was now, like, world famous? No, he would understand, she thought. She would call him. As soon as she heard he was back in Paris.

She made her way back to bed and pulled the sheet up. Noël had sprawled out since she got up, and she had to push him over a little. He grunted softly when she touched him, and rolled over onto his side with a *humph*. Eventually, she fell back to sleep—but it was a nightmare sleep that comes fully loaded with dreams so real that you're willing to swear they actually happened.

She was trapped in a dark corridor. It was hard to breathe. Someone was after her. She couldn't see anyone, but she heard the sounds they were making, someone or something approaching step-by-step. And from somewhere far away she thought she heard Antoine yell her name. And then something else. She strained to make out what it was. But it was like his voice was underwater, as if there was nothing for the sound to travel through. Something was coming closer and closer to her. He yelled again, and she thought she heard what he said this time. The figure came closer, closer, closer. Something rushed past her hand. Antoine yelled again and she heard it clearly. *Get out of there!* he yelled. Just then the corridor was lit by floodlights, and Simone was staring straight into…

She woke with a start, sweating and cold. Breathless.

It was later that morning when she heard the bad news. The moon mission was in crisis.

Antoine…

Simone and Noël sat frozen in front of the TV all morning and afternoon, while the live news broadcasts did their best to shed some light on what had happened out there. Experts espoused complicated theories, and the White House held the first of many press conferences, led by a president who couldn't offer anything other than a hope that it would all work out. No one knew for sure, and all they could provide was guesswork, graphic models, and predictions of what might happen. But no matter what, all the conclusions were the same: Unless the teens and the astronauts could get back on their own, there was nothing anyone could do.

Noël, who knew Antoine was Simone's ex-boyfriend and was one of the three teenagers, had been equally absorbed in the live coverage, but now he was starting to reach his limit. He was getting tired of the whole thing. They just kept playing the same footage over and over with little or nothing new to add. None of the attempts to reestablish contact with DARLAH resulted in anything, and there wasn't much else to do but wait.

"Why don't we do something else for a little while, Simone? I don't know how much more of this I can listen to. Wouldn't it be better if we got out and went for a walk? Maybe we could catch a movie or something? It's a shame to waste the whole day, don't you think?"

Simone kept her eyes on the screen for a full minute before she finally turned to look at him. Something she'd been thinking for a long time now was finally clear to her.

"Noël," she said, "it's over. I think it would be best if you went back home to your own place now."

CONTACT

The lunar rovers were not an inspiring sight. They were constructed without a body to make them as light as possible, and Antoine eyed the vehicles with a certain amount of skepticism. Nadolski, for his part, knew the rovers would suffice; they had certainly gotten the astronauts from *Apollo 15* and *Apollo 16* where they needed to go.

Antoine stood next to the LRV waiting for Nadolski to finish up some calculations. With his space helmet on, and that enormous suit, it was impossible to tell him apart from the fully grown commander. They both looked like experienced astronauts as they strolled around the vehicles. But inside Antoine's suit, there was no fully grown man. There was a French seventeen-year-old who had just met the most beautiful girl in the world. His previous life in Paris with Simone felt like a hundred years ago now. He suddenly realized he was having trouble picturing his friends. He'd already forgotten the shortest route between the Clemenceau Métro station and Lafayette, a route he previously could have walked blindfolded. Everything he used to be seemed to be disappearing, slowly but surely, from his consciousness. And it all was being replaced by the only thing that still meant anything: making it back home. Making it back home with Mia.

"Are you ready?" Nadolski said over the intercom, interrupting Antoine's train of thought. "If so, you can take the rover on the left there."

As if he were sleepwalking, Antoine shuffled over to the other rover and sat down behind the wheel.

"Stay right behind me and holler if you have any trouble," ordered Nadolski. "Steer clear of boulders and craters. We're heading north!"

And with that, they departed soundlessly over the gray plains, leaving DARLAH 2 behind them. Only the vibrations from the seat indicated that the vehicles were being pushed forward by engines. Antoine couldn't help but feel sort of spooked by the whole experience.

They made good headway, though the LRVs moved barely more than ten miles per hour. Because of the lower gravity, which made the rovers almost float above the ground, the speed felt much faster. As if he were at sea, Antoine was slowly rocked from side to side as the wheels rolled over the uneven terrain. Motion sickness was starting to kick in.

Minutes later, Nadolski floored it, forcing his rover up a gentle incline. Antoine turned just as they reached the top. He caught one last glimpse of the base where Mia was before they rolled down the other side.

How long had they been driving?

Nadolski wasn't sure, but it felt like it certainly must have been long enough. He had been checking the map constantly along the way. Maybe the rovers were just moving more slowly than he thought. After all, they had been sitting around unused for forty years. But on the other hand, it's not like they had been exposed to air or water, so strictly speaking they ought to be in the same condition they were in before.

At first he chose to ignore the nagging feeling and proceeded across the terrain, through the deep valley of the crater. But the feeling didn't let up, and that sense of doubt finally forced him to check his watch. He raised his hand to signal to Antoine that they should stop.

Nadolski studied the watch that was built into his suit. *What the f—?* Yeah, they should definitely be there by now. They should at least have spotted the area Coleman had shown him on the map before they left. He waved Antoine over.

"What does your watch say?" he asked.

"We've been driving for almost fifty minutes," Antoine told him. "Is something wrong?"

"We went too far," Nadolski declared.

"Too far?"

"Or the wrong way, I don't know. Something's not right."

"What?" Antoine asked, his voice full of uncertainty.

Nadolski wasn't quite sure how to respond. "We're, uh...

we're having a few problems with the map. But it'll work out. Nothing to be afraid of."

"Are you trying to reassure me or yourself?" Antoine responded, trying to laugh nonchalantly. He couldn't quite pull it off.

Nadolski pretended not to hear and went back to concentrating on the map. That Antoine was standing there waiting for him to say which way they should go made it even harder for him to stay focused. He had trained for this mission for years, and he knew there wasn't anything Antoine could do. It was up to Nadolski to get them out of this mess.

But that didn't change this impossible fact: He wasn't able to spot any similarities between what he was seeing on the map and what he was supposed to be seeing on the moon.

"Antoine, do you see a hill anywhere near us, maybe two hundred feet high or so?"

Antoine gazed around at the surrounding no-man's-land. "No."

"Well. We've been driving for fifty minutes, you said?" Nadolski asked. Antoine nodded. "Right. Let's see.... If we figure our average speed was about nine or ten miles per hour... that would mean that we've come about eight miles, plus or minus, right?"

"That sounds about right."

"Okay, here's what we'll do: We'll turn around and head back the same way we came for about fifteen minutes, then stop and get our bearings from there. We probably just drove right past the entrance. The whole thing is belowground, after all."

They walked back to the LRVs and turned them on, did U-turns, and followed their wheel tracks back the same way they had come.

At that moment Caitlin was sitting with Coleman in the red glow from the emergency power system in DARLAH 2's kitchen. Mia and Midori had been sent back to their room with the instructions to get a few hours of sleep. Coleman was doing his best to boil some water for the freeze-dried coffee he had found in the storeroom in module one. There was something about the smell of coffee that made everything feel safe. As if the fear he had felt when he realized that *Demeter* was unusable was somehow diminished by the scent of freeze-dried coffee. It must be because the scent reminded him of Earth. And that café on the corner of Second Avenue and Seventy-Ninth Street, where he always ate breakfast in the morning whenever he was back home in New York City. They would make it back home again. They would be rescued. They had to be.

His thoughts turned to Nadolski and Antoine. They would reach DARLAH 1 soon. With a little luck, Nadolski would be able to quickly activate the power station and start on his return trip without any more...problems. And after he and Caitlin reestablished contact with Earth, Coleman knew what he would do. He would invite everyone into the kitchen, and they would all enjoy sipping warm cups of coffee together. The kids, too. You were never really too young to learn to drink coffee.

He noted that the water was boiling and poured it from the kettle into two cups that he carried over to the table. Caitlin took one of the bags and emptied the contents into her cup.

Coleman passed her a spoon, and she stirred it around absent-mindedly a couple of times before she took a sip.

"Oh my God, Coleman, even the coffee tastes old."

He felt a pang of irritation at her remark. *What the hell is wrong with that woman? Is she starting to complain about petty things now, too? If you only knew what you are facing, Caitlin Hall. Believe me, old coffee is the least of your problems.*

"Well, the antibiotics and morphine down in the infirmary are, too," he responded coolly. "I don't suppose you would complain about it if you had to use them."

Caitlin set her cup on the table and pushed it away as if to emphasize her point. Then she added, "I know this is all old hat to you, Coleman. I'm sure you've known about DARLAH 1 and DARLAH 2 for years. If you know anything more than the rest of us about this power outage or the communications failure, you should just say so — now."

Coleman tried to chuckle for the sake of appearances but didn't quite manage to pull it off.

"There's nothing to know, Caitlin. We have problems here. We're trying to solve them as a team. That's it."

"I don't like your style, Coleman. I don't like it at all. You good old boys, with all your loyalty and your honor. If you know something about the shit we're standing in right now, Coleman... if you're trying to keep something secret..."

"Caitlin, I can't. Maybe I've read a few reports that aren't available to the public, caught wind of a few rumors here and there, but that's not going to help us now."

"Rumors about what?"

Coleman took his time sipping his coffee. "In a nutshell?

Rumors that we're not the first astronauts to encounter inexplicable problems on the moon."

"Excuse me?"

"I can't tell you any more than that. I don't want to. It can't do any good; it'll just make you worry more. For all we know, they're already planning a rescue mission."

Caitlin trained her eyes on him. She saw the same passivity as always, the same secretive half smile. "You believe that, Coleman?"

"No, Caitlin." Coleman put his head in his hands. "They think we're dead, don't you get that?"

She shook her head. "You're wrong. They would never assume that. They would make every effort…not to mention that you *know* it's a public relations nightmare if they don't…"

Coleman tuned out Caitlin's false hope. He knew that behind closed doors, the mission — and everyone on it — was presumed dead until NASA had some sort of confirmation otherwise.

Because behind closed doors, they knew what had happened here in the past.

The momentary, almost credible feeling that he'd had when he smelled the coffee that everything would work out was suddenly gone.

Nadolski followed the wheel tracks as closely as possible, but he still didn't recognize anything. He actually couldn't even remember having just driven through this same area a few minutes before. He was just about to check the map again when he heard swearing over his headphones. It was Antoine.

"Devereux, what's going on?"

It took a few seconds before he responded. "I think I ran over something."

"Stay where you are, I'm coming back."

"Okay."

Nadolski made a wide left turn and discovered the other LRV well over three hundred feet behind him. When he got back there he saw right away what the problem was. Antoine had hit a large rock with his left front wheel and broken the axle. The wheel was lying down flat in the gray dust.

"I'm really sorry about this. Really. I don't know what happened."

Nadolski looked at the damage. He couldn't do anything about it out here.

"What do we do now?" Antoine asked desperately, walking around the rover to pick up the loose wheel.

Old equipment, Nadolski thought. *Everything on this whole expedition is so goddamn antiquated.*

"It's not a crisis," Nadolski announced. "Both of the rovers were built to hold an extra thousand pounds of weight, so you can ride with me on mine. This was exactly what I was afraid—"

He didn't get to complete his sentence. Something in the dust caught his eye. He dropped down onto his knees and he felt a cold sweat trickling down his back inside the suit. Now it made sense.

"Devereux!"

Antoine let go of the wheel and returned to Nadolski as quickly as he could, but the enormous suit made his movements sluggish. Combined with the low gravity, he had difficulty keeping his balance.

"Do you see these tracks?" Nadolski asked. Antoine nodded. "Good. I'm just asking to make absolutely sure. It's been a long time since any of us has slept properly. And next I'll ask: Do you see these wheel tracks?" Nadolski pointed to another pattern running parallel to the first set.

Again Antoine said yes.

"These are the tracks we've been following since we turned around," Nadolski explained.

"And your point is...?" Antoine asked.

Nadolski looked at him. It was easy to see that he was worried, as if he already knew he was about to receive bad news.

"These aren't our tracks."

"What...do you mean? I don't understand. They're exactly the same, aren't they?" Antoine asked.

"No. Look at them carefully," Nadolski said. "This is one of our tracks, you see? And then look at the other one. You see that stripe in the middle? None of our vehicles makes that pattern."

"Maybe it's from another lunar mission?" Antoine volunteered. "Like when they installed the power station, for example."

Nadolski raised his hand to him. "No, Antoine. According to Coleman it was set up remotely without any astronauts on the ground. NASA has never been here. And neither have we, wherever we are. These tracks didn't exist an hour ago."

"What are you trying to say?" Antoine asked, his voice shaking.

"I'm trying to say I think we're in danger."

Just a few seconds later they spotted two figures about a

thousand feet away. They were walking toward them, slowly, but undeniably, closer and closer.

Neither of them was wearing a spacesuit or helmet.

They didn't struggle against the moon's low gravity.

They were walking as naturally as if they were walking on Earth. And they were coming this way.

There was nowhere to hide. It was impossible to run.

The last thing that Antoine noticed was that one of them looked like Nadolski.

And that the other one looked exactly like *him*.

Then everything went white and noisy, and Antoine Devereux felt himself losing consciousness.

Coleman drank his coffee and drummed the fingers of his other hand on the table. They should have been back a long time ago. He had already given them twice as long as he figured they needed, but he still hadn't seen them or heard from them. He had called them repeatedly over the intercom in one of the helmets, but as long as they were more than a mile or so away, they wouldn't hear him anyway.

Something must have gone wrong. Their attempt to get the power station operating must have failed. *Could it be…no…*

Coleman's throat tightened and his mind went black, as if someone had filled it with warm, viscous tar. He had to forcibly pull himself together to breathe normally. He hadn't felt like this in fifty years, since he was nine years old.

It had been a Saturday in July, he remembered. His mother had given him permission to visit a friend who lived on East Sixty-Fifth Street, even though he was too little to be wandering around New York City on his own. She'd given him cab fare and asked the doorman to help him get a cab. But he decided to walk instead and use the money for something else. Candy, maybe. He decided to go through Central Park, maybe stop by the zoo to see if there were any new animals. But on his way through the park, a figure suddenly crawled out of the bushes and grabbed him. Coleman was pulled behind a tree, and the next thing he remembered was the man holding a revolver to his head. Coleman tried giving him the cab fare from his pocket, but the man just laughed at him and cocked the gun.

"How old are you going to be when you die?" the man asked.

Coleman didn't answer, just felt the revolver chafing into his temple and the urine running down his pants leg.

"You're not going to get any older than this, you know," the man said and fired.

Coleman heard the gun click and knew the chamber was empty.

"Do you feel this?" The man pushed the gun harder against his head.

Coleman was sure it would puncture his skull. "I feel it," he whispered.

"This revolver holds six bullets. But there's only one loaded in it. How long do you think you'll live?"

"I don't know."

"I want you to count with me. All right?"

Coleman didn't respond.

"We already had number one, right?"

The man fired again. Again, the gun just made a clicking sound.

"Two."

Click.

"Three."

Click.

"Four."

Click.

"Five. Now's when it happens, you know."

That was when he felt it. The same feeling he had now, standing in a corridor in DARLAH 2. The feeling that there was no hope. And that all the goodness in the world couldn't save him from the evil standing right next to him.

There never was a sixth try. The man held the gun against his head for a long time, before suddenly lowering it and going on his way. Coleman sank into the grass, and the next thing he remembered was a young woman's face, her asking him if he was okay. She walked him home to his apartment, and his mom served her coffee. Coleman could still remember it, how the scent of coffee spread through the apartment and slowly made the world normal again.

He stopped in the dark corridor, not sure where he was actually going. From somewhere far away he heard footsteps, shoes running over the metal floor. *That must be the two girls*, he thought. *What are they up to? They should be resting.* Without another thought he turned around and headed back to the kitchen in module two. Caitlin was still sitting at the big, round table.

"I'm going to go out there to look for them," Coleman said.

She looked at him with concern. "Coleman, what are you saying?"

“It’s been more than four hours,” he said. “They should have been back ages ago. I’m afraid their attempt may have failed.”

“They took both of the LRVs, Coleman.”

“I’ll walk. Keep an eye on the girls,” he said, and then turned and left the room.

Coleman walked quickly to the equipment room, took down a suit, and pulled it on. He picked up an oxygen tank and attached it to his back before stepping into the decompression chamber.

This time it was his turn.

Coleman opened the metal box next to the hatch and typed a code on the keypad. It was a code only he knew. A green light appeared next to the keypad and he heard the little motor start humming. He depressed the button on the wall, and the hatch door lowered shut behind him. *Good, at least something still works,* he thought. Then he flipped one of the other switches on the wall, and the air was quickly sucked out of the chamber. The hatch to the surface opened and he stepped out.

SHOE

Mia was dizzy when she woke up. How long had she been asleep? She didn't know. Somewhere in the back of her head she heard music. Someone was singing. It took a few seconds before she realized she was still wearing her earbuds. Mia calmly sat up in bed and picked up her iPod. It was the Talking Heads. The song was called "(Nothing but) Flowers," and she knew it practically by heart. It was about a postapocalyptic world. The person in the song was ambling around in an open landscape, missing everything that didn't exist anymore: 7-Elevens, cherry pies, chocolate chip cookies, shopping malls, and real estate. She could picture the guy staggering around on an overgrown planet where the grass was three feet tall. *"If this is paradise, I wish I had a lawn mower."* She imagined his desperate search for signs of something he could recognize. "*This was a Pizza Hut, now it's all covered with daisies.*"

The moon was far worse, she thought, because nothing grew here. What if she had to spend a whole year here? Would that even be possible?

The music suddenly stopped.

She looked down at her player. The words LOW BATTERY appeared for a few seconds before the player went dead. She had been expecting that to happen. She was prepared for it, but it still hurt. From now on there would be no music in her world.

She quickly grabbed a pen and some paper to write down the lyrics in her notebook. That way at least she could keep the song alive a little longer. But the thought was interrupted by another one: *They must be back now. Antoine and Nadolski must be back from DARLAH 1.*

That got her out of her bed and into her clothes quickly. On impulse, she walked over to the little porthole window and looked out, perhaps hoping to see some sign of the two returning. But there was nothing to see. Nothing at all. Dead, gray surface as far as the eye could see.

But then, something else.

At first she thought it must be her sleep-deprived brain playing tricks on her. But she pushed her face right up against the glass and stared hard at what she thought she saw....

Footprints.

There were obvious footprints out there.

But that wasn't all.

The footprints were so clear, she could recognize the distinctive pattern.

Paratrooper boots, she thought, astonished. *The same as mine.*

"Midori? Midori!" Mia tugged at her roommate, fast asleep in her bunk. "Wake up!"

Midori slowly opened her eyes and looked confused. "What is it now?"

"There's someone here!"

Midori yawned and rubbed her eyes. "What do you mean? Are they back? Have we been rescued?"

"No, there's someone out there!" Mia pointed to the window.

Seconds later Midori was on her feet next to Mia, staring down at the moondust. She saw them, too.

Vividly clear footprints in the dust.

They ran through the corridors.

They ran past the computer room, through the hatches into module one, and didn't stop until they found Caitlin in the communications room. She was sitting down, hunched over the radio transmitters, trying to get them working. Breathlessly they told her what they had discovered outside their bedroom window and waited for her reaction. She raised her head and looked at them dully.

"Oh. Yes, I saw that," she said, and went back to the radios.

"What do you mean, '*I saw that*'!" Mia shouted frantically. "What the hell is going *on*?"

Caitlin looked at her blankly and shrugged. She said, "I saw that when I walked you guys back to your room."

"But..." Midori began. "What does that mean? What are we going to do?"

"There's nothing to be done, really. Not anymore."

Mia was furious. "Caitlin, what's wrong with you? There's someone out there, don't you get it? The hatch that got closed from the outside, Wilson and Stanton who couldn't get out. The lunar lander that was sabotaged."

"And Nadolski and Antoine, who never came back," Caitlin added in a somber voice.

Mia felt her heart sink like a sharp object scraping her up on the inside. "They didn't... come back?"

"No."

"But... have you tried to contact them?"

"Their intercom is way out of range. Coleman went out to find them."

"Thank God," Midori said with a hopeful sigh of relief.

But Mia looked around and then slowly asked, "How long ago was that, Caitlin?"

Caitlin's eyes seemed blurry.

"I don't know... many hours ago, I'd guess." It was as if Caitlin were in a trance. She didn't seem alarmed, or hopeful, or sad, or anxious. "I'm afraid it's too late to do anything for our dear Coleman. He was a great guy."

Mia grabbed Caitlin by the shoulders and shook her. "What the hell *happened* here? Why are you acting like Coleman is *dead*? And Nadolski and Antoine?"

"There's no reason to assume they're alive. Every person who has left this base has not returned. I'm so sorry, girls. I think it's just the three of us here now. We'll have to be brave, together."

The girls stared at Caitlin, dumbfounded. Was this woman on *drugs*? She suddenly changed topics and smiled. "Do you guys want anything while we're waiting?"

"While we're waiting for *what*?" Mia asked, almost hysterical now.

"Well, the emergency backup power will eventually run out, and the oxygen generator will shut off. After that the oxygen will disappear over a couple of hours. Maybe we should fix ourselves a meal. Or we could tell each other stories. I don't know." It was as if Caitlin had shut down all her emotions and was just coasting along in a dreamworld.

"You have totally lost your mind, Caitlin!" Mia wailed.

Caitlin ignored her cries. "Mia, tell me, do you still have any battery power left in your player?"

"No!"

"Okay. We'll have to get by without music, then. Of course, we could always sing. . . ."

"You're responsible for us, don't you get that!" Midori screamed. "You have an obligation to do everything you possibly can!"

Caitlin's response was apathetic and quiet. "There's nothing to do."

"So you've already given up, is that what you're saying?" Midori cried.

Caitlin fixed her eyes on Midori, and that scared her. "Yes. Haven't you?" came Caitlin's mumbled response.

Midori punched her in the shoulder, desperate. "It's not *fair*! It's just not fair!"

Caitlin stood up and grabbed Midori's arm, pushed it away, and hissed, "Well, what a shame. Poor you. Maybe you should've stayed home!"

Deflated, the two girls left the communications room. Mia insisted they should stop by the infirmary, although she wasn't really sure what she was looking for. But she had a theory, and after a few minutes of hunting it was confirmed: Several of the boxes of pills Coleman had shown them in the medicine chest were empty. *Caitlin. Caitlin has been here. She's started numbing herself to help her get through it.*

Mia examined the boxes. There were some pretty strong pills and morphine for severe pain. She showed them to Midori, who just shook her head without saying anything. After all, there really wasn't anything they could do for Caitlin, aside from leaving her in peace with her own indifference. Not at the moment anyway. But did that mean Caitlin was right? That there wasn't much they could do for themselves aside from wait? Wait for the electricity to go out? For the oxygen to disappear from the rooms and corridors? For all of them to suffocate and die?

They scarcely talked as they walked back toward the kitchen. They had a plan, but it wasn't a long conversation — just a few sentences from one of them, a couple of nods from the other.

As soon as they felt it getting hard to breathe, they would head to the equipment room. Then they would put on spacesuits and go out onto the surface.

They would find a suitable spot, maybe a hill, a place with a view of all of space. And there they would sit with their arms around each other until the oxygen ran out and the carbon monoxide poisoning sent them comfortably and quietly to their deaths.

CAITLIN

All she wanted was to sleep. She wanted to sleep and wake up somewhere totally different. Anywhere would be fine with her. Even if it was the middle of the desert somewhere in Mexico, without food or water, with a psychopathic mass murderer on her heels. Even if she had to crawl to safety on bloody knees through the wasteland, surrounded by snakes and coyotes. Anything would be better than sitting shut up in here with no possibilities.

The only thing Caitlin had to look forward to as she sat, half slumped over the desk in the communications room, was that the pills would let her avoid the worst of the fear.

After Coleman had left the base in his hopeless attempt to find Nadolski and Antoine, she had paced through DARLAH's corridors to keep her anxieties at bay. She ended up in the infirmary without thinking about it, and the large medicine chest with the bloodred cross on it had practically smiled at her, as if it were trying to say, *It's just fine; you don't need to be feeling this way.* She opened it and found everything from penicillin to adrenaline injectors, morphine, Valium, and a bunch of other analgesics and anesthetics, along with the usual first-aid equipment.

The room she was in was relatively large. The infirmary was part of module four and designed to accommodate several patients at the same time. In the middle of the room there were four tables, which were meant to serve both as hospital beds and autopsy tables. The walls were covered with cabinets that followed the almost oval shape of the room. It almost seemed to have been taken right out of an old sci-fi movie. Where she found herself in the role of scream queen right before the decisive scene.

What was all of this for? All the surgical blades, the microscopes, the plastic lab coats, the rubber boots? The drill, the hammer, and that awful set of rib shears?

What in the world did NASA think was going to happen to the people it sent up here?

And why were so many of the large cupboards locked, with no keys to be found anywhere?

This base, she decided, held many secrets that she would never find out the answers to. Didn't want to, really. The answers would surely terrify her. And now, she just wanted peace.

Caitlin grabbed a box of pills and an ampule of morphine, and clutched them in her hands. She felt guilty immediately.

I'll lose control if I take these.

What control? You lost that a long time ago.

I can't take this anymore.

You have to stay awake and alert, Caitlin.

Awake for what? It's not like anyone's going to come rescue us, are they?

You're responsible for those teenagers!

But I can't do anything for them. I'm just like them. I want to go home.

If you take these, you'll ruin whatever last chance you have of getting back home again.

What chance? There is no chance, is there? Not anymore.

Her frantic, quarrelsome thoughts had triggered a raging headache. *That does it.* She put the pills and the ampule in her jacket pocket and returned to the communications room.

Caitlin knew she should look for Mia and Midori, but just the thought of those two kids together somewhere in the base depressed her. They shouldn't be here. They should be back on Earth with their friends and families, not here in this godforsaken place. In a way, though, she was kind of envious of them; they were the same age, and they had each other. And she was totally on her own, without anyone to lean on.

She went back to module one with heavy footsteps.

Caitlin sat down in the one chair in front of the wall of radio transmitters and communications equipment. The countless small bulbs and screens that would normally have been lit were all dark and silent. She knew there was no point, but she still couldn't help herself and tried switching on all the equipment. And as expected, nothing happened. She collapsed in the chair, hiding her head in her hands, dejected.

What are you doing here, Caitlin?

She tried running back through her memories to figure out where all this had started.

She had been eighteen that summer, on vacation in Mexico with her boyfriend George, who was six years older than she was. They had spent the night on the beach, lying awake and staring up at the sky. There wasn't a cloud to be seen, and the absence of lights made it possible to see an overwhelming number of stars. Occasionally they saw a shooting star streak over their heads.

"Make a wish," George murmured.

"What was that?" Caitlin asked.

"Do you know what shooting stars really are?"

"Meteors."

George nodded and sat up, propped up on his elbows. "Yes, partially correct. But they're mostly space debris. You know, space capsules, satellites, all kinds of shit we've sent up there over the ages. There are cameras, pliers, and wrenches orbiting Earth right now. That's why it's hard to send up rockets these days. Because of all that debris."

"You're kidding, right? I mean, there's plenty of room up there if it's just wrenches and video cameras we're talking about."

"Well, that wrench is whipping around at a speed of seventeen thousand miles per hour. That's almost five miles per second. And it wouldn't be so cool if you ran right into that at seventeen thousand miles per hour, would it? And it's not like there's only one of them either. There're hundreds of things floating around aimlessly, in unknown orbits, so it's impossible to know for sure where they are. It's madness, Caitlin."

Many years later, after Caitlin had become an astronaut and started working for NASA and was preparing for the moon mission, she got to see a survey by the European Space Agency, ESA, of all the human-made objects orbiting Earth.

George had been right. There really were *a lot* of them. Too many. But he'd also been wrong. Because the number of satellites and wrenches and whatever it all was wasn't in the hundreds. It was in the thousands. There were twenty-two hundred satellites alone, supplying Earth's inhabitants with TV signals, GPS navigation, and so forth. And maybe that had been the beginning of her interest in space, which would last her whole life.

She thought about it often, that conversation they had had that night. If it hadn't been for that, she might never have become an astronaut, but something totally different instead. A doctor, maybe. Or an architect.

Suddenly one of the radios crackled. In a flash Caitlin was yanked out of her daydream back to reality.

The radio works!

The radio works!

She sat there frozen, listening to the crackling and the white noise. A small red light on the device had switched itself on. The receiver had power. She had no idea how that could be, but that wasn't bothering her right now. The most important thing was that it was working. *She could contact Earth!*

Joy and eagerness made her hands tremble uncontrollably. *Okay, careful now, careful now...*

She reached out with her right arm and gently but deliberately turned the search dial. The crackling stopped instantly, and for a second she was terrified that she'd ruined something. But then, after she turned the dial halfway around, it was there again, clearer now. There were voices. She heard voices.

Without wasting a second, she grabbed the microphone and set the radio to the emergency frequency.

"Houston, this is DARLAH 2, we have a problem!"

She waited a few seconds for a response, but none came.

She tried again. "Houston, Houston, this is DARLAH 2, we have a problem! We lost power at the base, and *Demeter* is damaged. Houston, do you read? This is Caitlin Hall from DARLAH 2. Hello?"

Nothing.

She switched frequencies and repeated the message to the receiver in Houston. But that one, too, was completely silent. She feverishly tried all the frequencies and settings. Every once in a while the original crackling would reoccur, sometimes with indistinct voices in the background, other times just white noise. Giving up, she sank back in the chair. And right then the voices became totally clear through the noise. It was coming from a news channel. She thought she recognized the broadcaster's voice.

"...NASA has been deflecting vehement accusations that the agency isn't moving quickly enough to enact a plan to undertake a rescue mission for the five astronauts and three teenagers stranded on the moon. The president of the United States is also facing heavy criticism for his call for a minute of silence to pay respects to the members of the moon mission. Speculation that the agency is withholding information is sparking rampant rumors that officials may indeed have evidence that there were no survivors...."

"No! *No!*" Caitlin screamed at the radio, frantically slapping the machine. "Don't give up now, we're still here, we're still alive, are you *listening*?" The news broadcast was cut short, and the speakers emitted an infernal piercing, grating sound for a few seconds before abruptly going silent for good.

She pushed her chair back, leapt to her feet, and started kicking the radio. "I can't *take* any more!" she shrieked, tears running down her face. Sparks were shooting out of the air vents, and the reeking smell of smoke started seeping into the room.

Without thinking, her trembling hands found the pills and the morphine ampule in her jacket pocket. She pushed out two pills and swallowed them without water.

For one last second she considered what she should do, if there were any good alternatives. But there weren't. With a decisive motion, she broke the tip of the ampule and stuck the needle into her thigh, through her pants, and squeezed.

The morphine started working in seconds. A heavy warmth spread through her body and wrapped her in a soft, thick blanket of gentle, carefree indifference.

THE SIGNAL

They'd been waiting for it to happen. But when it finally did, it still came as a total surprise.

The emergency power cut off.

Midori and Mia were in the kitchen when the reddish light they'd almost gotten used to over the last day finally disappeared. It was gone in a second, replaced by complete, utter darkness.

Midori had found flashlights in the storeroom a couple hours before and had set them on the table in front of them as they waited for the darkness. The light was much weaker than they had expected, though. In order to move safely from place to place they were forced to aim their flickering beams at the same point. The long, featureless corridors they had finally become accustomed to suddenly felt unfamiliar and labyrinthine and endless. But they continued on into it, though they weren't sure why.

With every step, Mia felt how much she missed Antoine, her friends, her hometown, her brother, Sander, even her parents. But she forced those thoughts to the back of her mind, hiding them away as best she could.

Mia and Midori didn't say much, and neither of them mentioned that they were walking around aimlessly, with no plan. It was best not to discuss it. Just keep walking, keep moving. Feel like at least you're doing *something* to keep yourself alive.

Because it would be time to sit down soon enough. And when they did, it would be for the last time.

They discovered Caitlin in the living room. She was sleeping on one of the sofas in there. Midori went over to her and made sure she was breathing. They let her be and proceeded back into the corridors again.

Mia suggested that they head for the computer room. That had previously been off-limits, but now that they were the only two left, there was no reason to abide by that rule. The hatch that had kept the room sealed off was now open, and they walked right in with no problem.

Mia looked around the octagonal room and her concerns were confirmed. All the equipment probably dated back to the early seventies. The main computer was located in the middle of the room. A chair was attached to the floor in front of it, and the walls and ceiling were covered with video screens and hundreds of small lights and buttons that at one time, Mia thought, would have lit up as brilliantly as an amusement park. She plopped down into the chair and groaned.

"We never had a chance with this equipment, Midori." She

thumped her hand against the computer a couple of times. The machine emitted a quiet, electrical *pfffsst* sound, and a light quickly glimmered across the screen before it went blank again. "This is the most outrageous thing I've ever seen in my whole life. What were they thinking? No one seriously had any objections? They actually thought this antique computer would keep working without any trouble for a hundred years? It's so unfair!" She thrust her foot out, kicking the machine harder this time. Again the computer made a sound and lit up.

But this time the light remained.

"Midori, look," Mia exclaimed, astonished. "There's still life in this thing!"

Two words glowed white against the black screen.

SYSTEM ACTIVATED

"Mia, what are you doing? Leave it alone."

"Don't you understand? I got it to turn on! All of DARLAH is out of power, but the main computer is still active. How do you explain that?"

Midori didn't have anything to say.

"There must be something else making it run," Mia said. "Its own power supply, somewhere or other."

"See if you can get anything out of it."

"What should I write?"

"I don't know. Hmm. . . . well, why not try to find out about the power? How can we get the power back on?"

"Okay, wait a sec." Mia leaned forward over the keyboard and typed.

POWER STATUS?

She hit *enter*, and a second later the response appeared.

MAIN POWER MANUALLY SHUT OFF
EMERGENCY POWER FAILED
AT 23:41 MTLT

Oh, shit. She felt the dread settling in her chest, and a wave of nausea rushed through her.

"Midori…the power didn't go out by itself. Someone shut it off."

"You don't know that."

"Well, look at this. It says right here. In black and white."

MANUALLY

The word glowed at them, almost scornfully. *Manually.* There was no misunderstanding that. Someone, or something, had been in here and programmed the power to shut off.

Mia leaned over the keyboard again.

TURN POWER ON

And the response appeared just as quickly as the first.

NEGATIVE
PRIORITY DP7 0271DE
ALL PERSONNEL ABANDON AREA

"What do you think it means, Mia?"

"It means the computer doesn't want to turn the power back on. Or else . . . it *can't*."

"What do you think Priority DP7 0271DE is?"

Mia waited before she answered. "I don't know. Whatever it is . . . I guess it means that we're on our own now."

Midori shook her head, as if she couldn't let herself comprehend the message. She changed the subject. "Ask how we can get out of here. Evacuation, rescue, whatever. Do it!"

Mia typed.

SHOW EVACUATION PLAN

She hit *enter*, but nothing happened. They waited. The computer began to emit a low humming noise, as if it were about to overheat. The screen flashed with static, but no words appeared. The humming turned into a buzzing so loud that it forced the girls to plug their ears. The vibrations rapidly intensified. The unit rattled, and their heads pounded until the sound abruptly came to a stop, and the computer went black.

After almost twenty seconds of silence, the answer appeared.

THERE IS NO ESCAPE

Again the screen went black for a second before more text appeared.

OXYGEN SUPPORT WILL
FAIL IN 224 MINUTES

"Who the hell is writing that?" Midori screamed in frustration, pushing Mia out of the way. She hammered out her question on the keyboard.

WHO IS THIS??

The answer was immediate.

011101110110010100100000
011000010111001001100101
001000000110110001100101
011001110110100101101111
011011100111001100101110

"That doesn't make any sense. Try again, Midori."

WHO IS THIS?

New characters appeared on the screen.

THIS IS ЬEQUJ5

Mia was going to rephrase her question in the hope of getting a clearer answer, but a new sentence appeared on the screen before she had a chance to type. A sentence that scared Mia more than anything:

DERE KOMMER IKKE TIL Å OVERLEVE

Instinctively she jumped back from the screen, as if the words themselves were going to attack her.

"What language is that?" Midori asked, looking at the letters.

"That's... that's Norwegian. It means..." She looked gravely at Midori. "It means '*You're not going to survive.*'" Midori gasped, and Mia shook her head in disbelief. "How does it know I speak Norwegian?"

The words remained for a few seconds before they were replaced by something else.

キミタチハ シヌ。

Midori pointed at the screen.

"Japanese! Oh my God, it knows who we are."

That very second, the screen died. Midori kicked it a few times to bring it back, but now it was as if it had never worked at all. They kept at it for ten or fifteen minutes, searched the room high and low without finding anything that could get it working again. But the computer in DARLAH 2 had had its say.

The girls left the computer room with an uncomfortable feeling that someone was keeping an eye on them in the darkness. Midori grabbed Mia's hand, and they moved step-by-step through the base.

"Where do we go now?" Midori asked.

"Away from here," Mia whispered, pulling her along decisively.

Midori was in tears. "There's nowhere to go. You know that."

"Yes, there is," Mia said, not sure she even knew what she was saying. "Come on. It's not far."

"What's not far?" Midori sniffled. "Where are we going?"

"Just stick close to me, okay?"

"Okay."

They entered a corridor neither of them had ever been in before. The air was different. Organic somehow. Mia was sure she recognized the scent of plants, dirt. "What is this?" she whispered.

Midori and Mia aimed the beams from their flashlights at the floor. Green plants were growing in front of them. Tomatoes. Cabbage. Grass. All of it completely overgrown and with an odor of rot.

"We're in the greenhouse. Outside the oxygen generator."

"Couldn't we just stay in here for a little while?" Midori complained, scarcely audible. "I don't want to walk anymore. I can't."

They stopped, listened. Nothing. Mia bent over and picked two tomatoes. She gave one to Midori.

"Here, eat this."

"What is it?"

"A tomato. Eat it now."

They bit into the tomatoes. And both spit their mouthfuls back out at the same time.

"Ew," Midori said. "That tastes old. Metallic."

Mia let the light from her flashlight fall on their tomatoes. A gray worm wriggled through big holes in the tomato's skin.

"Yuck!" Midori shrieked, tossing away her tomato. It hit the wall with a soft, wet *thump*. She could hear the rotten juice dripping from the wall.

"Midori? Is that you?"

The voice came from the corridor. It repeated the question a couple of times before Mia and Midori left the greenhouse and stepped back out into the corridor. In the weak light from their flashlights they recognized him right away.

It was Coleman. Midori heaved a sigh of relief. *He wasn't dead!* Caitlin had been wrong. And if Coleman was alive, maybe…

Mia's spirits soared for a precious moment.

"*Coleman!*" she cried. "Thank God you're here!" He nodded but didn't seem to know quite what to say. "We thought you went out to look for Nadolski and Antoine?" Mia prompted.

"I did," he said quietly as he approached. "I didn't find them."

Mia's heart was crushed by the news as Coleman continued. "Their wheel tracks stopped three and a half miles from here, but neither they nor the rovers were anywhere to be seen. So I turned around. I got back right before the emergency power cut off. Since then I've been fumbling around in the dark looking for you guys." He put a hand on Mia's head and stroked her hair. She didn't know if she liked that. "And now here you are," he added.

Midori didn't believe him. "But why did you come back at all? Why didn't you just keep going to DARLAH 1?"

"By myself? Without you two? No, Midori, I'm responsible for everyone who's left. Did you forget that?"

He was acting weird, that was for sure. Had Coleman been helping himself to supplies from the infirmary, too? Or had he just lost his mind? Hard to tell. Mia wasn't sure she could trust him, but decided to take the chance. After all, it was the only one she had.

"We discovered something," she said.

"Really? What?" He seemed curious but detached.

"In the computer room," Mia said.

"I thought I forbade you to go in there." Coleman was stern.

Mia shrugged. "It's not like that really matters anymore, does it?"

Coleman nodded slowly. "Still, you shouldn't have done that."

"We activated the computer. After the emergency power went off."

"That's impossible," Coleman said right away. "The computer room is directly connected to the power generator and the emergency power."

"Well, apparently not," Midori commented drily. "Anyway, it told us a few things."

"Like?"

"You mean you don't know?" Mia wasn't sure anymore if she could completely trust him. "I thought you knew everything about this base."

"So did I, but that was before computers started working without any power supply." Coleman felt his already considerable amount of anxiety growing.

"It told us about priority DP7 0271DE."

Coleman furrowed his brow. That wasn't one of the codes he was trained to recognize. None of the base's codes contained letters, he was sure of that.

"Not familiar with it," he replied.

"We don't know what it is either. But it told us to abandon the base."

"I'm not sure I understand...."

"I'm just repeating what it said on the screen. But there's more."

"More?"

Midori told him about what else they'd learned. The information about when the oxygen would run out. The message that there was no evacuation plan, that the power had been shut off manually, and that the machine knew they were from Norway and Japan. And then they told Coleman the code the machine had given in response to their question about its identity.

They could see how that last piece of information instantly stunned him.

"What did you just say?" he asked.

"6EQUJ5," Mia repeated.

"You're quite sure about that? Quite sure the numbers and letters were in that exact order? This is very important, you understand. Is there any chance at all that you could have mixed up the numbers or letters?"

"No," they both responded.

Coleman was quiet for a long time.

"I'm afraid we have bigger problems than we thought."

And then it hit Coleman that someone was missing. "Where's Caitlin?" he asked.

Mia and Midori told him about their suspicion that she had helped herself to sedatives from the infirmary. Coleman took the flashlights and used them to safely lead the two girls to the living room, where, they hoped, Caitlin was still sleeping. They followed him out of the greenhouse area and down the empty corridor in module three.

They stopped in the storeroom on the way to the living room. Coleman found some better flashlights in a locked cupboard.

"These should work for up to fifteen hours," he said, handing one to each of them. The flashlights were big and heavy. They reminded Mia of small versions of the theatrical lights her band used at concerts. They could only just barely carry them in one hand. Coleman took down two extras from the shelves and turned one of them on.

"I need to tell you two something," he began. "It might be important. It has to do with that code the machine gave you, 6EQUJ5. That's not just any code or an error. It's a signature. A signal."

"A signal?" Mia wondered.

"Yes, a signal. It's usually referred to as the 'Wow! signal,' after the mark the astronomer wrote in the margin on the signal printout. Let me try to explain: In Delaware, Ohio, there was once a giant radio telescope called the Big Ear. The radio telescope was part of the Perkins Observatory at Ohio Wesleyan University. It was mounted outside on a large, flat surface made of aluminum, about as big as a football field. And reflector walls were set up at either end that could catch and amplify incoming signals. Between 1963 and 1998, the Big Ear telescope was used to search for radio sources that could be coming from intelligent life in space. On fifty channels that were monitored by computers, the astronomers could listen for intelligent signals."

Mia and Midori were listening intently.

"The first fourteen years nothing happened. Absolutely nothing. They couldn't detect a single unknown radio signal. The computer printouts the astronomers reviewed every day didn't show anything other than a boring string of ones, twos, and threes. That means the signals the telescope was picking up belonged to frequencies and sources the researchers already knew about. Like planets or asteroids, for example. Because of course any object with mass sends out radio waves. So do people. But then, on August fifteenth, 1977, just after eleven o'clock at night, something happened.

"Dr. Jerry R. Ehman was sitting there, watching the printouts, when he suddenly discovered that the numbers on the paper had changed. First a four appeared, then a six. And suddenly a whole sequence, a code, a signal no one had heard before. With a totally different intensity. The meters were jumping around wildly. Instead of recording the sound source as a series of ones and twos, this code appeared: 6EQUJ5."

Mia and Midori were at first stunned, and then chilled, by hearing the code they recognized.

"No one could explain where the signal came from. It lasted for exactly seventy-two seconds before it disappeared. And after that it never turned up again. For almost twenty years they tried to locate that signal again. They used better equipment, more people and more time, but it was as if it had never existed. Dr. Ehman spent years studying that printout and those numbers. Little by little, he discarded most of the natural explanations. The signal couldn't have come from planets, asteroids, satellites, airplanes, or Earth. They simply didn't match the sound frequency. He was left with the big question: Could the signal have come from something intelligent, as if sent from a lighthouse in different directions and then randomly reaching Earth? At least that would make it probable that Ehman only

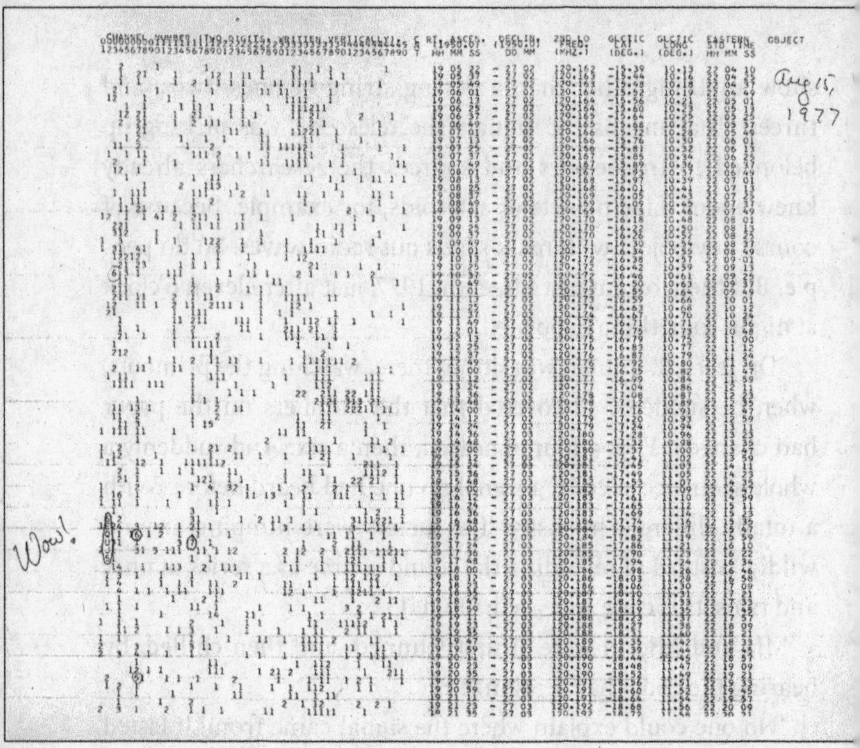
CHANNEL NUMBER (TWO DIGITS, WRITTEN VERTICALLY)
RT. ASCEN. (1950.0) HH MM SS
DECLIN. (1950.0) DD MM
2ND LO FREQ. (MHZ.)
GLCTIC LAT (DEG.)
GLCTIC LONG (DEG.)
EASTERN STD TIME HH MM SS
OBJECT
Aug 15, 1977
Wow!

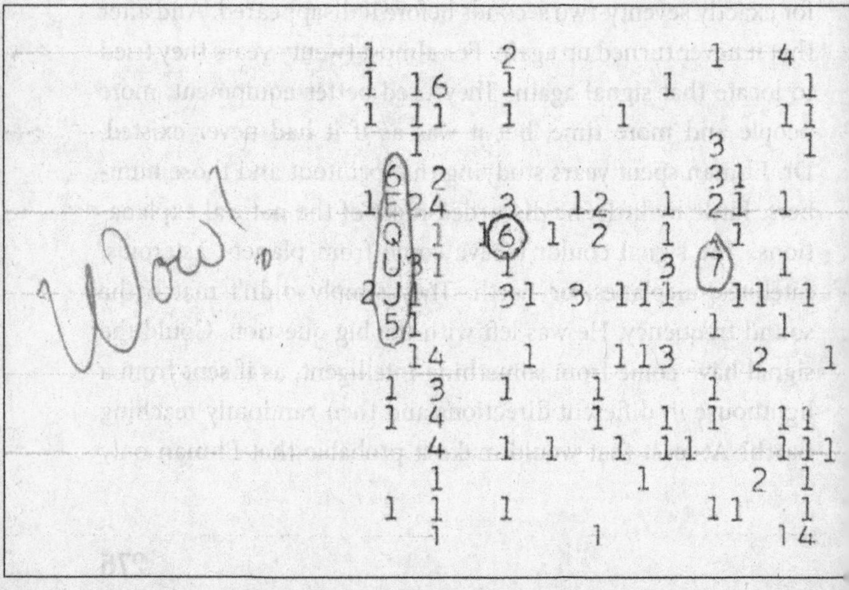
6EQUJ5
Wow!

managed to follow the signal for seventy-two seconds before it was sent in another direction. Regardless, the question of what 6EQUJ5 means has been discussed for more than forty years. But now? I'm afraid the discussion has just ended."

Mia looked at Coleman in the light from the flashlight. Suddenly she felt deathly afraid.

"What are you saying?" she asked.

Coleman's voice grew serious. "I'm saying we have to get out of here."

THE DARK

Coleman knew what had to be done. Standing over Caitlin in the living room, he gave her an injection. Mia had no idea what it contained, but its effect was obvious, because just a few minutes later Caitlin was sitting up on the sofa. She wasn't quite so bleary-eyed anymore, and her face had some color again. Coleman whispered something quietly to her. Neither Mia nor Midori could hear what he said, but the words seemed to snap her out of the darkness.

The four of them gathered around one of the tables. Coleman positioned the flashlights next to them so they could all see one another.

"I'm not planning on giving you false hope. The situation is critical, and now is the time to act. The oxygen generator will stop working in less than two hours. From then on the conditions in here will quickly become unbearable. Which means you will all have to abandon the base."

"But... where do you suggest we go?" Midori asked.

"DARLAH 1."

"Coleman," Caitlin began, "two of us tried to go there, and no one has heard from them since. Do you really think...?"

"It's our only option," he said, cutting her off. "It's a chance we have to take. If anyone has a better idea, I'm open to it, but right now this is the only thing that makes sense."

Midori glanced across the table to see if Mia seemed as scared as she was. But to her surprise Mia seemed just the opposite: calm, determined, focused. And seeing her like that helped. As long as Mia hadn't given up, there was hope.

"All right," Midori said. "Let's assume we make it to DARLAH 1. Just what exactly are we going to do there?"

Coleman pulled a map out of his inside pocket. It was the same size as the map of DARLAH 2. "There's an evacuation capsule at the end of DARLAH 1. To get to it, you have to go through the power station and two secure corridors. Five hatches total. Unfortunately, I've never seen it myself, so I can't explain to you exactly how it works. But it should be simple and self-explanatory. It's preprogrammed to return to Earth, a trip that should take four days. When you activate the rocket burner on board, the capsule will rise out of DARLAH 1 and climb to a height of fifty thousand feet. Then it will circle the moon until it gets up enough speed to start the trip to Earth. The capsule's control system will modulate the reentry angle and speed once it hits Earth's atmosphere, and parachutes will be released at twenty thousand feet to further slow its descent. Some radar on Earth is guaranteed to

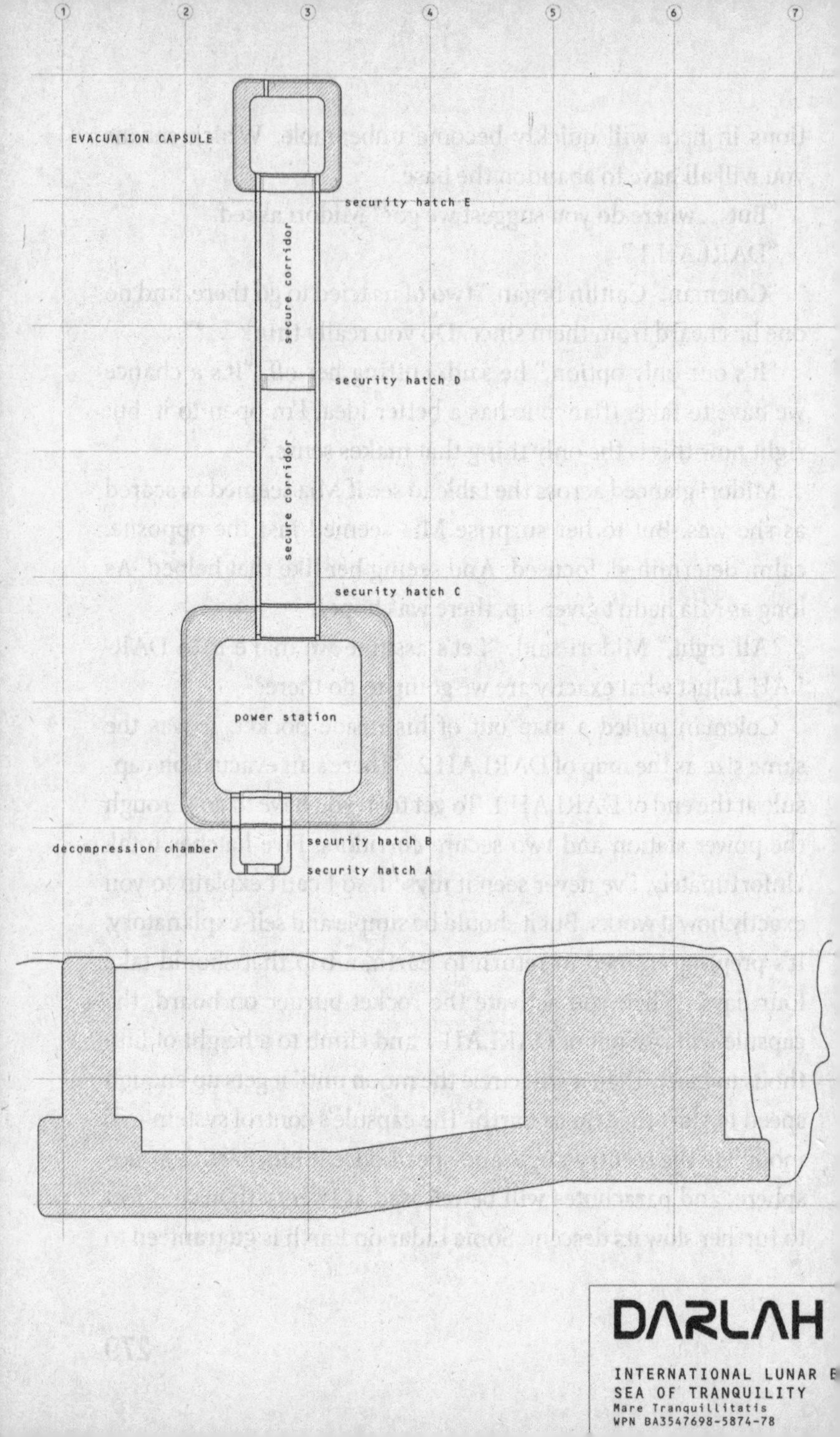
1
2
3
4
5
6
7
EVACUATION CAPSULE
security hatch E
secure corridor
security hatch D
secure corridor
security hatch C
power station
decompression chamber
security hatch B
security hatch A
DARLAH
INTERNATIONAL LUNAR
SEA OF TRANQUILITY
Mare Tranquillitatis
WPN BA3547698-5874-78

discover the capsule before you land. It also had a built-in radio transmitter that will activate when it lands, to make it easier to locate. With a little luck, you guys will be picked up within hours."

"'You guys'?" Mia asked, looking at Coleman with terror in her eyes. "Why aren't you saying *we*?"

Coleman smiled sadly. "The evacuation capsule only has room for three people."

"Then we need to find another solution!" Caitlin burst out, suddenly revived from her drug-induced stupor. "I won't accept that!"

"You're going to have to. There are no other solutions."

Mia couldn't believe what Coleman was saying. "There must be something we can do! Maybe we could... I mean, there must be a way we could squeeze four people into that capsule, or..."

"No, Mia. I'm afraid there isn't room." Then Coleman added, "I've made my choice. Now it's time to get you girls out of here."

Midori had been completely paralyzed by what Coleman was saying, but now she forced herself to open her mouth: "We're not leaving without you."

He gave her a cautious smile.

"I'm afraid I don't merit a ticket home, Midori. So I'm choosing to stay. It's the right thing for me to do. Someone has to go down with the ship, you know. And me?" He looked around the room as if he were actually fond of the place. "I'm the commander of DARLAH."

Mia was about to say something else, but Coleman motioned for her to be quiet.

"We're running out of time. Let's concentrate on doing what we have to do."

He pulled out a detailed map that showed the way from DARLAH 2 to DARLAH 1. He slowly pushed it over to Mia. She wondered if she ought to pass it on to Caitlin, but a quick glance told her that wasn't a good idea. Caitlin seemed to have withdrawn into herself again.

"You're in charge of this, Mia. Never let it out of your sight. You'll find suits and full oxygen tanks in the equipment room in module four. It's just over seven miles to the power station, and it shouldn't take you more than three hours to get there. Maintain an even pace and don't look back. Make sure you use the decompression chamber before you go into the station. Caitlin?"

"Yeah?" She was sitting, stiff and immobile, staring at the floor.

"Go to the kitchen before you leave. Eat some food and get enough to drink. You'll need it for this trip." He stood up from the table. "And now it's time for me to say my good-byes."

Mia should really hate him for having gotten them into this situation. After all, it was his fault. He and his people had been lying to them the whole time. But she couldn't. She looked at him, but all she saw was a man who'd made the wrong choice. She suddenly realized how much she liked him, how much she liked all of them she'd been up here with. Stanton, Nadolski, Wilson, Antoine... and now she was losing yet another person. She didn't know if she could take it.

Coleman came around the table to her and gave her a hug. "I

know what you're thinking," he whispered. "But I promise you, you guys can do it. In four days you'll be the happiest person Earth has ever seen. You'll breathe the fresh air in a whole new way. You'll stand by the ocean and feel the salty sea spray tingling in your nose. You'll be with people you know and love, and you'll appreciate how beautiful everything is. You'll see cars behind you in your rearview mirror, and maybe you'll laugh at the drivers' faces. Because they'll look annoyed, bored, angry. And you'll realize what they're missing. You'll live a long and happy life, Mia. Because when you get home, you'll realize that *anything* is possible. You mustn't ever forget that."

He let her go and went over to Midori and gave her a hug as well before moving on to Caitlin.

"I'm afraid the hospitality here on the moon was even worse than I'd hoped, Caitlin. I think it's best if you tell them not to send anyone up here again. I'm really, really sorry about that."

"Don't give it another thought," she snuffled.

"You're a good astronaut, Miss Hall. These girls need your skills. This is the most important mission of your life. Take good care of yourselves now, all of you."

And with those words, he picked up one of the flashlights and left the room.

The three women were left standing there in silence.

Coleman embarked on his very last stroll through DARLAH 2's dark corridors. With determined footsteps, he walked over to his bedroom in module two. He opened his closet, grabbed his pistol, and stuck it inside his jacket before turning around and heading for the greenhouse. He sat down by the big apple tree and set his flashlight next to him.

He would wait here. Wait until he was totally sure the other three had made it out of the base and were on their way to DARLAH 1. He would sit here, in position, with his weapon in his hands, until the oxygen level was so low that he was sure there was no other living thing inside these walls.

And then he would end it all.

OXYGEN

Mia's head felt foggy. It had only been an hour since the regular flow of oxygen from the generator had stopped, but she could already feel how difficult it was becoming to breathe. Every breath gave her the sense that someone had already breathed this same air and tapped it of all its sustenance. After the power went off, the temperature had slowly begun to rise. The sun, which was beating down on the moon's surface, ensuring temperatures of over two hundred degrees outside, was working its way through the base's insulation. And now that the cooling elements weren't working anymore, there wasn't much to keep the heat at bay.

Midori was sitting by herself in a corner of the kitchen, trying to eat an apple. Caitlin was studying the map. It was her idea to stick it out for another couple of hours before they left the base for good and started their trek to DARLAH 1. The sun was still too strong out there. Without an atmosphere there was nothing to protect them from its radiation, and therefore it was too dangerous to risk going out. Besides, Caitlin wanted to give them an opportunity to drink enough before they left. Turning around and coming back wouldn't be an option.

Mia was standing by the big window, looking out. In the reflection from the sun in the windowpane, she could see her own reflection, unclear and dim. She turned on her flashlight and pointed it at her face. The reflection in the window got clearer. She could see that she looked frazzled. The last several days had clearly left their mark. Mia thought she looked like a living ghost. She had obvious dark circles under her eyes, and her hair hung limply to one side. It was a depressing sight. She lowered the light, and her face disappeared from the glass.

"Mia? Are you sure you've had enough to drink?" Caitlin asked. Mia turned to her and nodded absentmindedly. She couldn't bear the thought of forcing herself to drink another drop of water here. It tasted metallic, old, rotten. It tasted like slow death.

She was impatient. Couldn't they just go? Get it over with? She wanted to get out of here as soon as possible and never come back. It had been a mistake to come here in the first place, the biggest mistake of them all. From the very beginning this place had been eating away at her, and by this time, there was hardly anything left. The only boy she had ever had a chance to love was out there somewhere with Nadolski, or alone. And she could almost smell the decay lingering in the walls. She had to focus to try to keep herself from imagining that it was the smell of Wilson, Stanton, and Coleman. She wasn't sure where they were, but they were nearby. She could feel it.

Again she raised her eyes and aimed the light at her face. She looked at the window. Her features were almost even clearer now. She could study the details around her nose, her mouth, her hair. She didn't look good. Resigned, she switched the flashlight off and lowered it.

That was when she noticed it.

Her reflection didn't disappear.

It stayed there in the window, even clearer than before.

For a second she allowed herself to just be fascinated by it. She made a face.

But her reflection didn't change.

And in a fraction of the next second she realized: *That isn't a reflection. That is you. Yourself.*

Out there.

Mia screamed. She dropped the light and staggered backward as she saw her own face in the window sneer at her. She lost her balance, bumped into the table, and knocked several plates off before she fell on the floor. Midori leapt out of her chair and came running.

"Mia, what is it?" she yelled. "Mia?"

Mia pointed to the window, and Midori cautiously walked over to it. She looked out.

"There's nothing there, Mia. Nothing."

"I saw…" Mia couldn't complete the sentence. She closed her eyes.

Caitlin was up. She came over to Midori.

"What's going on? Mia?" Caitlin stood at the window. "Did you see something? What did you see?"

Mia didn't have a chance to respond. A hundred, a hundred and fifty feet beyond the base, Caitlin spotted Antoine. *Antoine!*

He was standing there looking at her. He was wearing the same brown clothes he'd had on when she first met him. He waved at her.

"Antoine!" she shouted. "Antoine! He's out there. He's alive!"

Mia registered the name but couldn't quite comprehend it. Behind closed eyes, she was still seeing her own face, sneering at her malevolently. As if it knew something she didn't.

Caitlin was frozen, watching the boy outside. He waved again, then suddenly turned around and walked away from her.

"No, wait!" Caitlin yelled, then spun around and ran past the girls into the corridor.

"Caitlin, don't do it!" Mia shouted. "It's not him, do you hear me? It's not him. It can't be. *He's not wearing a suit!*"

But Caitlin wasn't listening. She was fueled by adrenaline and fresh hope and her own delusions. She ran like she'd never run before, out of module one, past the computer room, and into the equipment room. Without a second to lose, she climbed into one of the spacesuits, strapped on a full oxygen tank, and secured her helmet before she stepped into the decompression chamber. The power had made the hatches unusable, and she was forced to close the innermost door manually. She held on tightly to one of the handles along the wall and forced the outermost hatch up a few centimeters. A second later she felt the vacuum outside sucking all the air out of the room and pressing her against the hatch wall.

Once she felt the pressure equalize, she raised the outer hatch far enough to step out onto the surface.

Caitlin passed the closed hatch where Wilson and Stanton had died and continued around the exterior of module two. She was struggling not to hyperventilate. When she rounded the corner, she spotted him outside the kitchen.

Antoine.

She called out to him over the intercom, waved her arms. But he just stood there, motionless, looking at her. She stopped for a second, unsure. Why was he staring at her? Why wasn't he glad to see her?

Slowly he started walking toward her. With steady, rhythmic footsteps. Caitlin froze, unable to move.

Oh my God, she managed to think. *What the...?*

Mia was on her feet, standing next to Midori in the window.

They saw Caitlin standing perfectly still outside the window as Antoine rushed toward her at an alarming speed. He was virtually skimming over the surface, as if he weren't constrained by the laws of physics. In a flash, he disappeared right behind Caitlin. Mia strained to spot him again, but he was out of sight.

"That's not Antoine," she heard Midori whisper. "That's a copy!"

It felt like the next few seconds lasted an hour. Mia heard Midori speaking but didn't understand what she was saying. Out of nowhere Antoine's face popped up in front of the window, his mouth twisted in a repulsive sneer, and right after that he was gone.

Caitlin turned to face them slowly and made eye contact with Mia just as something grabbed hold of her and tore her legs off from under her. The look on her face was more one of surprise than pain. She formed a word with her lips, but it was impossible to understand what she was trying to say. Then in an instant she was pulled away, disappearing under the base, leaving the surface deserted and undisturbed.

Midori was in tears now, shaking uncontrollably and short of breath. The terrible sight of Caitlin's sudden death was sending her into shock. Mia wanted to just hold her, tell her that everything would be okay. But that wasn't true. It was going to get worse, much worse, if they didn't get out of this place.

Mia knew she had to act fast. It was too late to do anything for Caitlin, but there was one glimmer of hope left. Midori was squatting below the window, her head between her legs, sobbing silently. Drool was running out of her mouth.

"Wait here," Mia commanded. "Lock the door and don't open it until I get back, understand?"

"Where are you going?" Midori stammered.

"I have to find Coleman, if he's still alive."

"I don't want to be alone here!" Midori pleaded.

"It'll be fine. Just lock the door behind me and stay low."

Mia grabbed a knife from the kitchen counter and ran out into the hallway, through the bedrooms and the bathroom, and down the corridors. The beam from her flashlight flickered over the walls and ceilings as she ran as fast as she could. She checked the computer room and then ran to the infirmary in module four, but there was no one there either.

And then she suddenly stopped.

Music. She heard music.

But that's impossible. The power is out.

Mia started trembling. She knew that song. It was the Talking Heads.

Somewhere nearby she heard a girl's voice softly singing along to the words: *"Hold tight—wait till the party's over, Hold tight—we're in for nasty weather..."*

The music stopped as suddenly as it had started. Something moved in one of the corridors; she could clearly hear the footsteps. Then they stopped.

Mia listened. She slowly walked down the corridor, past the computer room again, and continued on toward module two, deliberately putting one foot in front of the other, holding her flashlight up in front of her. She saw nothing. She turned around and shone the light the other way. And now the light revealed a person at the very end of the corridor.

The person was identical to herself.

The figure was wearing the same clothes she usually wore, her black jeans. The jacket she bought at the flea market in London the year before, which she wore almost every day. It had the same hair. Exactly the same face. With the exception of the unrelenting sneer that hung over it. *And it's wearing my Italian paratrooper boots*, she thought.

"Hi, Mia," the figure said, taking a step closer. "Are you scared? It's just me. Don't you recognize me?"

Mia couldn't speak.

"Aren't you going to say hi?"

She didn't respond.

"I'm sorry about that business with your friends. But there really was no other way." Even the voice was the same as her own. Just calmer, with a slightly different accent. The figure took another step forward.

"Stop!" Mia cried, pointing the knife at her.

"There's nothing to be afraid of," she said, continuing to approach. "Were you happy to see Antoine again? I only did that for your sake."

Mia got down on her knees, holding the knife up in front of her, and let the figure come even closer. She was waiting until she was sure it was within reach. She waited as long as she dared.

Then she struck. With a powerful thrust, she drove the knife into the figure's thigh, and she could feel it forcing its way into the flesh.

But the figure just took a step back, pulled the knife out, and threw it away. "Why did you do that?" she said, sounding disappointed. "Come here, Mia. Come."

Mia leapt up to a standing position, whirled around, lost her flashlight, and ran back toward the kitchen. She felt an intense wave of pain as she smacked into a security hatch face-first. It knocked out one of her teeth.

"I thought you'd try to run," the voice said. "So I shut the hatch."

She was still coming closer. Mia became aware of something wet and sticky running down her forehead and realized she'd gotten a gash in her head. The pain was throbbing now.

"I was the one who cut the power, too. And I shut that hatch outside to stop your friends from repairing the generator. I met your friend Antoine a couple of miles from here, too. A handsome boy, very handsome. He was with someone else. Unfortunately I couldn't allow them to complete their task, so I... forbade them."

In a panic, Mia's hands fumbled their way to the bottom edge of the hatch and forced it up.

The footsteps came closer.

Closer.

She was only a couple feet away now.

Mia flung herself down onto the floor and rolled under the hatch before it fell down again with a loud, metallic *clunk*. She got back up and sprinted the last few yards to the kitchen.

"Midori, hurry! Help me shut this door!"

Mia threw her back against the door while Midori desperately rotated the wheel until it was tightly locked.

"What happened?" Midori whispered, looking at Mia, listening intently for any sounds, her eyes glued to the door.

Mia didn't answer the question, but her response was swift. "We have to get out of here."

DOPPELGÄNGER

"Come on," Midori whispered. "I know a place we can hide for now."

The creature out in the corridor had either disappeared or was lying in wait. Mia and Midori crawled across the floor without making a sound. They slid open the bolt that held the door to the dry storage room closed and crawled in there. Midori shut the door behind them and set the lights on the floor while Mia ripped off one of the arms of her T-shirt and pressed the piece of fabric against the bleeding, aching wound on her forehead.

Midori had regained her composure, but they were both exhausted, and the ever-decreasing supply of oxygen wasn't helping. In the glow from the flashlights on the floor, they looked like two ghosts, pale, their faces drawn.

"What's going on, Mia?" Midori asked quietly. "Is the lack of oxygen starting to affect us? Are we hallucinating? Maybe there's something about this base that's..."

"Killing us? Is that what you were going to say?" Mia asked. "Yes. Whatever it is, it really exists."

"But what in the world were you going to do out there?" Midori whispered, her tone just as accusatory as it was nervous. "You just left." She raised the flashlight so it lit up the middle of Mia's face.

"I was looking for Coleman," Mia said.

"Why? You don't even know if he's still alive, Mia. Didn't you hear what he said? He gave up."

"I'm sure he's alive. He's here somewhere or other. Somewhere he's sure he won't be discovered by... *them*."

Midori set the light on the floor in front of them. "But I don't understand why you want to talk to him again. If there was something else he could do or say to help, he would have told us before."

"I think he knows more than he told us," Mia said soberly. "And without that information we don't stand a chance of getting out of here alive."

"So what do you suggest?" Midori asked.

"He must be somewhere in module one."

"It's a long way over there, Mia."

Mia wasn't listening. "Get ready."

Seconds later they heard scraping sounds from the other side of the steel door out in the kitchen.

Mia slapped a hand over Midori's mouth....

Followed by the sound of the wheel that was keeping the door out there locked. Or at least *had* been.

The door opened.

Mia and Midori didn't move. They heard footsteps in the kitchen. Someone was slowly moving toward them. Mia pressed her hand harder over Midori's mouth. She wanted to shriek herself, fling the door open, and get it over with. But she sat there, her back so tense that her shoulders ached. Without making the slightest sound, she leaned over and turned off the lights.

They sat in the darkness and waited.

Thunk. Thunk.

Two knocks on the door to the dry storage room.

Footsteps.

Mia stared at the door, expecting it to open. Her head hurt so much it was almost impossible to concentrate.

Thunk. Thunk. A little harder this time.

Then it was quiet.

Mia's heart was pounding so hard that she was sure the figure on the other side of the door could hear it. She put a hand on her chest as if to muffle the sound.

But then they could hear the creature taking a few steps back from the door. Silence again. Then the sound of rapid movement, and the door to the kitchen banging shut.

The creature had probably left the room, but neither Mia nor Midori dared move for several minutes.

Finally Mia was the one to break the silence. She whispered as quietly as she could, "I think we'd better take our chances now."

"Wouldn't it be best to wait a little more?"

"We don't have time, Midori. DARLAH is almost out of oxygen—can't you feel it?"

"Yeah," Midori finally responded.

Mia squatted down and picked up one of the lights.

"Okay, Midori. Let's do it. We'll walk through the corridors to module one. Try to be as quiet as possible. If we meet anyone on the way, you run in the opposite direction and try to make it to DARLAH 1, whether you're with me or not. Good? Oh, and another thing—there's no point in attacking them. I tried. I stabbed one of them with a big knife. It had no effect at all."

Midori nodded silently and replied, "The same for you. If someone attacks me, you run."

As quietly as they could, they raised the bolt and opened the door of the dry storage room.

They shone their lights out into the kitchen. There was no one there, not a soul. The whole room seemed unusually desolate, as if no one had ever been there.

Mia took the first step and snuck toward the door leading to the corridor with Midori right behind her.

They stopped about every five steps and listened, letting their lights sweep over the corridor before they proceeded, and every time it turned out to be empty they were filled with an enormous sense of relief.

And then a fresh dread that the thing they feared was lying in wait somewhere in the darkness ahead of them.

They were past open security hatch M when Mia suddenly had an idea and stopped.

"What are you doing?" Midori asked anxiously.

"I want to check one place I forgot to look last time." She turned around and aimed her light back the way they had come.

"Are we going back?" Midori asked.

"Not all the way," Mia said. "Follow me."

Mia headed toward the computer room, stayed to the left, and continued down the corridor. She didn't know what made her so sure, but before she even set foot in the greenhouse, she knew she was right.

She heard the sound of a man breathing.

Slowly she ran her light over the dense foliage.

And there he sat.

Coleman. Up against the apple tree, with a pistol in his hand. He looked up at them sadly.

"You girls shouldn't be here now. Why are you still here? Didn't I tell you to get out of this place?"

They could see him wave the muzzle of the gun over his head. He seemed more disappointed than surprised to see them.

"There's someone here," Mia told him. "Someone else."

"What do you mean?"

And Mia explained. About Antoine showing up outside the window. About Caitlin going out to get him and disappearing. About Mia's double that she'd met in the corridor outside module two. Coleman listened, and when she was done, he lowered his head.

"Well, then, it's really started again," he said to himself.

"What's started? What are you talking about?" Mia asked. She moved slowly around the tree, bending over, as if ready to pounce. Her eye was on the open hatch door leading to the computer room. Midori was huddled under some large palm fronds up against the wall. Every once in while she would suddenly turn toward the dark glass behind her, as if someone had tapped her on the shoulder.

"What we've been afraid of all these years. What we came here to prevent."

His laconic explanation frustrated Mia. It reminded her of Caitlin, the way she'd been after she helped herself to the medications. As if Coleman had stopped caring now, too. But Mia knew better. It wasn't that he didn't care. He was just holding something back.

"What is it that you don't want to tell us?" she demanded to know. "Something is trying to kill us here, don't you get it? Everything you've told us is bullshit and you know it. What are you so afraid people will find out?"

"Oh," he responded. "There's plenty to be afraid of. You ought to understand that by now."

Coleman ran his hand across his forehead, wiping away the sweat. The dense foliage above him made his face appear even darker.

"Are you worried about NASA's reputation or something? That people will find out this mission wasn't a success? That you guys were up to a lot more on the moon than you told people, is *that* it? I'm sure most people have managed to figure that out on their own by now."

"No," he replied. "That's hardly it."

"So what the hell is it, then? You know all about it, don't you? You've known the whole time. And if you have even so much as a tiny speck of conscience left, I suggest you tell us what you know so that we can get out of here."

"I'm afraid I don't know everything, Mia. No one does. The fact of the matter is that we know hardly anything."

"But?" Mia prompted.

He took a deep breath. The smell of rot hung heavy in the steamy, overgrown nursery. "I thought it would be best if you didn't know anything. You must know that what I'm about to tell you now is top secret, sensitive information. It's important that you understand that."

The expressions on Midori's and Mia's faces clearly indicated they felt the idea of anything being top secret at this point was ridiculous. And Coleman had to agree, in a way.

He sighed heavily and set his weapon down in the grass. "The moon missions didn't end in 1972 because of a lack of funds or interest from the public, as people thought. The truth is that we no longer dared to send anyone to the moon. Have you heard about *Apollo 13*?"

They had. Nadolski had given a lecture on all the space missions in the Apollo program. After *Apollo 11*'s first moon landing, the nearly catastrophic *Apollo 13* mission in 1970 was the most well known. And definitely the most exciting. *Apollo 13* experienced an explosion in one of the oxygen tanks two days into the expedition. Almost without power and oxygen, the astronauts had been forced to continue on to the moon to make use of the weak gravitational field to fling themselves back toward Earth. It was definitely a miracle that they survived. And the sentence *Houston, we have a problem* was forever burned into space history.

"The world held its breath during the days that was going on," Coleman continued. "But for the wrong reason. Because there never was an explosion aboard *Apollo 13*. The whole thing was a lie, a complicated, convoluted, well-rehearsed lie to hide what actually happened. Because the truth is that *Apollo 13* landed in the Fra Mauro area according to plan. But something unforeseen happened."

"What?" Mia asked, suspicious, peering out into the darkness for signs that someone was observing them. But she didn't see anything.

"The pilot of the lunar lander, Fred Haise, came in contact with... *something* down in the Fra Mauro crater. It started when he observed an... anomaly... from the window of the lunar lander, and NASA ordered him to investigate it."

"But this doesn't at all match what the astronauts themselves said about the whole thing," Midori protested. "I watched the interviews. I read the biographies Nadolski gave us. I heard the tapes from the command module. You're lying."

"I wish I were. And I'm sure Haise wishes that what he told the world was true, too. But it isn't. Everything you've read, heard, or seen was made up. Fred Haise was on the moon, and he found something that shouldn't be there."

"What?"

"Well, the reports were unclear... until today. But it had to do with a figure. Someone or something that looked exactly... like... himself."

"Like what we saw!" Midori exclaimed.

"Yeah.... Fred Haise just barely got away, made it back to the lunar lander, and, along with Jim Lovell, left the surface of the moon after just a couple hours. A quick evacuation. But there's more. It happened on several of the moon missions. This was just one of many episodes. There were problems going back as early as *Apollo 11*. Midori, you found Buzz Aldrin's boots, right?"

She nodded.

"Well, they weren't left on the surface to reduce weight, as you were told. He threw them in the hopes of hitting something, something that was coming toward him. The truth is that for all these years, most of the folks at NASA believed that the astronauts' descriptions of seeing copies of themselves on the moon had to do with some type of reflection, an optical illusion brought about by the environment here. People believed that up until the event involving Haise in 1970. After that, everyone involved in Mission Control in Houston was ordered to sign a nondisclosure agreement, and since then they have been excluded from any further research findings. The top brass at NASA started cooperating with the military to build a base on the moon that could be used to study and potentially wipe out the phenomenon. NASA also got SETI researchers involved."

"SETI?"

"The Search for Extraterrestrial Intelligence. But that's not what we're dealing with here. I just thought I'd get that out there. We're dealing with something much, much more dangerous. Something that's completely unknown to us. It's unlike anything we know about, because it operates totally outside all normal patterns, completely emotionless. It's beyond all goodness, all evil. It just is. And it doesn't seem to serve any purpose other than pure destruction."

"You're saying it's not an alien? How can you be so sure of that?"

Coleman was quiet for a long moment.

"NASA captured one of them in 1972. Well, a piece of one. *Apollo 17* was attacked as it prepared to take off from the moon, and when they tried to close the hatch, one of the copy's arms was severed."

"So they're human?" Mia asked, feeling a strange surge of hope for a moment.

"No. Studies of the severed arm showed that it did not contain any organic material. It wasn't alive, never had been."

"So what is it, then?"

They were sitting next to Coleman now. Mia was keeping a constant eye on the hatch leading to the computer room. In this darkness they should have been staying well hidden or keeping in constant motion. They weren't doing either. They could be discovered at any time. But she had a feeling that what Coleman was telling them was important for them if they were going to have any chance at getting home.

"Have you ever heard the term 'doppelgänger'?" Coleman asked.

Mia had no idea what he was talking about. It sounded like the name of some insect. "Say that again?"

"Doppelgänger. It's German. It means 'double goer,' a ghostly counterpart of a living person, a double, a wraith. The term is used when people see copies of themselves or people they know, even if there's no logical explanation. Like when you see someone you know on the street, but you know they're actually at home. Or if you see yourself in the mirror and suddenly discover a copy of yourself, standing behind you. It has happened. There are hundreds of reports of it. And I don't mean people seeing someone who looks like someone they know. I'm talking about *exact copies*."

"But what do they want?" Midori asked.

"The problem is no one knows *what* they are. Is it some kind of optical illusion, or do the doppelgängers really exist? For a long time people believed they were illusions, but that was until the French report on Emilie Sagée turned up."

Midori suddenly stood up and squeezed against the wall, as if her hands were trying to press their way through until they came in contact with the blackness outside. She was staring at the opening that led to the oxygen generator.

"How do we know it's not in there?" Midori asked, gesturing.

"Sit down, Midori. It would have had to walk right past me," Coleman said.

"The French report?" Mia prompted.

"Right. A French woman, Emilie Sagée, was a teacher at an exclusive private girls' school called the Pensionat von Neuwelcke in Latvia in the eighteen hundreds. The story was first told by Julie von Güldenstubbe, who was one of the girls in Sagée's class. Emilie Sagée was well liked by all of the students. But shortly after she came to the school, rumors started that Sagée could be two places at once. For example, some of the girls might say they had just seen her outside the main entrance, while others claimed that they had seen her in the library, at the other end of the large building. These types of episodes were constantly dismissed by the other teachers.

"But everything changed on March twenty-second of that year. Güldenstubbe and twelve other girls were in math class when an *extra* Sagée suddenly appeared next to their teacher.

The two women were completely identical. Sagée was standing there with her back to the class, writing on the blackboard. So she couldn't see that a totally identical woman was standing next to her doing the same thing, just without any chalk in her hand. After Güldenstubbe left the classroom and reported this to the school's headmaster, all of the girls were brought out of the classroom. One by one they were questioned about the event, and all of them reported the same details."

Both Mia and Midori were impatient. It was dangerous to stay in one place too long; they were painfully aware of that. And every single minute they spent in this oxygen-poor darkness diminished the chances that they would ever get out of here alive. But they also understood that they no longer had any choice. Mia had been right that Coleman clearly was withholding information before, and if they were going to have any chance at all, they needed to find out as much as they could before leaving DARLAH 2.

Coleman noticed that he did not seem to have the two girls' complete attention, but he decided to go on with his story anyway: "The next few weeks, Sagée's doppelgänger was observed more and more often. One of the events took place in the cafeteria. The doppelgänger was observed sitting next to Sagée, but like in the classroom, her hands were empty. As the teacher ate, the copy just mimicked her movements. Unlike before, however, the students weren't the only ones to witness this episode. The waitstaff also witnessed the doubling.

"Over the course of the spring, the doppelgänger's behavior changed. It seemed to have its own free will. For example, the teacher would get up to stand in front of the class, while the doppelgänger would remain sitting. But the most important episode came at the end of May. The school's forty-two students were sitting in the large auditorium doing needlework, and through the large windows along the one wall they could clearly see Emilie Sagée outside in the garden. She was walking back and forth among the beds, picking flowers. Minutes later the teacher overseeing the students' needlework left the auditorium to go get something from his office. But his chair didn't remain empty. A second later the students discovered Sagée sitting in it. Confused, they glanced out at the garden again. Emilie Sagée was still walking around picking flowers. . . ."

Coleman stopped, vigilant. He was listening for sounds from the corridor and was obviously nervous. Mia and Midori gave each other desperate looks.

"Should I continue?" Coleman asked.

Mia nodded quickly.

"After that day, it became too much for the students. One by one they left the school, and by the beginning of fall semester, the number of pupils had dropped from forty-two to twelve. The school didn't see any other option than to dismiss Sagée. She left the school a week later, and no one knows what happened to her. But there's been a lot of research into the Sagée affair, and dissertations written on it. The problem is simply that all of their conclusions are vague. People think this is something similar to a ghost. But not one in a white sheet with a chain around its leg. A living ghost. A nonexistent entity. It's not really important right now what they call it. I'm afraid what we're dealing with is a more dangerous version of the doppelgänger."

"What do you mean?"

"An evil twin that's out to take over your life without anyone noticing. It kills you and mimics all your habits, so that it can approach new victims. Sagée's doppelgänger was frightening but harmless. But ours? Five out of eight people are dead, Mia. Do you understand what I'm saying?"

"Well, that's it," Midori concluded, her face deathly pale. "We're going to die."

Mia didn't respond.

"What *did* actually happen out there in the corridor, Mia?" Coleman asked.

Mia took a breath and then explained everything she could remember. About the music coming out of nowhere. The person showing up in the corridor and talking to her. That it looked and sounded just like her. Mia told them what the figure had said about the others.

They listened to the silence in the base. Whatever was out to get them could be hiding anywhere. It could be in the same room as them, right then, right there, without their knowing it. Coleman took a breath of the oxygen-depleted air in the room. It wouldn't be long before the conditions would no longer sustain life.

He contemplated the situation. For a long time. Then he said, "I...have an acquaintance who's a...pastor. I've known him since I was a boy. He...well, I'm not a religious person, but I really respect him and listen to what he says. One night I plucked up my courage and told him about what I'd learned about the moon landings, the parts that only I, the astronauts, and a few other people at NASA knew about. I must have talked for over an hour without stopping, and when I was done he looked at me for a long time before he said, in all seriousness: 'You know, Aldrich, when God cast Lucifer and his other enemies out of heaven and down into the abyss to a new place he called hell, he never specified exactly where hell was, did he?'"

"So... you think the moon is... hell?" Midori said.

Coleman shrugged off the terrifying notion by saying, "It's just one idea. But if it were... and it were possible to get rid of hell for good... wouldn't you give it a try?"

"Is that what NASA is trying to do? That's just... ridiculous!" Mia replied. "I'm not religious, anyway. I don't believe in that kind of thing."

"Me, either," Coleman said. "But that's beside the point. The point is that what we're experiencing here could be anything," he continued, "a kind of... phenomenon, a physical, real manifestation of the doppelgänger. An existence we're not aware of. Something we should have left alone from the beginning. The problem is that certain powerful individuals with influence at NASA, which is staffed almost exclusively by agnostics and scientists, began to lean toward some of these more radical religious notions during the late nineties. Which brings us back to the Wow! signal that the Big Ear radio telescope picked up in August 1977. It's true that it surprised NASA, as well. But even years later, as we continued to study it, we never had any doubt that it came from the moon. We just didn't dare to tell anyone about that. Because we didn't know anything about the reason. Was it a mistake? Were we meant to hear it? Or was it a random intercept of some internal communication? But now we know what it was: a sign. A signature that even back then reminded us that we weren't alone, and that there was something to fear out there. 6EQUJ5. This thing we're facing, no matter what it turns out to be, one thing is absolutely certain: It must never make it to Earth. That would mean an end to everything."

The three of them sat there in silence for a while. It wasn't possible to believe what Coleman was saying, was it? Did it actually make sense? And if so, what should they fear most? This place or the people on Earth, who, with all their insane, radical theories, had decided to send teenagers up here anyway?

We shouldn't have come looking for Coleman at all, Mia thought. *He doesn't have any answers. Just more complications.*

"Coleman, there're only three of us left now," Midori said before Mia had a chance to confront him with what she was thinking. "There's room for you in the evacuation capsule. Please come with us. We'll have a better chance of making it to DARLAH 1 if we all go together."

But he was unwavering, even now, once he'd become convinced of what was going on around them.

"Sorry, Midori. I'm really sorry. But I have to finish what I started here. It's time for you two to get going. Every single minute you spend here with me puts you in greater danger. They could find us at any time, which is why it's critical that you guys keep moving from now on. Go to DARLAH 1. Go home!"

It was pointless trying to convince him. Reluctantly they stood up and hugged him.

"One more thing," Coleman said. "So far you've only seen Antoine's doppelgänger. And Mia's. But that means there could be others out there, too. If you get separated at any time, you have to make sure you're not mistaken. According to the reports from NASA and the other books I've read about the phenomenon, doppelgängers cast a shadow facing the wrong way. Sometimes you'll also be able to see it in their eyes. The bottoms of their irises are black. They may seem like they're good friends, giving you helpful advice, but the advice is usually misleading or dangerous. This allows them to create confusion. And that is exactly what they want. Because that gives them time to prepare their attack. Will you remember all that now?"

They nodded to him. "And you? What will happen to you?" Mia asked.

"I'm just going to sit here a little longer. And think about things." He gave them a little smile. "Don't be sad. I was meant to die here. I know that now."

There wasn't anything else to say. Coleman had to do things his way. And Mia and Midori had a job to do. With a final farewell to him, they exited the greenhouse and stepped out into the pitch-black corridor.

"Are you ready, Midori? Or do you want to stay here longer?"

"I'm ready."

"Good. Then we'll run to the equipment room on my signal. I have the maps for DARLAH 1. Whatever you do, don't let me out of your sight. You hear me?"

"Got it."

"Three," she whispered. "Two. One." And then: "GO!"

They ran through the base like crazy, working their way in the darkness toward module four. The hallways were pretty much devoid of oxygen, and with every breath they took they felt like they were suffocating. Mia ran as fast as she could without turning around, without stopping to see if the coast was clear. She just ran, with Midori on her heels, and the only thing she could think was *I'm never coming back to this base again, I'm never coming back here again, I'm never coming here again, I'm never coming here again.*

They reached the equipment room, and both seemed almost surprised that they'd gotten there without incident. Without a word they helped each other with their suits. They picked the fullest oxygen tanks and strapped them on. Boots and gloves were secured; all seams and openings in the suits were checked. They worked as fast as they could, but still the minutes ticked by, and they both kept staring, terrified, at the black hallways they had come from.

"Caitlin left the outer hatch open," Mia yelled to Midori through the built-in speakers. "We'll only have one chance when we open the inner hatch. Give me a sign when you're ready."

Midori gave her a quick thumbs-up.

"Let's go! Grab on to something!"

Midori locked her arm around one of the solid steel pipes along the wall, and Mia grabbed a similar one on her side. With her free hand, she raised the hatch to the decompression chamber, and the last of the oxygen from DARLAH 2 was sucked out with remarkable force along with everything that wasn't fastened down. Papers, boots, spacesuits and helmets, loose wires, and oxygen tanks were flung out into weightlessness and went swooping and bobbing out over the surface. Mia and Midori hunched over, making themselves as small as possible to avoid being hit by any projectiles.

"IS IT EVER GOING TO STOP?" Midori yelled at Mia.

"Hang on, Midori! It can't be much longer now!"

But it felt long. And longer. As they clung fiercely to the pipes, Mia focused on thoughts of home. Her band, which had surely decided to keep Kari as their vocalist by now. Her parents, how scared they must be for her. Had they already given up? And Sander. What was he doing right now? Was he sitting still outside the visitors' center at Johnson Space Center with his hands on the protective helmet he wore when he was outside, his eyes trained on the skies, waiting for his sister to come back?

Finally, they felt the worst of the force relenting and they were able to let go. Together they raised the hatch all the way up and left the base.

"That way," Mia yelled, pointing toward the flat, deserted landscape.

There was a man sitting under the apple tree in the greenhouse. There was no oxygen left for him to breathe.

It's time, he thought as he began to suffocate. *Aldrich Coleman, you've waited a long time to complete this race. It had to come sooner or later, didn't it? The sixth and final shot.*

This time, there wouldn't be any *click* from the weapon. He closed his eyes and imagined he was back in Central Park again. He could almost smell the scents of that Saturday morning long ago. He could feel the presence of the man who'd held the revolver to his temple and cocked it. Five times. But it was different now. He wasn't scared anymore. It was his turn now. He was the one in control. He got to have the last word.

Coleman picked the pistol up from the dry soil. It was heavy, heavier than he remembered, and its weight just reinforced the somberness of the situation. He put the muzzle to his temple. Pressed the trigger.

There was no *click*.

Had there been any air left inside, the sound of the shot would have sent an echo through the entire base.

MIDORI

They headed north. The whole surface-scape reminded them of a world after an atomic war where nothing existed anymore. No life. Just dust. Dead, immobile dust.

Every once in a while Mia would turn around to make sure Midori was still following her rapid pace. The inside of her helmet was covered with condensation from her breathing, and small drops of water ran down over the glass. The sun was exactly above them and they both felt the broiling heat, despite the cooling systems in the suits. They kept going. Mia glanced at the map. Yup, they were on the right track.

"Come on," she yelled behind her.

"I'm doing the best I can," Midori wheezed. "You're moving too fast."

"We can't slow down now. Come on. You can do it. It's not far."

She was lying. It *was* far. An hour, at least, according to Coleman's information. According to the map, they had to go beyond the hill ahead of them. And that was still a good three miles away, if not farther.

"Stop!" Midori shouted. Mia turned around abruptly and looked back. Midori was lying on the ground.

"I can't get back up...the suit...it's so heavy."

Mia hurried back to her and grabbed her arms.

"Wait a minute. Push off with your legs...*now*." Mia pulled up hard as Midori heaved forward back into a standing position.

"You have to lean over a little when you're walking," Mia said. "Like you're underwater and—"

She couldn't finish her sentence. Something else had caught her attention. There was something in the moondust ahead of her.

Not an object, but a message. Like someone had written it with a finger in the dust. She recognized the letters and numbers, and it sent a sickening feeling through her.

6EQUJ5. The same code she'd seen on the machine in the computer room.

She hadn't made the connection then, but now suddenly everything was clear.

"Midori? I think someone has been keeping an eye on us from the very beginning."

"What are you talking about?"

"Look"—Mia pointed at the writing on the ground—"the same code. Have you seen it before?"

"Yeah, in the computer room."

"I mean, before that."

Quickly Mia told Midori what she knew. She'd been sitting with Antoine in his room in Houston one night. Midori had been out having dinner with her parents, so it had been just the two of them. Antoine had told her this absurd story about how he had been the only person on Earth to see a plane crash into the English Channel. The story had made an impression on her, but if she hadn't already been falling in love with him, she would probably have thought he was a little crazy. Because it was even stranger that Antoine was so obsessed with the two letters he'd been able to make out on the tail of the plane before it had hit the surface of the water: *QU.*

And only now did she notice the uncomfortable similarity.

Why hadn't this occurred to her earlier? The insignia that had appeared out of nowhere on the back of Murray's coat that night in Central Park had been 6E, hadn't it? One second there was nothing there, then two characters, and then it was as if an invisible arm had slithered into the park and moved the brush over his coat.

"That was no coincidence, was it?" Mia said after she told Midori the whole thing. "Maybe it was actually meant as a warning? Something to make us decide not to come here. But the question is, where did the last part of the code show up?"

Midori scraped her boots back and forth on the ground, rubbing out a couple of the characters.

"The plane I took from Narita to New York left from gate J5," Midori said numbly. "We had trouble finding the gate. The people we asked said it didn't exist. And a woman in the bathroom told me not to go. But we still did."

"6EQUJ5," Mia concluded softly. "We should never have come. We should have stayed home, with the rest of the world."

"There's nothing left to say anymore, Mia."

"Maybe. Maybe not."

Mia turned away and studied the map again. And when she looked up she spotted something white in all the gray. It was a hundred meters ahead of them. It was impossible to see what it was.

"Come on," she commanded, hopeful that it might be an entrance to DARLAH 1. "Let's keep going!"

They approached the white objects ahead of them. Mia's heart sank.

They were Nadolski's and Antoine's bodies. Still in their suits. They were lying side by side, and their helmets were gone. The LRVs they'd brought were gone, too. Not even a wheel mark remained to be seen.

Mia bent down over Antoine. She brushed the gray dust off his face. It was already disfigured by the scorching sun that, without any atmosphere to penetrate, had been attacking his skin for many hours. His eyes were wide open and bloody and halfway out of his head. The dust had dried up his eyeballs.

Nadolski was the same way. But one of his arms had been ripped off at the elbow, and the exposed arm stump was gaping at them. All the oxygen they'd had in their bodies had been pressed out the instant their helmets were removed and the vacuum outside got the upper hand. The two people seemed almost inflated.

But, strangely, the sight didn't turn her stomach at all. She wasn't afraid. She just felt a vast, exhausting sadness that almost made her give up. She tried to close Antoine's eyes, but they were bulging too much for his eyelids to cover them. She scraped together some dust with her big gloves and covered his face instead, and crossed his arms over his chest.

"Sleep well, my friend," she said quietly, and stood up. "We have to leave you now, Antoine. We're going home."

She took Midori's hand and led on.

At some point, after they'd been journeying for what seemed like hours, Mia stopped, certain they were nearing their destination. "It should be here somewhere," Mia said, surprised, with the map in her hands. "Midori, what do you think?"

There was no answer.

She turned around and saw that Midori was lagging behind. She was trudging along fifty yards behind her.

"Are we there?" Midori asked.

But Midori wasn't the only one coming. On the horizon behind Midori, Mia saw another figure approaching quickly.

She knew what it was.

Her doppelgänger.

"Midori, hurry, it's coming!"

"I can't do it," Midori groaned.

"Run!"

"I can't!"

The doppelgänger was closing in. It wasn't wearing a spacesuit. It was wearing Mia's normal clothes. It sneered and picked up its pace.

"Midori!"

She made up her mind quickly. Mia ran back to Midori and

pulled her up the last hill and down the incline. She was dragging her over the ground as if she were a doll, staring intently at the map the whole time.

I don't understand. It should be right here! Mia was about to lose it.

She desperately looked around for anything that could resemble a building or an entrance. But there were only rocks and dust. Gray, dead matter.

She looked at the map again.

She had never focused on the thing as a whole before.

According to a thin line on the diagram, the base was underground. Only an opening dug out around the entrance would reveal its location.

She grabbed Midori and pulled her back to the first place they'd stopped.

In front of her, on the hill, the doppelgänger came into view. It was still coming toward them.

"Midori, you have to run on your own. I can't do it for you. Midori? Midori!" Mia yelled.

She punched Midori hard in the side with her fist.

"Ow! Okay, I'm coming!"

Mia let go of her and scanned the surface around her in all directions. Nothing. Nothing. *Nothing.*

But there.

There it was.

A hole in the ground.

"Midori, I've got it! It's *here*! Come *on*!"

The news gave Midori a surge of energy, and she arrived panting at Mia's side. They ran toward the opening and

immediately discovered the ladder. It extended sixty feet below the surface.

"Hurry. *Hurry!*" Home suddenly seemed within reach. It was all Mia could think of. Adrenaline pumped through her body with a force she'd never felt in her life.

Mia flung herself into the hole, grabbed on to one of the rungs, and clambered down. Quickly glancing up, she confirmed that Midori was right above her. And then she jumped off the ladder and landed on the bottom.

Dazed, she stood up and examined the enormous steel hatch. It was twice as big as the one for DARLAH 2, but aside from that it looked the same. She pushed the button next it, and to her enormous relief the door slid open without difficulty. She waited a few seconds until Midori was down, and pushed her into the decompression chamber ahead of herself.

"Shut the door!" she screamed at Midori. "Shut the goddamn door!" Midori planted a blow on the button on the inside, and the door closed.

"We're in," Mia said, breathless and exhausted.

"Yes," Midori replied with a sudden calm, watching Mia. "Now we're in."

Midori planted her hands on a handle in the middle of the wall labeled OXYGEN and pressed it down. A hissing stream of air flowed into the room through large vents, making it possible for them to remove their helmets. As the chamber filled with air, she opened the hatch into the power station. The light was on, but it was still dark compared to the strong sunlight outside. Mia turned on her light and followed Midori.

The power station was built into a gigantic cavernous hall

with enormous turbines stretching up well over a hundred feet to the ceiling. Row upon row of computers and gauges lined the walls, but it wasn't long before they were able to spot the two main breakers. As Mia reached out to flip them on, Midori suddenly knocked her hands away.

"Why did you do that?" Mia asked.

Midori smiled. "Just felt like it."

"We're not here to play around." Mia quickly flipped the breaker handles up. All the buttons lit up immediately, and the turbines started rotating with a deep, rumbling sound.

"Aren't we? Why are we here, then?"

Mia aimed her light at Midori to see her better.

Then she noticed it. A wave of panic shot through her.

Midori's body cast a shadow facing the wrong way.

Mia took a step back.

Then another one.

She slowly, slowly moved toward the decompression chamber.

"Where are you going?" the doppelgänger asked.

"No... nowhere."

"You can't leave now, Mia. Your friends are here, after all."

"What the hell do you mean?"

"Caitlin. Nadolski. Antoine. They're all here, all of them. Don't you miss them?"

Mia broke out in a cold sweat.

"I know what you're thinking," it said, cocking its head to the side. "You're wondering what happened to Midori, aren't you?"

Mia kept backing toward the decompression chamber.

"Unfortunately, she couldn't be here. When you left the kitchen to look for Coleman, well... yes, let's just say she had to go." Midori's face broke into a disgusting sneer. "And by the way, that thing with the knife was pathetic. Did you really think that would make any difference?" She sneered again, and this time the sneer grew grotesquely large. It nearly extended from ear to ear.

"*Watashi kirei?*" the thing said. Now Mia could see blood running from the corners of its mouth. It had *ripped*.

"Wha-what did you say?" Mia gulped.

"Am I beautiful now?"

Oh my God, Mia thought. *Get me out of here!*

"Midori was so fond of her ridiculous urban legends. So I thought I would pay tribute to her with that one."

The doppelgänger stuck its hands into its mouth and stretched it even further. The nauseating sound of tearing flesh and muscle could be heard as the skin on the face was torn from ear to ear. The doppelgänger's teeth gleamed red. Thick drops of blood landed on the floor with small splashes.

"There's no way out. You know that—right, Mia?"

Mia kept her mouth shut, taking the final steps backward into the chamber.

"We'll go say hi to your friends when we get home," the doppelgänger said, snuffling through the ruined mouth and holding her hands out to Mia. "We'll take good care of them. For a while, anyway."

Mia calmly put on her helmet, all the while watching the doppelgänger make its way fully into the chamber.

Then, with a lightning-fast motion, Mia flung out her hand and slammed the hatch button before flinging herself to the floor and grabbing hold of a pipe. The outer hatch opened, and the vacuum outside sucked the creature out.

It slammed hard into the rock wall and sank to the ground, immobilized. Papers and equipment from the power station whooshed past her at lethal speeds. Mia dragged herself up and stretched out her foot as she clung to the steel pipe. With a well-aimed kick, she hit the button again and the outer hatch closed again.

She was alone.

DEPARTURE

She was hearing noises all the time. It was no longer easy to tell if they were imaginary or real. Footsteps approaching from all directions, hideous voices mumbling unintelligible sentences. Chanting.

The negative pressure of the air release had sucked her flashlight out into space, and she could no longer fully make out her surroundings. Only the dim light suspended from the power station ceiling far above was helping to give her a vague sense of where she was. Mia kept her eyes firmly locked on the safety hatch at the innermost point of the large hall. She found the door release and pressed it. The hatch opened with a hollow sound.

Mia stared into a long, dark corridor. The very sight of it made her feel sick.

You have to go through there.

You have to go through there, Mia.

I don't know. I don't know, I don't know....

The evacuation capsule is on the other side of that corridor.

How far could it be? A hundred yards? No more than that, at any rate.

You can do it. You can walk a hundred yards.

You're going home. You will come back from here.

You can do it.

Run, Mia!

She hurled herself into the darkness.

She fumbled her way forward in a panic. The darkness was all-encompassing, but the sense that she wasn't alone propelled her swiftly down the corridor. To navigate, she swept her right hand along the side wall as she ran. She was sure the walls were moving closer together with every step.

I've got to be there soon.

It can't be far now.

This corridor was only supposed to be a hundred yards long, right?

It felt like hands were reaching out of the darkness, trying to grab her.

She kept going deeper. Deeper. Deeper.

Stopped.

She was at the end.

Her hands felt the door. It was impossible to see anything, but she groped around for the steel wheel. Grabbed hold and turned it. It wouldn't budge. She tried again. Stuck.

No. No, no, no.

It's not fair.

Not now.

Come on, damn it!

She put all her weight into it and suddenly it yielded, rotating, and the door opened. It was almost too easy. As if someone on the inside had helped her open it. Dim light shone on her.

Mia cautiously pushed the door open and went in.

The room was smaller than the power station, about the size of a classroom.

And a gray, cone-shaped vessel stood in the middle of the room.

The evacuation capsule.

The capsule was sitting on a small rocket launchpad, connected to a number of hoses and instruments. Mia moved closer to see it. It wasn't more than ten or eleven feet high at its highest point. The hatch was up near the top on the back. On the opposite side there was a small, round window of thick, heat-safe glass.

She peered in through the window. It looked like a small airplane cockpit with two seats, side by side, in front of an instrument panel. One more seat in back, up against the wall. Coleman had been right. There wasn't room for four people. Hardly even for three.

"What do you think? Do you like it?"

Mia whipped around when she heard a voice that sounded like her own, her eyes searching feverishly in the dim light. Nothing.

"Unfortunately, I can't let you go, you know," the voice spoke again. "That would be... wrong."

Something moved in the corner.

The doppelgänger crawled out of a maintenance duct under the floor, as if she were a giant spider.

"Who... are... you?" Mia stammered, jumping away from the capsule.

The doppelgänger grinned repulsively at her.

"I'm Mia. Don't you remember? I'm *you*." She emerged from the dark corner, moving toward Mia. An identical copy, down to the smallest detail. Except her eyes. The bottom portion of the doppelgänger's irises were pitch-black.

Mia's eyes flitted wildly back and forth between the evacuation capsule and the doppelgänger.

It came closer. In a few seconds it would be close enough to grab her.

Mia looked around, desperate for something to hit it with. But aside from the capsule, the room was empty.

She only had one chance.

Please, she said to herself. *I've made it this far. Please let me make it home. Let me do that so...*

The doppelgänger lunged toward her.

Mia struck out blindly with her arms, feeling herself hit it hard in the face.

Hands grabbed hold of her and pulled her down to the floor.

Please.

She struck again, not sure if she hit, but still managed to get up—run to the capsule—tear open the hatch. The doppelgänger was standing right next to her.

She flung herself into the capsule, shut the hatch again, and sealed it.

The other Mia screamed. She hammered on the door with the fierceness of a wild animal.

Mia frantically stared at the control panel.

Which one is it?

Which one?

A desperate face was pressed onto the window. The look was one of pure hatred.

Fingers clawed at the glass.

Mia feverishly pressed random buttons.

There was hammering on the walls of the capsule.

Voices.

Footsteps.

Screams.

And inside the capsule, there it was! A red button to the far right:

EMERGENCY LIFTOFF

She pushed it, and the panel lit up. The rocket engines started rumbling. It took mere moments for her to strap herself into one of the seats.

More screams from outside the capsule, more hammering hysterically against the hull.

Mia heard the blast of the rocket engine igniting. The capsule

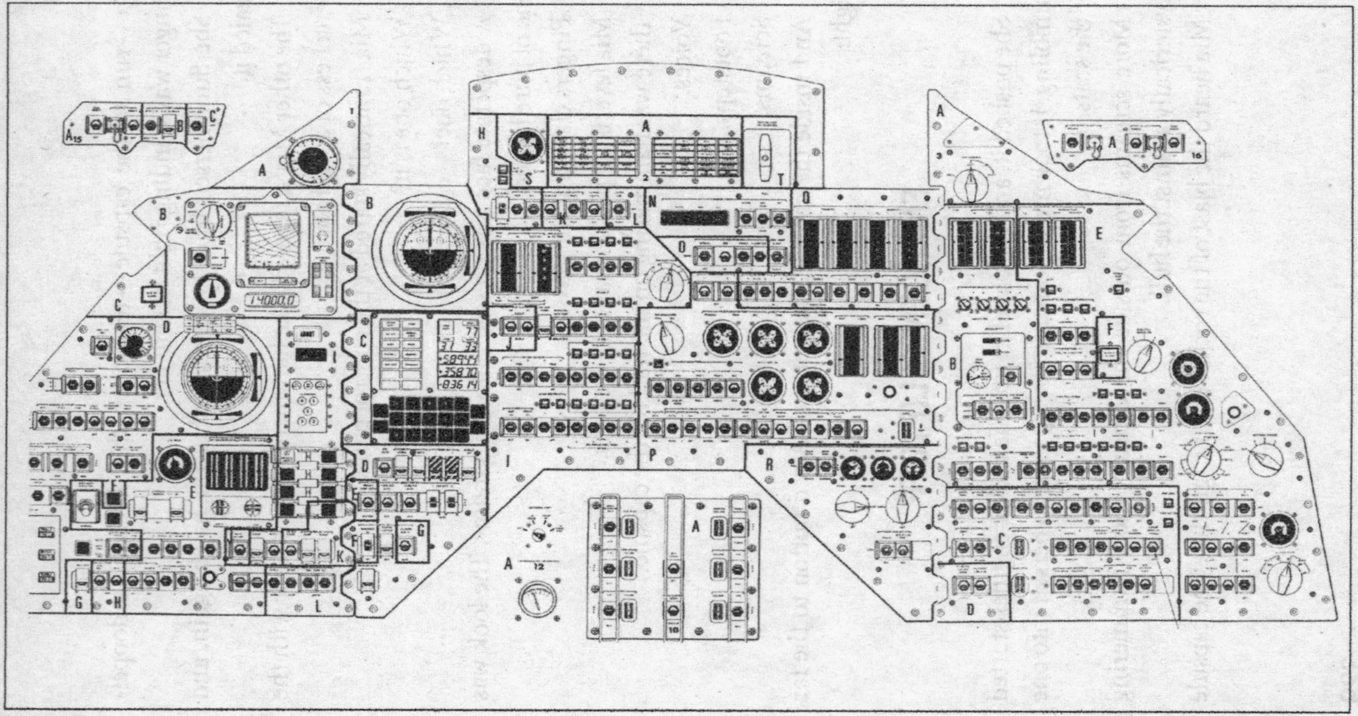

shook violently, and Mia clung to the controls and closed her eyes.

She was going up. She was going up!

Seconds later, the capsule lifted off from the platform. The cables ripped loose, and the capsule was launched out into space with ferocious force.

3

AFTERWARD

THE ATLANTIC

NORAD—the North American Aerospace Defense Command—picked up the evacuation capsule on its radar a few minutes after noon. Since NORAD couldn't immediately confirm what type of object it was, for a few minutes officials thought it was a meteorite. Or an enemy rocket. The secretary of defense and the Joint Chiefs of Staff were contacted, and they considered shooting the object down. But closer scrutiny showed that it was moving too fast to be an enemy missile. It had to be something from space.

NASA also detected the capsule, and although the agency couldn't immediately confirm what the object was, there was reason for hope. Hope that the team members NASA had lost contact with five and a half days ago had survived, and that they had made it back to Earth on their own. If that were the case, it would be nothing less than a miracle. But that was exactly what NASA needed right now. A miracle from above. Something that could silence the noise from all the TV channels, newspapers, and talk radio programs that were reporting incessantly on the tragedy and turning it into an international scandal, claiming that the organization had been reckless, greedy, and inhumane to put young people's lives at such risk.

But now all that could change. Instead the media would be full of tales of heroism. There would be interviews with and news bulletins about the brave astronauts who had managed to bring them home again. There would be footage of sobbing mothers and fathers hugging their sons and daughters. In the best-case scenario, all the attention might even boost the support for space travel.

The NASA bigwigs were aboard the U.S. marine rescue helicopter that took off from its base an hour later, heading for the waters off Newfoundland, where the capsule had apparently landed. Even before the helicopter reached cruising altitude, the NASA team members had already started working on the speeches they were planning to deliver to the press once the crew was safely aboard.

Mia slept most of the four days the trip took. It wasn't until the capsule entered the atmosphere that she was jolted completely awake again. Then the parachutes released to slow its descent. The capsule swayed gently as it sailed downward and touched down somewhere on the surface of the Atlantic Ocean.

Mia undid her seat belt and made her way over to the window

and looked out at the water. The sight of the seemingly infinite blue ocean was overwhelming.

She walked stiffly over to the exit and released the emergency opening. The explosive bolts in the hatch made the hinges release and the door fall off, disappearing into the ocean. Mia sat in the opening and felt the wind on her face. She turned her face into the sunlight and felt the salty sea spray wash over her each time a wave hit the capsule.

She sat there rocking for several hours without thinking of anything in particular, as if all the stress had wiped her mind clean. She just sat and stared, as if she had never seen water before.

Late that afternoon the first fishing boat showed up nearby. Astonished, weather-beaten, bearded fishermen were standing on the deck of the *Sea Harvest* trawler, looking in awe at the girl sitting motionless in the capsule's door opening. Captain Tyne ordered the crew to launch the tender, and a few minutes later they raised Mia aboard. She was wrapped in blankets and brought to the captain's cabin, where Tyne himself kept her company.

Mia didn't say much. She told him where she'd been and that something had gone wrong. That was it.

Captain Tyne gave her a concerned look.

"I'll explain everything later," Mia said. "I promise. I'm just not feeling that great right now."

They set course for shore, and the coast guard helicopter that flew over them an hour later had no idea who was on the boat below. She stayed in the captain's home in a little fishing village on the Newfoundland coast while they tried to make contact with NASA and wait for the representatives to show up.

But when morning arrived and Mrs. Tyne brought a breakfast tray up to the attic room where Mia was staying, the girl was gone. The bed was neatly made and the curtains drawn. There was no trace of her aside from a note on the nightstand.

Had to move on. Thank Capt. Tyne for me again. I'm doing fine now.

Mia

The helicopter hung quietly in the air less than a dozen feet over the capsule as the divers prepared and jumped into the water. They searched the capsule and did countless dives in the vicinity to find any trace of survivors. The NASA representatives took the announcement—"There's no one here"—with somber expressions.

Disappointed, one of the bigwigs opened his briefcase and took one last look at the various drafts of welcome home speeches he had written. Then he whipped open the side door of the helicopter and tossed the pages out. They fluttered down and floated limply on the surface like dead fish.

Before they turned around to head back to the base, the two NASA officials stuck their heads out the opening to get one last glimpse of the space capsule.

What was floating down there wasn't the command module *Ceres*. It was labeled with another name.

DARLAH 1.

They were going to have trouble explaining this to the rest of the world.

It was easier to get to New York than she had thought, although it took time. That night, after Captain Tyne and his wife went to bed, she got dressed and snuck out the front door without a sound. At the pier, she hid among the cargo crates until morning came and then snuck on board the first ferry out. After hitching a few different rides to Ottawa, she managed to convince an older married couple she'd met in the bus station that her wallet had been stolen; they gave her enough to take an express bus to New York City.

Mia arrived at Port Authority Bus Terminal in Manhattan early the next morning. She asked a nice elderly woman for some change for the phone booth, and dialed the number of Johnson Space Center in Houston.

It was a short conversation. Mia was happy about that. Her mother couldn't get a coherent word out; she just sobbed, and her father had to take the phone. She told him where she had been found and about her stay in Newfoundland but didn't mention anything about what had happened on the mission. She just repeated that she was fine.

Her father yelled into the phone, as if he were afraid that she might disappear again any second. "Go to the Four Seasons Hotel. I'll call right away and arrange a room for you. A suite! Your mother and I are in Houston. We'll head to the airport and get tickets to New York as soon as we hang up. Don't go anywhere, okay? Stay at the hotel, order whatever you want from room service. Are you sure you don't need me to send a doctor to see you?"

"No, it's fine. Thanks anyway."

"Your mother and I will be there tomorrow night at the latest. Hopefully sooner. We can't wait to see you—"

"I ought to get going, Dad. It's cold here."

"Cold? Well, okay—get going, honey. To the Four Seasons, you hear?"

Mia hung up and walked the last little way to the hotel. Outside its front doors she passed a newspaper stand and noticed the headline in the *New York Times*.

It didn't faze her. No one would recognize her, and none of that mattered anymore. They didn't even give her a second glance as she approached the counter to check in.

NEW YORK, WEDNESDAY, JULY 27th, 2019

DARLAH Capsule Recovered - Sole Survivor Found

Rescue mission deemed impossible.

CONEY ISLAND

Her father had already managed to book her a room, and with a sigh of satisfaction she took the elevator up to the suite on the fifty-second floor with a fantastic view of the park. But Mia didn't stay in the room and wait for her family, as she'd promised.

She had already done enough waiting. After just a few minutes in the room and a quick shower, she left the hotel, heading for Central Park.

Murray didn't show up until close to eleven p.m. He came pushing his shopping cart and didn't spot her until she stopped him.

"Hi," she said.

He looked at her for a long time. It was as if he were running through a big library card catalog in his brain. And finally he found a card with her name on it.

"Mia?" he said, astonished. "You're back."

She smiled. "Thought I'd say hi."

"I heard about you on the radio," he said. "Down at the Salvation Army. They said you all died. They said you didn't have a chance."

"That's true. But I survived."

"Yes, by golly if you didn't," he said, putting his arm around her. "And your folks?"

"They're coming tonight. At the earliest."

"Four Seasons, wasn't it?"

"That's right," Mia said. "Same as last time."

"Great. I'll walk you over there."

"I have another idea. Come on."

Murray left his shopping cart in his usual spot and followed her to the subway station on Lexington Avenue.

"Do you have money for the fare?" she asked.

"Are you kidding? Do I look like I have money?"

They waited until no one was looking, crawled under the turnstile, and jogged down to the platform. She gave Murray clear instructions not to read any of the signs along the way so that he wouldn't figure out where they were going. Every time the train stopped at another station, he held one hand up over his eyes and used the other and his shoulder to cover his ears so she could tell he really wasn't cheating. They took the subway to the last stop, and Mia held Murray's hand as he closed his eyes and followed her up into the warm evening air.

"Now you can look," she said. Murray opened his eyes.

"Coney Island," he exclaimed. "You brought me to Coney Island! I haven't been here in . . . all these years."

"Do you remember telling me how you guys used to sleep on the beach here?"

"Yes, I remember. They don't do that anymore. No one sleeps on the beach anymore."

Mia pulled him along, down toward the water. "But tonight is different. Tonight someone is going to sleep here on the beach at Coney Island."

Murray's eyes went glossy. "Thank you," he said. "Thank you. This is the best gift anyone's ever given me."

The path down to the beach was littered with trash. Around them were the remains of what had once been an amusement park — ruined carousels, parts of old trucks, and a lone, motionless Ferris wheel.

They found a spot next to an old wooden boat on the beach, and Murray spread his coat out on the sand so they could lie on it.

"Welcome back," he told her.

"Same to you," she replied.

Murray fell asleep faster than anyone else in New York that night. Just over a minute after he laid his head down on the sand he was out. But Mia didn't sleep.

She sat up the whole night, staring straight ahead, until the sun came up out over the water. *I'm on Earth*, she thought. *I'm home.*

* * *

Murray was groggy when he woke up. He didn't know where he was at first and yelled a couple expletives at no one in particular until he noticed Mia and remembered the previous night.

He got up and ambled down to the edge of the water to stand next to her.

"How's it going?" he asked.

She turned to him. "It's going to go great. For me."

And then she sneered at him. A repulsive sneer.

He studied her face more closely now, and suddenly he didn't feel right. He couldn't quite put his finger on it. "Your eyes," he said finally. "You ought to get them checked, I think. It looks like there's something wrong with... uh... with... them. They're... totally *black*."

She shrugged, her sneer deepening. "Unfortunately, I can't let you come with me back to Manhattan."

"I... yes. Wait, what do you mean?" Murray replied, confused. Instinctively he took a step away from her and stumbled backward.

Mia was instantly standing over him. He felt himself begin to panic.

The sun rose out of the ocean and shone on them. It lit up the whole beach and sort of gave Coney Island its color back.

Murray had just enough time to see her hands coming at him, and then he felt an intense, blinding pain in his head, as if his skull had cracked just over his eyes and split in two.

Then everything went black.

* * *

She left him like that, without batting an eye. She slowly turned and walked toward the Ferris wheel and what was left of the once-famous amusement park. Far away, on the other side of the East River, she could see the Manhattan skyline, just as the first rays of morning sunlight struck it.

She stood there watching the city for a little while before she started walking toward the entrance to the subway station.

THE DISTANT ONES

The doorman at the Four Seasons bowed to her and opened the door as she entered the building. Without saying a word to anyone, she walked through the lobby and into the private elevator and took it up to the fifty-second floor. She slid her key card into the lock and stepped into the luxurious suite.

It wasn't so much a hotel room as an enormous apartment: the Ty Warner Penthouse suite, with nine rooms occupying just over four thousand square feet, taking up the entire fifty-second floor of the hotel. The biggest room had a panoramic view of Central Park, and any human would have been absolutely enchanted to see the crisp morning light filtering through the trees in the park. But she didn't even notice. She just walked from room to room, and then into the library, where she found a red armchair and sat down.

She waited.

Sat motionless and waited.

The hours passed.

And if anyone had been there in the room to see her, they would have been terrified. Because she wasn't just sitting still. She was completely immobile, staring blankly ahead.

The phone rang six hours later. As if just a couple of minutes had passed, she got up, walked over to the little table, and answered it.

"Miss Nomeland, this is the front desk. Your parents are here."

"Send them up," she replied.

"Of course."

She went to the door, looked in the mirror. Her eyes were dark, her hands looked gnarled, as if her body had aged fifty years. She studied her features with interest and then turned attentively to the door.

There was a knock. One knock, two knocks.

Then she heard a key card being put into the lock, and the door opened. There they stood. Three people: a man, a woman, a boy. Her parents and brother.

Her mother dropped her bag and ran to her, flung her arms around her and wailed.

"We were so afraid for you, Mia. We've been so dreadfully afraid." The mother only just managed to get the words out. Days of not knowing whether her daughter was alive or not had clearly left their mark on the mother's face. It was gray, dry, like a newspaper with only tragic headlines, and her hair was messy and unwashed. She obviously hadn't slept for days. "I love you so much, do you know that?" her mother sobbed, hugging her again even harder. "I thought we'd never see you again."

The father was just behind the mother, also hugging her with tears in his eyes. And then this kid.

Sander, his name was. He was standing a couple feet away, watching her with a distrustful look. He was clutching a tattered stuffed lion in his hands.

"Weird eyes," Sander mumbled. "Weird eyes."

But no one else heard him.

"Sander is exhausted," she heard her mother say. "It's been almost twenty-four hours since he's slept, poor guy. You know, we had trouble at the airport, delays, or a strike, I'm not quite sure. Well, and then NASA suggested we take a private flight and, well... it's been a long day."

"Sander, are you tired? Do you want to go lie down for a while?" the father asked. "They have super-great beds here, you know. Just for you. And now you can sleep securely, pal, because now Mia is safely back with us. Aren't you happy now?"

"Yeah," he replied, giving his lion a good hug.

"Don't you want to give Mia a hug, too?"

"No," he said quickly, turning away.

The mother looked at her, stroked her cheek.

"It's been so long since Sander saw you, you know. He's not used to you being gone for so long. Maybe you want to help him get ready for bed," the mother suggested, "make sure he brushes his teeth and all that? I'm sure it would mean a lot to him. Then Father and I will order us some food. What would you like?"

"Nothing."

"Nothing? Are you sure? Maybe you ate already?" The girl

shook her head. "Well, I'll order something anyway, and then you can see if you want it or not."

She took a step toward Sander and held out her hand. Reluctantly he took it. He noticed that it was cold.

"Come on, Sander."

He obediently shuffled along behind her into the bathroom. She closed the door and turned on the tap. She found a hotel toothbrush and unwrapped it, squeezed a stripe of toothpaste onto the brush.

"Why don't you let me hold your lion for a minute while you brush your teeth?" she said.

He shook his head and stared at the closed bathroom door. Slowly he took the brush from her and began moving it across his toy's tattered mouth.

"Did you miss me while I was gone?"

"I'm scared, Mia," he replied.

"I'm not Mia."

The tattered stuffed lion fell out of his hands when she grabbed him. He didn't have a chance to make a sound.

She then proceeded to open the bathroom door and reenter the hotel room, where his parents were waiting.

"How did it go?" the mother asked.

"It went good," she answered, smiling, as a girl who looked just like her emerged from the bathroom behind her.

The doppelgängers swiftly slinked out of the suite. Four identical copies of Mia moved from room to room with such ruthless efficiency that before long there were legions of copies sweeping through the hotel. Most of the guests opened their doors when they heard the knock. They would peer out the peephole and see a young girl out in the hallway. The last thing they were expecting was to be attacked without mercy.

One by one, the doppelgängers took elevators or stairwells down to the first floor and exited the lobby, climbed into a cab or simply strolled down the sidewalk. None of the hotel employees in the lobby or the guests who were busy checking in noticed that the same person appeared to keep leaving the Four Seasons Hotel over and over again.

With one exception.

A bellhop, who was impatiently waiting to carry in the luggage of a slow Japanese couple, thought he saw one teenage girl pass him three times. He wondered about it but quickly brushed it off as déjà vu. He was tired, anyway. And then he was asked to bring the luggage up to a room on the thirty-first floor.

The bellhop pushed the button to call the elevator and glanced up at the lighted display, which indicated the elevator was on its way down to him, something he'd seen hundreds or thousands of times before. It would be the last time.

A quiet *ping* was heard as it reached the lobby and the doors opened.

LOG NO_88.723.
NAME OF SHIP: RV PROVIDENCE
CREW: 8
ORIGIN: SECTOR 12, EARTH
FINAL DESTINATION: EUROPA
CURRENT LOCATION: THE MOON, QUADRANT 60 (MARE TRANQUILLITATIS)
DATE: 08/17/2081
TIME OF TRANSMISSION: 21:14 UTC

PRIMARY MISSION: DEEP-SEA INVESTIGATION OF MOON EUROPA, AREA #878
CURRENT ASSIGNMENT: INVESTIGATE QUADRANT 60, LUNAR SURFACE

1.
ENCOUNTERED SUBJECTS BELIEVED TO HAVE CONNECTION TO THE DP7 EVENT ON EARTH IN 2019.
SUBJECT #1 (DCSD) IS FEMALE, APPROX. 16YRS. FOUND 600FT FROM MOON BASE DARLAH 2 MAIN HATCH. CLOTHES: NASA SPACESUIT. FRACTURED HELMET FOUND 5FT FROM BODY. CAUSE OF DEATH: EXPOSURE TO VACUUM. SUBJECT VISUALLY IDENTICAL TO FIRST OBSERVATIONS OF DP7 ON EARTH. TISSUE SAMPLE SHOWS SUBJECT IS HUMAN. FOOTPRINTS (NO SHOES) FROM UNIDENTIFIED SUBJECT FOUND IN CLOSE PROXIMITY TO BODY.

2.
EXTERIOR INSPECTION MOON BASE DARLAH 2: BASE LOOKS INTACT. NO VISIBLE EXTERNAL DAMAGE, INTEGRITY OK. DISCOVERED SUBJECT #2 (DCDS) BETWEEN MODULES 2 AND 3. CAUSE OF DEATH: UNKNOWN. SUBJECT #2 IDENTIFIED AS LT. HALL (LMP).

INTERIOR INSPECTION MOON BASE DARLAH 2:
MAIN HATCH LEFT OPEN. MAKESHIFT CRYSTAL RADIO RECEIVER DISCOVERED ON FLOOR INSIDE DECOMPRESSION CHAMBER. NO POWER OR OXYGEN PRESENT THROUGHOUT BASE. SUBJECT #3 (DCDS) IDENTIFIED AS CAPT. COLEMAN (HCOM) FOUND IN MODULE 3/GREENHOUSE. CAUSE OF DEATH: SELF-INFLICTED GUNSHOT WOUND TO HEAD. BASE OTHERWISE LOOKS INTACT, NO INDISPUTABLE SIGNS OF STRUGGLE. SUBLEVEL POWER GENERATOR (MODULE 4) REVEALS SUBJECTS #4 AND #5 (DCSD), IDENTIFIED AS S. WILSON AND P. STANTON. CAUSE OF DEATH: ASPHYXIA.
LUNAR ROVER VEHICLE SEEMS TO BE MISSING FROM MODULE 4.

FURTHER INVESTIGATION SUGGESTED.

RV PROVIDENCE CONTINUING TO EUROPA.

>>>>>>>>>>>>>>>>>>>>END OF REPORT...

SEE APP. NEXT PAGE

APPENDIX TO LOG NO_88.723.

DESCRIPTION: ITEM FOUND IN LEFT SIDE POCKET OF SUBJECT #1. ITEM IS A HANDWRITTEN NOTE, SIGNED BY DECEASED.
PARTS OF THE MESSAGE DIFFICULT OR IMPOSSIBLE TO DECIPHER.

IT READS AS FOLLOWS:

I REMEMBER. IT IS STRANGE, ISN'T IT, HOW SO MANY ANIMALS PREFER TO DIE ALONE, HIDDEN AWAY FROM THEIR FAMILY, THEIR PACK. THEY JUST SEEM TO WANDER OFF AND DISAPPEAR WHEN THEY FEEL THE TIME IS NEAR. WHY WON'T THEY LET ANYONE STAY WITH THEM THE LAST FEW MINUTES? I ALWAYS FOUND THAT HARD TO UNDERSTAND. UNTIL NOW.
I NO LONGER BELIEVE THEY DO IT TO SPARE THEIR FAMILY THE SADNESS OF BEING THERE WHEN IT HAPPENS. I THINK THEY DO IT TO SPARE THEMSELVES. LOOKING INTO THE KIND EYES OF THOSE YOU'VE LOVED, THOSE YOU SPENT ALL YOUR GOOD DAYS AND ALL YOUR BAD DAYS TOGETHER WITH WHILE YOU'RE TRYING TO GENTLY SLIP AWAY MIGHT BE TOO HARD TO TAKE, AND YOU END UP STRUGGLING FOR EXTRA TIME, WILLING TO PROLONG YOUR OWN SUFFERING JUST TO MAKE IT EASIER ON THEM.
BETTER, THEN, TO LEAVE SILENTLY, UNDISCOVERED, IN THE DARK OF NIGHT. ALONE. IN MANY WAYS, I'M GLAD NONE OF YOU ARE HERE WITH ME WHEN I (INDECIPHERABLE) MAYBE IT'S FOR THE BEST FOR MANY REASONS. (INDECIPHERABLE) IT'S ON ITS WAY TO YOU NOW, SO (INDECIPHERABLE, TWO LINES OF TEXT HAVE BEEN VIOLENTLY CROSSED OUT) DAD, TAHNK YOU SO MUCH FOR TEACHING ME HOW TO (BUILD?) A RADIO. YOU PROBABLY WOULD HAVE WANTED ME TO REMEMBER YOU FOR SOMETHING OTHER THAN THAT, BUT THAT IS THE IMAGE THAT SEEMS TO HAVE (STUCK?) WITH ME. YOUR FACE WHEN YOU MADE THAT RADIO WORK, HOW PROUD YOU LOOKED THEN. AS A KID. & I LOVED YOU FOR IT. (I?) WAS ABLE TO BUILD ONE MYSELF. DIDN'T LOOK AS GOOD AS YOURS, THOUGH. BUT I MADE IT WORK.
AND SO I'VE HEARD THAT THERE WILL BE NO RESCUE MISSION COMING MY WAY AND THAT "A CLERGYMAN WILL ADOPT THE SAME PROCEDURE AS A BURIAL AT SEA, COMMENDING THEIR SOULS TO 'THE DEEPEST OF THE DEEP,' CONCLUDING WITH THE LORD'S PRAYER." I'M AFRAID NO PRAYER WILL DO ~~ANY OF US~~ ANY GOOD NOW. SORRY ABOUT THE WRITIN. USING A PENCIL WITH THESE GLOVES (INDECIPHERABLE) AS I WOULD HAVE LIKED. OR MAYBE IT'S (MY?) HEAD, I'M RUNNING LOW ON OXYGEN, ~~HEADACHE~~ IT TAKES TIME TO GET WORDS WRITE. WILL LEAVE DARLAH 2 NOW, FIND A GREAT SPOT OUTSID (INDECIPHERABLE) CAN WATCH THE EARTH UNTIL I (INDECIPHERABLE) IT WILL A BEAUTFUL LAST (SIGHT?). THERE'S NOTHING MORE I CAN TELL YOU. IT WAS A GREAT RIDE. ALL OF IT. YOU AR ALL BEAUTTYFULL. ~~NO ILIED. I WISH YOU WEREHERE. NO ANIMAL.~~ THE LETTER.
MOM. SANDR. I'M SORRY IM SO SORRY. I HAVE TO (GO?) NOW.
MIA (SIGNATURE)

>>>>>>>>>>>>>>>>>END OF MESSAGE...
>>>>>>>>>>>>>>>>>END OF TRANSMISSION

AUTHOR'S NOTE

The signal 6EQUJ5 was actually received on August 15, 1977, at the Big Ear Radio Observatory (now known as the Ohio State University Radio Observatory) in Delaware, Ohio—and the details in Coleman's story on pages 274 to 277 concerning the signal's reception are actual facts. It is also worth noting that on August 20 and September 5, 1977, two spaceships named *Voyager 1* and *Voyager 2* were launched from Kennedy Space Center in Florida. In addition to taking pictures and solar measurements, they carried a message: a gold-plated record containing images, music, and sounds from our planet, compiled in the event that the ships were ever discovered by an extraterrestrial civilization. Thirteen years after the launch, *Voyager 1* passed Neptune's orbit and left our solar system. *Voyager 1* and *2* are continuing their journey into space at a speed of seventeen kilometers per second, and they remain the man-made objects that are farthest from Earth. If no one discovers them in the meantime, *Voyager 1* won't reach Alpha Centauri, the closest star to our solar system, for at least forty thousand years.

ABOUT THE AUTHOR

JOHAN HARSTAD (born 1979 in Stavanger, Norway) debuted in 2001 with the prose collection *Herfra blir du bare eldre* [*From Here You Only Get Older*]. The following year he published a collection of short stories titled *Ambulanse* [*Ambulance*], and in 2005 he published *Buzz Aldrin, hvor ble det av deg i alt mylderet?* [*Buzz Aldrin, What Happened to You in All the Confusion?*], which has been published in thirteen countries, including the United States, France, Germany, Russia, and Korea, and was a *Kirkus Reviews* Best Fiction of 2011 book. In 2007, Harstad published the novel *Hässelby*, which earned him the Norwegian Youths' Critics Prize. He has also written four plays. *172 Hours on the Moon* (originally published in Norway as *DARLAH: 172 timer på månen*) is his first young adult novel, for which he received the 2008 Brage Award, one of the most prestigious literary awards in Norway. The book is currently being published in ten countries in Europe, Asia, and America.